Suddenly the earpiece in his neurohelmet rang out. "Sledgehammer One to Specter One, I have bogies at the back door in number. Repeat, they've come around to our rear flank and will be here in five minutes."

Damn! Archer had half expected that Colonel Blucher would pull such a move. There was still time to spring his trap, just much less of it. "Understood. Specter One to all Sledgehammers, roll to the south and engage. Specters, wait until our Hammers are with us and then charge down the hill."

Off to his right and left the ground quaked as the ground and hover armor roared past his *Penetrator* and the other Specter Command BattleMechs and straight into the approaching Arcturan Guards. The Lyran Alliance 'Mechs stopped moving up the hill and seemed to freeze for an instant, aware that they were suddenly outnumbered and outgunned and were about to be rushed by a tidal wave of 'Mechs and armor.

On an open combat frequency, Archer barked out one command clear to all of his people: "Charge!"

BATTLETECH®

MEASURE OF A HERO

Blaine Lee Pardoe

A ROC BOOK

ROC
Published by New American Library, a division of
Penguin Putnam Inc., 375 Hudson Street,
New York, New York 10014, U.S.A.
Penguin Books Ltd, 27 Wrights Lane,
London W8 5TZ, England
Penguin Books Australia Ltd, Ringwood,
Victoria, Australia
Penguin Books Canada Ltd, 10 Alcorn Avenue,
Toronto, Ontario, Canada M4V 3B2
Penguin Books (N.Z.) Ltd, 182–190 Wairau Road,
Auckland 10, New Zealand

Penguin Books Ltd, Registered Offices:
Harmondsworth, Middlesex, England

First published by Roc, an imprint of New American Library,
a division of Penguin Putnam Inc.

First Printing, July 2000
10 9 8 7 6 5 4 3 2 1

Series Editor: Donna Ippolito
Mechanical Drawings: Duane Loose and the FASA art department
Cover art by Doug Chaffee

 REGISTERED TRADEMARK—MARCA REGISTRADA

Printed in the United States of America

PUBLISHER'S NOTE
This is a work of fiction. Names, characters, places, and incidents either are
the product of the author's imagination or are used fictitiously, and any
resemblance to actual persons, living or dead, business establishments,
events, or locales is entirely coincidental.

To my wonderful wife, Cyndi, and my children, Victoria Rose and Alexander William. To my parents, who supported my interest in gaming and writing when it made no sense at all. To one of my favorite authors—Harry Turtledove, who provides me with countless hours of entertainment. And to all of my friends who put up with this very weird hobby of mine—being an author.

And, as always, to my alma mater, Central Michigan University.

What makes a hero? Circumstance, timing, the willingness to do something more than is expected and anticipated; yes, all of these things factor in. But there is more. A true hero is not a once in a lifetime phenomenon. True heroes perform heroically over and over again, and do so with such a degree of style and personality that they are remembered. They walk among us, police officers, firemen, members of the armed forces, and perhaps that person in the room with you now.

In developing Archer Christifori as a character, I read about men like Frank Luke, Felix von Luckner, Joshua Lawrence Chamberlain, and other true heroes. They contributed to this book without ever knowing it. I like Archer; he's seasoned, not embittered, and has done his part for king and country when the book starts. That takes a lot.

I must acknowledge the contribution of good folks like John Kendrick, who got me out at least once a week or so searching for long-lost Civil War relics in the woods of the Piedmont in Virginia. It was the best relaxation I could hope for. Thanks to all of the other BattleTech novelists and Bryan Nystul who helped put together what the Civil War is and will be. Donna Ippolito deserves some thanks simply for putting up with all of this on such short notice.

Thanks go out to Cullen Tilman for getting me whitewater rafting in West Virginia with North American so I could include that chunk in the book. And I fully acknowledge the contributions to this book by other good friends like Greg Johnson, the Hosicks, the Druhots, the Hunts, and Rivenburgs.

Finally, to the Sons of Virginia who died during "The War of Northern Aggression" and the tales they left about a real Civil War and its impact on our history. I think we've finally lulled the Yankees into a feeling of overconfidence. As the saying goes, "There is nothing 'civil' in a civil war."

Detail of the Inner Sphere
Circa 3062–63

Coreward
Spinward
Anti-spinward
Rimward

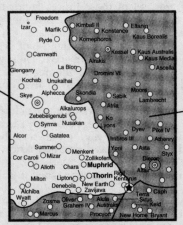

SKYE PROVINCE

DRACONIS COMBINE

Freedom
Izar
Kimball II
Marfik
Konstance
Eltanin
Ryde
Komephoros
Kaus Borealis
Carnwath
Kessel
Kaus Australis
Alrakis
Kaus Media
La Blon
Ascella
Glengarry
Dromini VI
Kochab
Unukalhai
Skondia
Moors
Alphecca
Sabik
Lambrecht
Skye
Atria
Alkalurops
Ko
Zebebelgenubi
Lyons
Syrma
Nusakan
Dyev
Pike IV
Alcor
Gatatea
Imbros III
Athenry
Summer
Yoni
Asta
Styx
Cor Caroli
Mizar
Menkent
Dieron
Alioth
Chara
Zollikofen
Altair
Muphrid
Rigil
Milton
Lipton
Thorin
Kentarus
Denebola
New Earth
Terra
Caph
Alchiba
Zavijava
Sirus
Reid
Wyatt
Zosma
Oliver
Alula
Australis
Procyon
New Home
Bryant
Grahem IV
Marcus

SKYE PROVINCE
DRACONIS COMBINE BORDER
LEGEND

8 PARSECS

40 PARSECS OR 130.4 LIGHT YEARS

SCALE: 1/8 INCH = 1 PARSEC = 3.26 LIGHT YEARS = 19,164,277,860,000 STATUTE MILES

MAXIMUM JUMP: APPROXIMATELY 30 LIGHT YEARS
FOR NAVIGATIONAL PURPOSES USE 9 PARSECS = 29.34 LY

Prologue

Task Force Bulldog Field Hospital
Lootera, Huntress
Kerensky Cluster, Clan Space
8 April 3060

Archer Christifori was uncomfortable, but moving only made things worse. With three broken ribs and numerous sprains, just about any position was painful. They'd given him painkillers, but the drugs left him trapped somewhere between agony and consciousness.

He stared up at the ceiling fan that spun overhead, wondering just how long he would be stuck in this field hospital. He hoped it wouldn't be more than a few more days. He yanked at the sheets with his right arm—the uninjured one—for what seemed like the hundredth damn frustrating time, attempting to find a position that was bearable.

It had been one hell of a week. Months of tedious space travel from the Inner Sphere to Clan space, shattered in sudden, quick terror. Task Force Bulldog had arrived in the Huntress system only days before, and not a moment too soon. Operation Serpent, the other arm of the campaign to end the Clan invasion, had been ground down to only a handful of operational units. So far from home, the Serpents lacked the men and materiel to complete the destruction of the Smoke Jaguars.

Archer's unit, the Tenth Lyran Guards, were part of Bulldog when it came to Huntress. He remembered the approach of his DropShip through the planet's stormy skies. He and the rest of his unit were mounted up in their 'Mech cockpits, awaiting the signal for the drop doors to open. Their orders were to cover the retreat of the Northwind Highlanders, who had been fighting the Jaguars in the thick, stinking mud of the Dhuan Swamp.

As he drifted in and out of consciousness, he heard footsteps in the hall. It wasn't the soft padding sound of nurses' shoes, but the familiar jingle of spurs, the unmistakable trademark of officers of the Armed Forces of the Federated Commonwealth. He lifted his head to see who was approaching, and several blurred figures entered his field of vision.

"Major Christifori," he heard one of them say. Archer blinked to focus his eyes.

"Sir," he managed to respond, bringing his good right arm up for a salute even though he was flat on his back. He immediately recognized Prince Victor Davion, his commander and the overall commander of Task Force Bulldog, but not the other officers with him.

"I've read the after-action reports submitted by Colonel MacLeod on your relief and rescue mission, Major," the Prince said with a slight smile. "That was one hell of a stunt you pulled."

Archer shook his head slightly. "Not really, sir. Just following orders."

The Prince cocked his head slightly. "I don't recall

giving the order to drop right into the middle of the Smoke Jaguar advance, Major."

Archer closed his eyes slightly. Memory flooded back through the haze of his drugged brain.

> The DropShip quaked. "Captain Strong, bring us in right between the Northwind Highlanders and the Jaguar," Archer ordered.
>
> "Roger that, Major," came Strong's reply in Archer's headset. "You are one minute to drop and counting. LZ is hot."
>
> He switched to the Command Company's frequency. "There's not a lot of time, so listen up. Our mission is to relieve the Highlanders. These people have paid for this operation with their blood, and we're here to make sure they live to celebrate the victory. I want a wide dispersal directly between the Jags and the Highlanders. Form a battle line with Command Lance on the left flank, Striker in the center, Stalker on the right.
>
> "Your orders are simple. No Jaguars are to punch through to the Highlanders."
>
> "Sir," said Lieutenant Moss, "they outnumber and outgun us. Second Company will be up in twenty. Shouldn't we wait?"
>
> "Those folks have already been through hell. We're gonna finish what they started. Remember, no Jags get through."

Archer's eyes cracked open slowly. "Your orders were to relieve the Northwind Highlanders, sir. If I had waited, good warriors would have died. Too many had already."

The Prince nodded. "I'm not criticizing what you did, Major. I'm praising it. Not only did you assume a good piece of ground, you also took the initiative without hesitation. According to the reports filed by your commanders, you personally engaged a total of six Smoke Jaguar 'Mechs at once. That was a hell of a feat.''

Archer drew a long deep breath, part of him still caught in the memory.

"I have multiple bogies closing fast, all weight classes," said Lieutenant Friscoe over the commline. His voice was tinged with fear.

The short-range sensors of Archer's Penetrator *didn't paint a happy picture either. There were too many Jaguar 'Mechs, and they were pursuing the Highlanders like a pack of rapid dogs.*

"All right, people, this is where we pay back for the Serpents. The Clanners have trashed their own engagement rules, so keep your heads on straight. Your orders are to engage multiple targets—engage them all. Fire at anything that even tries to break through the line."

The first oncoming 'Mech was a Jaguar Vulture, *its mottled gray camouflage already burned and gouged in several places. It crested the ridge off to his left, moving along the flank of his line. It didn't even try to engage him. It was pursuing the Highlanders withdrawing through the surrounding marshland, and its birdlike gait made it seem to bob across his field of vision.*

Archer twisted his Penetrator's *torso and jabbed the joystick forward so that the targeting reticle drifted over the running* Vulture. *He locked a trio of his medium pulse lasers onto the same target interlock circuit and kept his 'Mech moving forward to keep the distance steady. He triggered the lasers, and the air filled with bright emerald bursts as the beams stitched into the side and rear of the Jaguar OmniMech. The beams found their mark, rocking the 'Mech and peppering armor plating. The Omni's running gait slowly ground to a halt as the Clanner turned to face his attack.*

Archer moved farther up the hillside as a Dasher *also attempted to burst past. Ignoring a* Vulture *also coming at him, he locked onto the light-brown* Dasher

*and let go with his extended-range lasers. The tempera-
ture in his cockpit spiked, if only for a moment.*

*"DropShip Hill, this is Ironclad. What is your
ETA?" he said, the sweat running into his eyes inside
his neurohelmet.*

*"Ironclad, this is the A. P. Hill. We'll be on top of
you in twelve."*

"Make it five . . ."

"The report overstates the engagement, sir," Archer said. "Second Company's DropShip was only a
few minutes away. My right flank folded, but the
center and left held. I just wanted to shoot at as many
Jags as possible to get them tied up on me rather
than the Highlanders."

"The rest of your company was eventually forced
to pull back, but you held your ground."

Archer flushed red at the note of respect in the
Prince's voice. "Sir, you've been in command of the
Tenth Guards for a long time. You know that combat
situations tend to be fluid."

"But not like this, Major. When you were recovered, you'd already punched out. Your 'Mech had
suffered almost eighty-nine-percent armor loss.
Around you were six OmniMechs and three Elementals, and according to your *Penetrator's* battlerom, you
killed them all."

The Warhawk *stumbled as Archer's only remaining
large laser sliced into its knee, popping the actuator in
a muffled explosion of white and gray smoke. It plowed
into the mud and sod of the hillside with such force
that his own mangled 'Mech quaked under the impact.
Archer hobbled past the fallen* Dasher *he'd downed a
few minutes before and swept the field both visually
and with his short-range sensors.*

A gray- and black-striped Galahad *was climbing up
the ridge along the right flank of his position. It had*

*been damaged long before the arrival of his unit. It was
a survivor of the long fighting for Huntress and was
battling for the survival of its Clan—its way of life.
The Galahad aimed its gauss rifles up the long slope
almost wearily. Archer understood the feeling. The last
ten minutes of fighting had left his unit falling back
and his 'Mech was more scrap metal than machine.*

*He targeted his own four remaining medium pulse
lasers and the one functional ER laser at the Galahad.
He somehow managed to fire first, releasing a wave of
emerald bursts and bright scarlet beams on his foe. Two
pulse lasers missed, sizzling into the muck and sod near
the feet of the 'Mech. The large ER laser sliced into the
Galahad's head, right into the cockpit.*

*It replied by firing a pair of gauss rifle slugs, silvery
balls of metal accelerated via magnetic pulses to super-
sonic speeds. One missed totally, but the other dug into
the tissue-thin armor of the Penetrator's right torso.
The 'Mech sagged backward as warning lights flared,
and a ripple of heat swept over Archer like a hot, wet
blanket. Warning lights flickered on his damage display.
His 'Mech was dying around him.*

*He could barely keep the 'Mech upright as he main-
tained his target lock. He locked his medium pulse lasers on the Galahad just as his 'Mech stepped on one
of the Elementals he'd killed only a few minutes into
the fight. Archer fired, and so did the Jaguar MechWarrior. He did not wait for the impact. He wrapped his
hands around the ejection control and pulled the ring
as hard as he could. There was a rush of cool air, the
grinding of metal, and a flash of light that was all he
remembered after that.*

"Yes, sir," Archer said simply. "I guess I did kill
them all."

The Prince patted him gently on the shoulder and
smiled. "We've finished mopping up here, Major. Tomorrow we head for Strana Mechty, where I'm going

to end this invasion once and for all. But for now, Major Christifori, it is my distinct pleasure to award you the Star League Medal of Honor for consummate courage in the tradition of the first Star League Defense Force." He held out the medal, which glittered in the glare of the overhead lights.

Archer gave a weak wave of his one good hand. "Sir, with all due respect, this belongs more to Task Force Serpent. They fought the Jags for months. I only fought for a few minutes. One of them surely deserves the medal more than me."

"Don't fret, Major. I've handed out so many of these to members of Serpent today that I'm almost tired of the task. Only two members of Bull Dog were nominated for the honor, and the commendations came directly from the Serpent commanders. In your case, Colonel MacLeod of the Northwind Highlanders put up your name. He observed your actions from a position deeper into the swamp."

Archer was stunned. He looked at the medal in his open palm.

"It was forged from armor melted off Jaguar 'Mechs," Prince Victor said, closing Archer's fingers around the medal.

"My sister," Archer stammered. "I'm going to give it to her." The medal was cool against his skin, and it felt like it belonged in his hand.

"She's been running the family business back on Thorin all the time I've been away. She's had to carry on all alone. I couldn't even be there when our parents died. We're the only family either of us has, and I promised that this would be my last campaign."

Prince Victor nodded. "Family is important. The AFFC doesn't want to lose you, but there is more than one kind of obligation in this life. I, too, have a sister who means a great deal to me," he said, obviously referring to Yvonne, the youngest of the Davion siblings. His sister Katherine seemed more interested in vying for her brother's power than any blood bond between them. "Your sister will be very proud of you. You're a hero. The Medal of Honor hasn't been awarded in over three centuries. It's a great tribute, and it makes me even more proud that you are a member of my personal command—the Tenth Lyran Guards."

"She deserves this more than I do," Archer murmured drowsily, still thinking of Andrea.

The Prince nodded. "My father once told me that medals and decorations were not so much for those who wear them but for the rest of society. It gives them something to admire, something to aspire to." Archer thought he saw a longing look in the Prince's blue eyes, as if he wished his father were still alive to see all his son had done.

"Hanse Davion was a great man," Archer said. "If he said it, then it must be so." His voice was slurred, still fighting the pull of the drugs. "Sir," he managed at last, "thank you."

"No, Major," Victor Davion said, clasping Archer's good hand, which still held the medal, "thank you."

BOOK ONE

One Man's Rebel Is
Another Man's Patriot

". . . Doctor Talman, as a long-time observer of the political situation in the Inner Sphere, I'd very much like to hear your thoughts on the recent troubles in the Federated Commonwealth. Take the problems on Solaris VII, for example."

"Well, in my opinion the incidents broadcast from Solaris were presented completely out of context by the media."

"Doctor, isn't that skirting the issue? I was asking you to comment on the Archon's order to suppress the Davion supporters, which seems to have fueled a new wave of protests throughout the old Federated Commonwealth, all of which have been put down with an iron heel."

"You and your viewers will have to draw your own conclusions, Ms. Forrester. History is replete with examples of capable and well-loved leaders forced to go beyond the rule of law in the interests of keeping the peace. The Solaris situation was only a minor incident which the media has blown all out of proportion."

—Holoclip from a *Face the Planet* interview with Dr. Stephen Talman of Thorin University, Donegal Broadcasting Company, Lyran Alliance 30 August 3062

= 1 =

Ecol City, Thorin
Isle of Skye Province
Lyran Alliance
23 October 3062

Archer Christifori stood watching as one of his transports, the *Union* Class *Angelfire*, lifted off from the spaceport tarmac. The corporate logo of Christifori Express—a planet with rings and the initials C.E. in yellow underneath—shimmered in Thorin's dull yellow sun. He always came down to watch whenever one of his transports was headed out. His father had done it before him, and it seemed like a good tradition.

His communicator beeped twice, and he tapped it on to receive. "This is the *Angelfire*," he heard the DropShip captain say. "Dockmaster has given us the green light, Mister Christifori."

Archer raised the communicator to his lips. "Good luck on your run, Captain Fullerton. And see if you can lay your hands on some Glengarry Ale while you're there."

He cut the signal and watched as the massive fusion drives ignited under the ship's ovoid form. The *Angelfire* lifted slowly into the morning sky, rising on the white-hot flames of its thrusters. A few seconds later, he heard the roar, a thunderous noise that vibrated in his chest. It made him proud to watch the ship rise steadily upward into space.

A hand on his shoulder broke the spell, and he turned to see his sister Andrea. She was shorter than him by at least a head, but her body was strong and muscular.

"So, Lee Fullerton's on his way," she said, tilting her head to watch as the ship became no more than a small dot in the bright blue sky.

"It'll be a profitable run. Shipping spare parts and ammunition for the Lyran military is suddenly a booming business."

Andrea scowled slightly. "If our Archon wasn't so busy suppressing Davions, she wouldn't be needing to ship spare parts to her regiments."

Archer smiled fondly; he'd heard it all before from Andrea. She opposed the way things were going in the Lyran half of the Federated Commonwealth and blamed the Archon. Katrina Steiner had been busy consolidating her power in the past couple of years, and Andrea believed she was putting her ambitions above the welfare of the Lyran people.

Though Katrina was still immensely popular, she

didn't have the situation entirely under control. She'd managed to take the throne of the Federated Commonwealth away from her brother while he was off fighting the Clans, but now he was back. Victor, too, had his faithful supporters. Not only was he the firstborn of Hanse Davion and Melissa Steiner, he was also a genuine war hero. He'd made no move to retake the throne, but he wouldn't have to look far for help if he decided to do so.

Katrina had always favored the Steiner half of the realm, especially these days. When push came to shove, she always seemed to decide against the Davionists. Protests had become more and more frequent in the Davion strongholds of her far-flung realm, and Katrina had allowed her troops to brutally put down the Davion nationals. Even normally quiet and complacent Lyrans like Andrea Christifori were shocked. This wasn't soldiers fighting soldiers, but warriors killing civilians in the streets.

"I think you've made your feelings well known," Archer said quietly. His sister had penned more than one long and scathing editorial published in the capital city paper. The most recent appeared two weeks ago, and people were beginning to rally around her criticism of the Archon's actions.

"I wish you would, too, Archer," Andrea said. "You're the one who's popular and well-known on Thorin. If you spoke out against the Archon, more people would listen." He saw that she still wore his Medal of Honor on a long chain around her neck. It was like a cornerstone between them, a linchpin.

Archer had been given a hero's welcome when he came home to Thorin for good. To have won a Medal of Honor, which no one had received since the days of the old Star League, had made him an instant celebrity. There had been parades and even balls in his honor, which he attended with Andrea on his arm. Various corporations had offered him lucrative endorsement contracts for their products, but Archer had turned them down. His name and face were not for sale. Men and women had died so that he was still alive, and he wasn't going to make a profit on their sacrifices. The only honor he'd accepted was command of the planetary militia.

"I was a MechWarrior, Andrea, not a politician. I don't approve of the Archon sending in troops to crack down on people who have a right to speak their minds, but that doesn't mean I want to stir up trouble. Besides, there's no reason for me to get involved in this."

Ecol City wasn't the only place where anti-Katrina sentiment had emerged. Protests and disturbances had broken out on both of Thorin's continents, especially since the Steiner-Davion war had erupted on the streets of Solaris VII. It had been so much like the Inner Sphere in miniature that it triggered strong feelings on both sides. Archer could almost sense the coming storm. How soon before it broke wide open, sweeping everything before it?

He glanced at his watch and shook his head. "I have to go."

"Yes, our new keepers have arrived," she said bitterly.

"The presence of the Fifteenth Arcturan Guards on Thorin doesn't make them our keepers. Their posting here is simply part of their rotation in the theater. Trust me, the military rotates units all the time."

"And now you've got to go and kowtow to their commanding officer," she chided.

Archer stiffened slightly. "Not quite, Andrea. I'm in command of the Thorin Militia. Colonel Blucher is regular army—which puts him in charge of the defense of the entire planet. On paper, I report to him. According to his dossier, he's a respected career man, which means he and I will get along just fine."

"Then answer me this, Archer. We're far from the

Clan front, far from any other government who might wish to capture our world. In fact, Thorin hasn't been attacked since the Second Succession War, and you know it."

"Your point?"

"What are they here to defend us from?"

Archer frowned slightly and turned away without answering. He had an appointment to keep.

The Fifteenth Arcturan Guards were garrisoned in a small fortress first erected some three hundred years ago in what were now the southern suburbs of Ecol City. The original had been gutted by orbital bombardment when the Lyran Commonwealth invaded Thorin during the First Succession War, but the fort had been rebuilt. Even so, the dull granite outer walls still bore deep burn marks and in some places were cut all of the way down to the ground. Over the decades, the city around the fort had rebuilt, too, though the area was rundown, a far cry from the nicer northern suburbs. Archer knew that the fortress could house a full battalion of troops. His own base was on the western edge of the city, nearer the countryside. For Archer the fort had a special meaning. It dated from the days of the first Star League, and he was one of the handful of Thorin troopers to become members of the newly resurrected Star League Defense Force.

He showed his papers to the guard, who looked them over quickly, then motioned him through the gate. Archer crossed the reinforced ferrocrete of the courtyard with a strict military gait, his boot heels clicking smartly. At the entrance to the enormous 'Mech bay, he paused to observe the bustle of activity. Inside, standing in gantries, was a full company of BattleMechs. Technicians scrambled over them like busy spiders performing their work.

It had been six centuries since the BattleMech was

first created, forever altering the face of warfare. Roughly humanoid in shape, standing nearly three stories tall, 'Mechs moved at speeds upwards of ninety kph, and carried enough firepower to equal a platoon of twentieth-century armor. A 'Mech could level a city block with missiles, lasers, and autocannon in the blink of an eye. Even after years of piloting them in battle, Archer still felt a sense of awe at the raw power they represented.

As he stood there, a somewhat shorter man approached from the interior of the cavernous bay. Where Archer's militia uniform was light green, this man wore the darker green dress uniform of the Lyran Alliance Armed Forces as well as the taller black boots. His black hair was shorn close, and spots on either side of his head had been shaved for better contact with his neurohelmet. The rank insignia on his shoulders identified him as the man Archer had come to meet—Colonel Felix Blucher.

Archer saluted as the colonel approached.

"Leutnant Colonel Christifori, I presume," Blucher said, with a slight Germanic accent.

"Sir."

The colonel studied his face. "I've heard a great deal about you, Leutnant Colonel. Your record of service during the Clan invasion and in Task Force Bull Dog is well known."

Archer nodded once slightly. "You have me at a disadvantage, Colonel Blucher. I only know you from the brief dossier provided, and that was scant on detail."

Blucher gave him a thin smile. "I was only recently given command of the Fifteenth Arcturan. After Colonel Wright's accident, they brought me here from the Skye Theater."

Archer looked past him into the 'Mech bay. "That's some impressive equipment you've brought with you, sir."

Blucher nodded. "Yes, First Battalion tends toward heavier equipment. Even for old soldiers like you and I, these machines still hold a touch of magic about them, don't they?"

"Yes, sir." Archer longed, if only for an instant, for another time, another place. "I've brought you the TO&E for my command." He handed the file to the colonel.

"You mean my command, don't you?" Blucher asked coyly.

Archer was caught a little off guard. "Of course, Colonel. As the ranking regular army officer on Thorin, we are yours to command."

"No offense taken. I tend to favor formality, however. Something of a character flaw, I'm afraid." Blucher glanced at the file, then closed it and slid it under his armpit. "Looks like you've got roughly a battalion of troops."

"We have a company of ground armor and aerospace elements and a full company of BattleMechs as well as infantry," Archer said.

Blucher fixed him with his deep blue eyes. "And what are their loyalties, Leutnant Colonel?"

That question caught Archer even more off guard. "They are loyal, sir," he said finally.

Blucher smiled and clapped Archer on the shoulder. "My apologies for being so blunt, but you must understand that I am here to ensure that Thorin remains a peaceful part of the Lyran Alliance. Surely you've heard the reports of disturbances on a number of our worlds fomented by factions who oppose the Archon."

"My people are loyal to the government," he said firmly.

"Then there will be no problems," Blucher returned. "What I must ask you next is more personal. I mean no offense by it, you understand, but I was given some intelligence concerning this world that forces me to do so."

"Go ahead, sir."

"What about your own loyalties, Christifori?"

Archer didn't flinch. "I am a loyal citizen of Thorin. Politics don't interest me, sir. As for these rebellious acts, I'm not in favor of anything that places innocent lives at risk.

"If you're asking me if I back the Archon, I would have to say that I question some of her recent actions, but only because I'm not in favor of any threat to our rights as free citizens. But my loyalty has never been in question either now or in the past." As if to emphasize his point, he glanced down at the three rows of ribbons on his uniform, including the one with the Cameron Star that was his Medal of Honor.

"I understand fully, Leutnant Colonel Christifori. However, I understand that your sister has written an inflammatory editorial against the Archon that was published recently. That aroused concern among upper command that you might be siding with some of the rebellious groups on Thorin. They wanted a full investigation of you, but I convinced them that it would be better if you and I talked first rather than jump to conclusions."

"Did you get the answer you were hoping for?" Archer couldn't help the trace of anger in his voice.

"Yes, I did. Though, as a fellow officer, perhaps you will permit me to advise that you caution your sister about her writings. This is not the right political climate for voicing dissent."

"My sister is all I have left of my family, sir. Our parents both died while I was away defending the Inner Sphere from the Clans. I never had time for a wife, or even a life outside of the military. She's all that I have now. I want to protect her, not try to keep her from expressing her opinions. Though you say this is not the time to voice dissent, she would say that this is exactly the time to do so. If you have a problem with her, I suggest that you speak with her directly."

"That is not necessary. I just wanted us to start off on the right foot and be honest and straightforward in our dealing with one another."

"Fair enough. Now if you'll indulge me, sir, I have a question for you," Archer countered. "What are your thoughts on what's been happening on our worlds?"

Blucher raised his black eyebrows as if he were impressed with Archer's boldness in shifting so swiftly from defense to offense. He actually chuckled slightly as he began to speak. "Leutnant Colonel Christifori, I am a military man from a long line of military officers. A Blucher has served in the Lyran armed forces ever since the days of the original Star League. I prefer my fights to be against other soldiers. I didn't bring this battalion to Thorin or my other two to Muphrid to bully private citizens.

"Don't get me wrong," Blucher added firmly. "I'm more than willing to defend the Lyran Alliance against any enemy, even those from within. I wouldn't look forward to it, I wouldn't relish it. But I swore an oath to the Archon. She is the law of the land and our rightful leader and my duty is to serve her.

"There, now you have my answer. Was it what you expected?"

Archer didn't speak for a moment. "I had no expectations, Colonel."

Blucher reached out to shake his hand. "You and I are not so different. We're both soldiers at heart. You're militia now, but you spent plenty of years on the front lines in some of the bloodiest fighting of the last century. We've both faced down our enemies from the cockpits of our 'Mechs. We've both faced death and won.

"Over time, Archer, I believe that we two will get to know each other well and even become friends. That is my sincere wish."

Archer tightened his grip on his new commanding officer's hand. "We do have a lot in common, sir," was all he felt he could honestly say. His eyes drifted over to the fortress as the morning detail began to raise the Lyran Alliance flag. The wind was not blowing, and the flag hung limp on its grommets.

The image struck Archer as ominous. Was it, he wondered, a sign of the times?

Three hours later he was in his office, flopped in the chair at his desk, his posture far from military. He loosened his tie and unbuttoned the top two buttons on his shirt while surveying the battlefield of his desktop, whose terrain consisted of mounds of paper, invoices, purchase orders, and requisitions, all of it seeming to require his attention.

There was a time when life had seemed simpler, but this was a new day. He was still an officer, though only on weekends. Since returning home, he was enjoying the responsibility of running the business with Andrea, but it lacked the excitement and risks of his earlier career. As he stared at the assorted piles of hardcopy, mentally debating which one to tackle first, a light rap came at the door. It opened before he could respond, and his sister entered the room.

"You look beat," she said. "Paperwork getting to you?"

Archer grinned. "A former CO once told me that the day we have a paperless office is the day they invent a paperless toilet. That's not it, though." He pushed some of the papers to one side with a grimace.

"The new Lyran CO and I had a little talk, that's all," he said. It had been a long day of going over the troop dispositions, unit rosters, and so on for his unit and the newly arrived Arcturan Guards. Then he'd spent the last hour or so mulling over his conversation with Colonel Blucher. He kept a cool demeanor in Blucher's presence, but for anyone to question his loyalty disturbed Archer profoundly.

"Trouble?"

He shook his head. "No, he simply wanted to make sure we were on the same side."

"And what side's that?"

Archer shrugged, leaning his arms on the spot he'd cleared in front of him. "I think that's part of the problem, Andrea. The lines are a little blurred right now."

She took a chair opposite his dark wooden desk. "I hope my opinions didn't get you into trouble."

Archer shrugged slightly. "Well, it *did* come up. Your words seem to have rattled the Colonel just a little. Imagine, you, a revolutionary." He chuckled.

"He said that?"

"No, not in so many words, but he seemed to think you were taking too many chances."

She reached over to take one of his hands. "I'm so sorry, Archer. It was never my intention to get you interrogated about my activities or my opinions."

He smiled to reassure her. "Don't give it another thought. I've learned that it's healthy to keep a commanding officer a little in the dark about some aspects of your life. Besides, I more than owe you five minutes of verbal flak."

2

Civil disturbances and protests have increased in frequency and volume in the Federated Commonwealth, some even calling for Archon Katrina Steiner to step down. Also reported is the occasional anti-Victor rally, though these almost always take place in Lyran space. The nobility has prospered under Katrina's rule, while the common man seems to feel he is getting less and less of the pie.

—Dana Powell, *Newswatch: Atreus and Beyond*, Station WFWL, Free Worlds League, 30 October 3062

Ecol City, Thorin
Skye Province
Lyran Alliance
1 November 3062

The shell that had once been a restaurant and bar still spewed a thin haze of smoke as Felix Blucher stepped through the security cordon surrounding the rubble. He caught the hint of dust and ozone in the air and the odor of something rotting in the debris. It smelled like long-spoiled food, though only two days had passed since the explosion.

The Foolery's location a mere block from the fort had made it an instant favorite of the Arcturan Guards. All that stood now were the rearmost wall and the common wall shared with the business next door, whose shattered windows were still being swept off the streets. The rest was a sprawling mound of broken bricks, concrete, piping, wiring, metal, and the odd personal effect lost during the explosion.

Blucher had dined there only a few days earlier, and could just as easily have come again the night the explosion killed everyone in the building. Including some of his own people. Worse yet, it looked like this was neither an accident nor random violence. From what he'd read in the preliminary report, there was some evidence of sabotage.

His aide de camp, Leutnant Luther Fisk, came up alongside him as Blucher surveyed the damage, one booted foot propped on the overturned cornerstone of the building. Blucher caught a whiff of the man's cologne. It was expensive, and in the colonel's mind, somehow not befitting an officer.

"What's the report on our people?" he asked without preamble.

"One dead, three in critical condition," Fisk said.

"And the civilians?"

"Eight killed, two injured." Fisk spoke as though he were talking about livestock rather than humans.

"What a waste," Blucher said more to himself than his aide. "Any leads on who did it or why?"

Fisk shook his head slightly. "I don't have specifics, Colonel, and the locals all claim they haven't a clue who might be responsible. But you and I know."

"We do?" Blucher said, feigning ignorance.

"Who else but Davion loyalists? This was a deliberate act of terrorism. They've been protesting our posting to Thorin, and now they've killed some of our people."

Blucher turned to look at his aide. "A hundred people with picket signs calling for fair treatment hardly constitutes a raging terrorist movement. You're spouting theories, Leutnant. I need facts, not speculation."

"I'm just following the logic," Fisk said. "There hasn't been a terrorist act on Thorin in decades. Now we have protesters calling for the Archon to step down, followed by vicious attacks on our troops."

Blucher swept his arm out toward the mound of rubble. "Has forensics got anything?"

"They believe a bomb set off the gas pipes in the basement."

"They believe? Aren't they sure?"

Fisk hesitated. "Well, they found evidence of explosives—gunpowder. No fragments typical of a bomb, but the investigation continues."

Blucher shook his head. "That's not evidence. It could be that nothing more than some ammunition stored in the basement set off the explosion."

"Well, Colonel, our intelligence people have been tipped that this was a deliberate act—the work of one or more cells of an organized resistance movement here on Thorin."

"Any hard, tangible evidence?"

"None yet, sir, but it's only a matter of time."

Blucher rubbed his temple as if it would ease his mind. He didn't like this, didn't like it at all. A political appointee, Luther Fisk was ambitious, eager to pressure him into territory he wasn't ready to enter. Fisk was a young man with a powerful father, not a real military officer whose main concern was the welfare of his troops, his command. He cared more about politics and how he might or might not benefit from any given situation or action. To Blucher, who had dedicated his career to performing with honor, that attitude stank of dark alleys and smoke-filled rooms.

Yet, this time, the young officer was probably right. This thing had all the markings of a terrorist attack. It also fit the pattern of reports of sabotage against Lyran troops garrisoned on other worlds. But they had nothing firm to go on. Whispers in the dark, rumors, dark lies, wild guesses—that wasn't enough. Felix Blucher was a pragmatic man who needed to see solid evidence before making up his mind.

"Here's what we'll do, Leutnant. We'll issue a press release saying that we suspect a terrorist attack, but that we're still investigating. We will stress that we're here to maintain the peace on Thorin, a world the Archon values as a former jewel of the original Star League. You will draft it and have it on my desk tomorrow morning."

Fisk licked his lips nervously. "Sir . . . may I speak freely?"

Blucher gestured for him to continue.

"Colonel, we have an entire battalion on Thorin. The Fifteenth is a first-rate command. Why not deploy them as a policing force? We could say it was to protect the interests and lives of civilians in case we are dealing with terrorists. A heavily armed presence on the streets would calm the truly loyal citizens and at the same time would send a clear message to those responsible."

"Leutnant, I am a serious student of history. I understand what you say, but perhaps you haven't considered all the implications.

"Putting our troops on the streets will not scare off dedicated terrorists, if that's what we've got here. All it will do is make our people easier targets for further attacks. Besides, BattleMechs are mighty weapons of war but make lousy riot-control gear. If we used them in such a capacity, it will surely set off another incident, one that may make all of us pay in the long term."

"But the loyal Lyrans on this world—"

"Will see this for what it is, a tragic explosion that took the lives of civilians and soldiers alike. True, they will not see a BattleMech on every street corner, but the tradeoff is that when they wake up tomorrow, they *will* see Thorin as it was the day before."

"Colonel, you've read the report from intelligence. They've identified several rabble-rousers beginning to emerge among the civilian rank and file, people calling for the Archon's resignation. Are you going to ignore that as well?"

"You're right, Fisk. We've got a number of people with the potential to become rebels. That's the reason we won't supply them with a reason to revolt. I will draft an order today that these individuals be brought in so we can talk with them. It won't be an interrogation, nor will they be held for any period of time. I want to meet with them, tell them where we stand, come to terms early on if possible."

Fisk was shocked. "Sir, it would be easy to arrest them. Calling this a terrorist attack would give you all the cause you need to hold them indefinitely. How does the old saying go? 'Kill the head and the body will die?' Arrest them now before they escalate, and we can crush a rebellion before it starts. Other regimental commanders are doing it, and the Archon has not reversed their actions."

Fisk's argument was tempting, almost seductive, but not enough to make Blucher take that leap. "As I said, I am a student of history. If you wish to fuel a rebellion, try to blow it out. Like a flame, the more you blow, the more it spreads. If we arrest these people without just cause, they'll only become martyrs in the eyes of the man and woman on the street. We'd be giving those who haven't yet decided where they stand a powerful reason to oppose us. No, my order stands. And it must be done discreetly. No press, no squads of soldiers breaking down doors. This is simply a friendly invitation to speak with the planetary garrison commanding officer. We will do nothing that will further fuel thoughts of rebellion. Understood?"

Fisk looked dejected. "Yes sir," he said. "But you did read through the list of names, didn't you, Colonel?"

Blucher nodded. "Yes, I did."

"You know that the sister of Thorin's little war hero, Leutnant Colonel Christifori, is on the list of suspects."

Blucher didn't like Fisk's tone, which was almost mocking, but again he let nothing show. "I know, Leutnant. You will put her lower on your lists. Leutnant Colonel Christifori is a well-known public figure on this world. I want to first advise him of our plan, so he won't think we've blindsided him."

"With his sister out publicly damning the Archon, perhaps he should step down as the militia commander."

"Use your head, Fisk. Archer Christifori is a man you don't want standing against you. He is well-loved here, a respected businessman, a war hero. Thorin is like a small town, and Christifori is a big fish in this small pond. Attack that image and you attack everyone who admires and looks up to him."

"Sorry, sir," Fisk said, apparently realizing he'd overstepped his boundaries. "As your aide, it is my duty to point out options, that is all. I meant no disrespect of you or of the militia commander."

Blucher rubbed his chin reflectively, thinking how to handle this. "I'm sure you are motivated by only the highest motives, Leutnant, and I commend you for your eagerness to resolve a difficult problem. But I am in command here, and there is a reason for that. We will conduct operations on Thorin and Muphrid my way." The colonel didn't have much use for Fisk, but was hopeful he'd come around. Otherwise he'd continue to stir up trouble, and who knew where that might lead?

"So, Fisk, I hope we understand each other. We must arrange for a formal tribute to the soldiers who died here, with the whole battalion present to send them off with honors. And then you will track down the relatives of the civilians who also died. Send them flowers with my condolences." Blucher turned away from the scene of so much destruction and began to walk away, his boots making cracking sounds as he crushed more rubble underfoot.

"I will take care of it, Colonel. Where will you be, sir?"

"In my quarters," Blucher said, not looking back. "I have a task to perform that I have grown weary of in my career. I must write the families to tell them that their sons and daughters will not be coming home."

He continued to walk away swiftly, leaving Luther Fisk standing alone amid the sprawl of debris.

═══ 3 ═══

Precentor Martial Victor Steiner-Davion today issued a statement condemning the Archon's recent measures aimed at preserving peace in the Federated Commonwealth. The government, however, assures all citizens that civil authority and the public welfare have been greatly enhanced by these measures. Making the streets safe and ensuring the orderly progress of public life are among the Archon's highest priorities for her people.

—Official palace press release, Donegal Broadcasting
Newsline Feed, 5 November 3062

Fauquier Foothills, Thorin
Skye Province
Lyran Alliance
6 November 3062

Archer angled his *Penetrator* along the hillside, slowly winding his way up toward the top. The slope was steep, rising at an almost fifty-degree angle in many places. Light filtered down from the trees as he moved, almost like a strobe light inside his cockpit as he stepped from shadow to light. The trees dotted his path enough to provide cover from the air, though that had not been the problem over the last two days. The problem was the Fifteenth Arcturan Guards and their relentless pursuit.

The wargame had been organized as a way to integrate and coordinate the workings of the two units. Archer was in command of the Thorin Militia against Colonel Blucher commanding the Guards. They had chosen the venue of the Fauquier Foothills because it was isolated, offered a wide variety of terrain, and because neither side had the advantage of knowing the lay of the land too well. The hills were rounded, with some gray rocks jutting out every so often. Trees were scattered over them, but otherwise the typical forest growth wasn't present.

The exercise had started out well. In the low hills to the south, Archer had managed to ambush Blucher's supply train. The 'Mech battle computers had been rigged to simulate combat damage, which was good for the Guards. Had the weapons been fully armed and loaded, the explosion of the supply train would have been visible from Thorin's orbit.

Then things had taken a turn for the worse. Archer's infantry companies had gotten bogged down in a nearby swamp and been cut off from the main force. Archer had tried to punch through to relieve them, but without success. The infantry held off Blucher for hours, buying time for Archer to get his force to this spot, their fall-back position. It was the highest terrain around. To the east and west, the hills and rock formations prevented a flanking maneuver. To the north were narrow defiles and a rugged logging road if he had to retreat further into the mountains. To the south, the long, sloping hillside led down nearly five kilometers. It was the only avenue of approach, the only logical place to attack.

And Archer was ready.

"Specter One to Specter Four," he said slowly as

he stopped his *Penetrator* and turned down the south side of the hill. "Report."

The radio voice of Leutnant Val Kemp off to his right came through Archer's neurohelmet. "Specter One, all's quiet here." Kemp had been in the militia for eight years after a stint in the AFFC, but had somehow managed to avoid actual combat. He was polished, but lacked real-life experience. Until then, these exercises would have to suffice.

"Specter One to Sledgehammer One, are the hammers locked and loaded?" This time he was reaching out to Second Company. Thus far in the exercise they had not yet had a taste of the Guards. Almost totally a ground armor force, the Second had been sent ahead to this position early on. It had taken them time, but Archer would need them when the fight came. Under the command of Hauptmann Alice Gett, they would be weary but ready to fight.

"We're in position and holding. I have Sledgehammers Five, Six, and Eight covering the back door if we need it," Gett replied firmly.

"Contacts, multiple, fast-moving," rang out a voice that Archer recognized as Specter Nine, Senior Warrant Officer Kane Livernois. "Repeat. I have enemy 'Mechs coming in from the south in large numbers."

Archer felt his heart begin to race, and he began to sweat inside his coolant vest, which was beginning to stick to his bare chest. He had been here before, on a number of battlefields.

"Specter One wants numbers, Nine," he said. Remain calm, he told himself. Some of his troops were true weekend warriors and didn't get nearly the time he would have liked in the cockpit. The last thing he needed was for them to panic and fall back too soon.

"I am showing two full companies, if not more," came back the nervous tone of Livernois's voice. "They're closing right . . . aw crap!" There was a roar in the speaker from a 'Mech taking a blast. Livernois was under attack.

"Fall back, Nine. Everyone else, fire and move back up the hill. Just like we planned. Keep firing, keep moving. Watch your pacing and speed." He peered down the hillside and saw distant forms suddenly light up on his secondary display, where he had the long-range sensors sweeping down. *Here they come. . . .*

The massive shape of an *Atlas* grabbed his attention as the battle computer spat out its technical stats. Archer ignored the data. He knew an *Atlas* and what it could do. Others came into view, a dark gray *Champion* and a *Cicada* moving up the hillside. His short-range sensors showed that Specter Nine's smaller *Stealth* lit its jump jets, attempting to escape the advancing line of Guards. Their simulated fire raked the 'Mech as he landed on the far right flank. A Guard *Wyvern* moved alongside it and opened up with its lasers and short-range missiles. While the dummy warheads went off in a cloud of white powder indicating hits, the powered-down lasers also bathed the already-damaged *Stealth*.

Archer didn't wait to see the results. He trained his own extended-range large lasers on the *Atlas*, and the instant the targeting reticle turned green, he opened fire. From what he saw, his powered-down shots dug into the right arm and torso of the one-hundred-ton 'Mech, doing little more than searing off simulated armor. The *Atlas* seemed to pause, as if it were surprised by the attack.

Archer grinned to himself inside his neurohelmet. "You weren't expecting me hitting you at seven hundred-fifty meters, were you?" he said out loud, grinning with satisfaction. Inner Sphere ER large lasers had a maximum range of 570 meters, but Archer's *Penetrator* had been refit with Clan-technology weapons before he left Huntress. The old girl still had a few tricks up her sleeve.

"Specter One, this is The Brain." That was Hauptmann Katya Chaffee. A former MechWarrior who'd been gravely wounded in the Clan invasion, she was now in charge of the militia's intelligence operations and had an active role in the battle that was unfolding. "I cannot account for all of the Guards. I show two lances not in our sensor range."

"Roger that, Brain," Archer replied. If they weren't here, they must be coming at him from somewhere else. "You think they're coming to the rear?"

"If I was a Lyran, that's what I'd be doing," she said, sounding as if she were reading, thinking, and talking all at the same time.

"Thanks, Brain. Time to think on our feet." He switched his comm channel to broadband so that his whole command could hear him. "Specter One to all Specters. Continue to fall back. Sledgehammer One, you'd better send some help to the back door, just enough to keep them bottled up. The Brain tells me that all the bad guys are not present and accounted for." Then he sidestepped his *Penetrator* just as a simulated gauss rifle slug from an Arcturan *Hollander* missed its mark, sending up a white cloud of smoke off to his left as he moved.

Leutnant Val Kemp's *Crab* had taken too long to draw itself out of the wave of attacking 'Mechs. Archer couldn't see it with his eyes as much as he could tell from his tactical display. Its large lasers sliced away at the upper body of the towering *Atlas*, but the damage still only mangled armor plating. Archer joined in with his extended-range weapons, again hitting the arm and the center torso, but not enough to help Kemp. Instead of just falling, his severely damaged *Crab* barreled down the hillside, plowing into a *Cicada*. Both 'Mechs went sprawling down the steep slope, knocking down several trees as they slid and skidded away.

A large laser hit laced up the right leg of Archer's *Penetrator*, and his battle computer rang out as it computed the fake damage and portrayed it on his tactical display as a ripple of yellow and light red lights.

Archer didn't flinch. He knew his 'Mech; the armor had held. He reached the last stretch of rise on the hill and turned again to the skull-like, grinning head of the *Atlas* that was lumbering slowly after him and his battered militia. It was as if the Guard BattleMech was coming straight at him. It let go with its gauss rifle, sending the dud-slug into Archer's right torso, rocking the 'Mech back slightly and sending a cloud of white powder into the air. Again the damage display gave him a saffron color on the damage readout. Beads of sweat formed on his forehead, and when he licked at his dry lips, he tasted the salt from his perspiration. Keeping his lock on the *Atlas*, he opened up again on the 'Mech's upper body, once more burning away precious armor.

Suddenly a voice rang out in his earpiece. "Sledgehammer One to Specter One, I have bogies at the back door in numbers. Repeat, they've come around to our rear flank and will be up here in about five minutes."

Damn! Archer had half-expected Blucher to pull just such a move. There was still time to spring his trap, just much less of it. "Understood. Specter One to all Sledgehammers, roll to the south and engage. Specters, wait until our Hammers are with us and then start to charge down the hill, just like we planned it."

To both his right and left the ground quaked as the ground and hover armor roared past his *Penetrator* and the other Specter Command BattleMechs, racing straight into the approaching Arcturan Guards.

The Lyran 'Mechs stopped moving up the hill and seemed to freeze for an instant, aware that they were suddenly outnumbered and outgunned and were being rushed like a tidal wave breaking over them.

On an open combat frequency, Archer barked out one single command to all his people: "Charge!" His own *Penetrator* joined the mad rush down the hill.

The mock battle drill ended almost an hour later. It had been close, and when the points awarded by the judges were calculated, it was declared a dead draw. The charge had broken the Arcturan Guards, but only for a few minutes. Their attack on the rear of the ground armor had done more damage than Archer would have liked, but it had bought the time he'd needed.

To Archer, it was really a victory. For a planetary militia unit—a band of weekend warriors—to fight a regular army unit to a draw was quite an achievement. He stood with his command staff at the mud and vine-covered feet of his *Penetrator*, laughing and talking about the fight. Katya Chaffee was sitting on the foot of the 'Mech, splashing her face with water from her canteen. Second Company commander Hauptmann Gett kept looking at a portable datapad, studying the tactical feed of the battle, trying to explain to Archer how they could have pressed the fight even further. His troops didn't really consider the exercise a victory because it wasn't all they'd hoped for.

For a few minutes, Archer allowed himself to laugh and be a soldier again. After years in the field, where he'd often longed to be a civilian once more, he found himself reveling in being a warrior. There was a magic about the camaraderie, the invisible bond between members of a unit who understood each other, working together as a team. He almost didn't notice the two officers heading in his direction.

Like him, they wore coolant vests and shorts, and both were carrying their neurohelmets. Colonel Blucher he recognized instantly, but the other man he didn't know.

Archer saluted as Blucher stepped up. "Colonel Blucher, that was a good exercise, sir," he said.

Blucher returned the salute. "It was at that, Leutnant Colonel. You gave as good as you took. My troops have been humbled by the performance of your militia troops."

It took a lot for a fellow warrior, and a superior officer, to concede victory with such grace. Archer smiled and gave his CO a slight nod. He looked over at the stranger and extended his hand. "I don't believe I've had the honor."

Colonel Blucher smiled somewhat sheepishly. "May I introduce my aide de camp, Leutnant Luther Fisk." Fisk did not shake Archer's hand, but instead gave him a formal military bow, a gesture Archer thought more suited to the royal court than actions in the field.

"My pleasure," Archer replied, dropping his hand.

"Actually the pleasure should be mine, sir. You are a well-known hero." There was something hostile in his manner. Archer sensed immediately that the junior officer didn't like him. It was in his eyes, his gestures, the way he stood.

"Reports of my heroism are greatly exaggerated," Archer replied.

"You performed well today, though, sir. The Colonel and I were reviewing the battle and noticed that you hit us at a range neither of us had anticipated."

Archer smiled and thumb-pointed to the *Penetrator* looming up behind him. "That old girl still has a few surprises in her, Leutnant Fisk. She's packing a pair of refit Clan extended-range large lasers. Lighter weight, better range."

"Indeed," he said coolly. "That information was

not provided as part of the exercise briefing. It seems that your little surprise gave your militia a somewhat undocumented advantage."

Archer felt his anger rise. He was being told that he'd cheated, and by a junior officer. "I'm sorry it was overlooked, Leutnant," he said, stressing the rank. "Somehow the file must have been overlooked by you. You see, that BattleMech was my ride when we fought on Huntress. She's fought on a dozen planets here in the Inner Sphere and on the Clan homeworlds. There wasn't anything left of it, so at the Prince's command it was rebuilt using some of the captured Clan tech."

"Prince Victor?" Fisk asked.

"Yes, Leutnant." Archer allowed himself a touch of indignation. "Is there a problem?"

"Far be it from me to imply you behaved in any way improperly, sir," Fisk hedged. "I simply was not aware of it." His tone had made no secret that he wasn't an admirer of Victor Steiner-Davion.

"Of course," Archer said slowly. "I would hate to think that you would imply that someone of my background and rank would not obey the rules of the engagement." He lowered the tone of his voice, leaving little room for Fisk to squirm away.

Colonel Blucher stepped between them. "Leutnant, it doesn't matter. It was an excellent exercise and showed that we have a lot to learn from each other. That was the purpose, after all. Besides, if I catalogued every 'Mech on both sides that had some sort of unofficial modification, it would take a terabyte of data." He took Archer's elbow lightly. "Archer, why don't we allow Leutnant Fisk to get to know your command staff. I have something I'd like to discuss with you—in private."

Archer cocked his eyebrow slightly and nodded. "Hauptmann Chaffee," he said to his intelligence officer, "please take Leutnant Fisk around and introduce him to the unit." As Katya started the introductions, he followed Blucher some distance away to the shade of a massive oak tree. "Is there a problem, sir?"

"No, Leutnant Colonel, not a real problem. I just wanted you to hear this first from me. You know about the explosion at the restaurant a few days ago, I presume?"

"Yes. It was hard to miss on the news."

"We're still unsure if it was sabotage or merely an accident. The truth of the matter is that we may never know. I have begun gathering a list of citizens who have publicly expressed opposition toward the Archon. They are not suspects, but I have begun meeting with them one on one, to discuss our presence here and attempt to convince them that it is in everyone's interest for our relationship to be a positive one."

Archer knew there was more to it than that. "I've heard that on some planets the local garrison commanders have imprisoned such suspects."

Blucher shook his head. "I doubt that will be necessary here. I don't rule it out, but I don't intend to provide those who dislike the government or the Archon with a reason to make trouble."

"Is there a reason you're telling me, sir?"

Blucher gave a short sigh, but it expressed clearly enough his present discomfort. "Archer, your sister wrote another editorial last week calling for the Archon to step down in favor of her brother."

"She was within her rights to do so under the law," Archer said slowly.

"Yes, she was. But at the same time, her name has appeared on my list. I will be meeting with her, just as I have with several other citizens whose political position runs along similar lines."

"Why are you telling me, sir?" Archer asked again.

Blucher looked hard into his eyes. "You are a well-known pubic figure on Thorin, Archer. And you serve under my command. I wanted you to know before you found out somewhere else. I would prefer to have you understand my motives rather than blindly react to them."

Archer gave a long, drawn-out nod. "I appreciate the heads up, sir. You understand, however, that I feel a strong obligation to discuss this with my sister."

Blucher nodded. "Yes, I thought you might. As I said before, it's a simple interview, nothing more—nothing less."

4

On the world of Clinton, an anti-Steiner protest quickly escalated to a small riot, and Lyran Alliance garrison forces were called upon to quell the disturbance. Led by a Pro-Davion separatist named Drancy MacLaw, the rioters failed to obey orders to disperse, resulting in eighty-five arrests and twenty-three deaths.

—Reported by *Word from the Underground*,
    pirate broadcast, Thorin, 5 October 3062

Ecol City, Thorin
Skye Province
Lyran Alliance
9 November 3062

Leutnant Luther Fisk ordered his driver to stop the vehicle several houses away from the Christifori home. Peering out the window, he was surprised to see it wasn't the kind of neighborhood where you'd expect a national hero to live. The houses were unpretentious dwellings with trimmed hedges, narrow, sloping yards, and surrounded by shade trees. It was nothing like the majestic surroundings where he'd grown up.

He holstered his pistol, as did the two soldiers with him. Dressed for urban warfare, the trio looked distinctly out of place in their sleek black vehicle. With their heavy shin and knee pads, blast-vests, visored helmets, and shoulder and elbow pads, they were outfitted more for a riot than a routine pick-up. Another car was dropping off two more soldiers on the next street over to make sure Andrea Christifori wouldn't try to escape via the rear door.

At this moment, Fisk couldn't help thinking of his father, Count Francis Fisk of Odessa, and how different he was from Colonel Blucher. The colonel was too soft, while his father had always taught that a leader must never be afraid to use force to maintain order. Fisk didn't like the colonel. He seemed hesitant to use the power he possessed. Luther Fisk was not.

He knew that Blucher had forewarned Christifori that his sister was on the list of suspects. Fisk believed that was a mistake, that the colonel had overplayed his hand, lost the advantage of surprise. It was true the Christifori girl hadn't fled, but that didn't prove her innocence. Anyone who would dare to speak out against the government, against the Archon, was a person who could not be trusted. Maybe she hoped to get close enough to the colonel to assassinate him, maybe she had the press waiting for some sort of propaganda ploy. He was not about to let her gain the upper hand of the situation. They key to this type of operation was to always maintain control.

"Just like we did with Newburgh yesterday," he said to the two troopers. "Our mission is to escort Andrea Christifori to the fort for a meeting. She is suspected of subversive activity, but our orders are simply to bring her to the Colonel for a discussion. Understood?"

The two big infantrymen nodded. Fisk opened the door and climbed out, flanked almost instantly by his two troopers. He brought up his wrist communicator and spoke into it. "Unit Two, are you in position?"

"Yes, sir," came back the reply.

Fisk nodded to the two troopers with him. Side by side they followed Fisk up the long driveway to the front door of the house, where all three unbuttoned their holster straps. Fisk rang the doorbell and could hear the faint sound of the bell tones on the other side, followed by the sound of footsteps that grew louder as they approached. The door opened halfway and a female figure peered out at them. She looked like a younger, smaller version of her brother, and appeared to be in top physical shape. At the sight of the infantrymen, her face flushed. Fisk guessed it was from anger rather than embarrassment.

"Good morning," he began. "I am Leutnant Fisk of the Fifteenth Arcturan Guards of the Lyran Alliance. I trust that you are Andrea Christifori?"

She nodded and opened the door a bit more. Her dark brown skirt fluttered in the light morning breeze. "I was told you would be coming," she said, a hint resentfully.

"Colonel Blucher has asked that you accompany us back to the fort. He would like to discuss with you the anti-government editorials you have written."

"You are so afraid of my words that you brought armed soldiers?"

Fisk stiffened at the jibe. "You must understand, miss. Some of the people we are sent to escort are not likely to be as cooperative as you. Besides, these troopers, like myself, are here for the protection of Thorin."

She cocked an eyebrow and crossed her arms in defiance. "I was unaware that we had asked for protection, Leutnant. Or better yet, perhaps you're simply protecting us from our rights as free citizens?"

"We could prattle here all day, Miss Christifori. The Colonel is waiting."

"Well, come in if you wish while I get my things." She opened the door all the way and turned to walk down a long hall. Fisk followed her across the hardwood floor, the two infantrymen close behind. Their boot heels echoed loudly, out of place in the otherwise serene surroundings.

In the dining room she walked over to a credenza, then turned and looked at Fisk. "It must be terribly rough on you, Leutnant Fisk."

"What's that, ma'am?"

"Supporting a leader like the Archon and working to keep someone of her ilk in power. Pulling these police-state tactics of dragging people in for interrogations. It must be hard for you to sleep at night."

Fisk's eyes narrowed. She'd pay for her arrogance. If not today, then sometime soon.

"I assure you that I sleep well. This is not an interrogation, but a simple conversation with the colonel. Have you forgotten that the Archon is our rightful ruler? My support of her is total and all the justification I require. Now then, if we can get going . . ."

She turned back to the credenza and opened a drawer. "There's something I want to bring to your Colonel," she said, reaching into the drawer.

Fisk caught a flash of silver, the shape of a knife in her hands along with some papers. There was no time to stop, to think, to process the image. There was only time to react! Luther Fisk drew his pistol and leveled it at her from the side as she began to turn. Yes, that was definitely a knife. The other two soldiers drew their weapons as well.

Fisk didn't remember pulling the trigger, but the next thing he knew there was an explosion and blood spraying outward. Andrea Christifori was thrown back as the first, then the second bullet entered her body. She reeled, as if in slow motion, into the credenza, then twisted down to the floor. His brain was locked on the image as the infantrymen came closer, weapons still drawn, covering the fallen form. It was unnecessary. Fisk was sure she was dead.

He couldn't hear them or the sound of Unit Two bursting in through the back door of the house. One of the infantrymen dropped and checked her pulse, but Fisk knew it was no use. Numbly he took a step forward and stood looking down on her crumpled form.

In her hands were folded-up copies of the newssheets that had published her editorials. Lying near her was a silver letter opener, not a knife. His mouth gaped open as he saw what it was. She must have accidentally picked it up with her bundle of papers. Fisk dropped to one knee and stared at his victim. No sounds reached his ears, which were still ringing from the explosions of the gunshots in the tight confines of the room. There was something around her neck half-hidden by the way her hair fell forward. Lifting away her bloodied hair, he saw the Cameron Star around her neck, splattered with her blood. The smell of gunpowder still stung the air as he stared at the medal. He knew what it was and who it belonged to.

Fisk also knew he was in trouble now. Even his father might not be able to protect him. This whole thing had been a mistake, but no one would believe that, not even Blucher. Worse, there would be those on Thorin who might use this incident against the garrison and the government. They would martyr her, all because of him. He kept staring at the Medal of Honor as he wondered what to do next, what to say.

"I thought she had a weapon," he said, pointing to the harmless letter opener. "She was so damn belligerent. You saw it, didn't you?" he asked, looking up at the two infantrymen. One of them nodded. "I saw the blade, sir," he said, moving the letter opener closer to her open hand with the toe of his boot. He didn't even call it a weapon.

Yes. That was it. Fisk found the dark idea in some back corner of his mind. "She was one of them, a leader of the resistance against the Archon. She must have thought she could attack me or smuggle that knife in to use on the Colonel." He reached over and picked up the newspaper clippings she had been holding and tossed them across the room in a rage.

"You've done well," he said, rising to his feet and running his hand nervously through his hair. "The first shot to defend this world for the Lyran Alliance was just fired here."

His confidence grew with his own words. He locked eyes with his two men and saw that they understood what he'd left unspoken. He just hoped their stories would mesh with the tale he had just handed them.

5

Royalty was out in style last night as Archon Katrina Steiner, wearing a stunning blue Signori dress, attended the National Unity Ball held in her honor. Count Nicholas of Odessa presented the Archon with an exquisite white-gold brooch inset with emeralds. The Archon, true to form, donated the jewelry to the Solaris VII Survivor's Fund, which was established to help Lyran citizens recoup their losses from the rioting on the Game World over a month ago.

—Holovid clip from *You Are There*, Donegal Broadcasting Syndicate, 8 November 3062

Ecol City, Thorin
Skye Province
Lyran Alliance
9 Novemberr 3062

"Catherine," Archer called through the open door of his office to his administrative assistant.

"Yes sir," she responded politely, coming to the doorway. Catherine Daniels had been an employee at Christifori Express since his father's time. She was old enough to be a grandmother in years, but looked much younger.

"I want to send an HPG message to Muphrid, to the attention of Captain Fullerton. Inform him that as soon as he makes the necessary transfers, he is to proceed to Lipton to pick up some additional cargo. There is a current manifest in my system folder. Attach it to the message as well."

She noted his request on her handheld noteputer, then looked up and smiled. "Right away, Mr. Christifori," she said, going back to her desk and closing the door behind her.

Archer had returned to reviewing the firm's current invoices when he heard her muffled voice on the other side of the door talking with someone. Something in her tone caught his attention, a note of urgency. He wheeled his chair back and had just started to rise when she knocked, then cracked open the door.

"Mr. Christifori," she said, "there's someone to see you, sir, and he says it's urgent." Not waiting for permission, she opened the door and a soldier dressed in the formal dress of the Fifteenth Arcturan Guards entered the room and gave him a quick salute—unnecessary since Archer was in civilian garb. He returned it almost numbly as a premonition took hold of him. Something was wrong. Something serious.

"Leutnant-Colonel Christifori?" the soldier asked crisply.

"Yes, Sergeant Major," Archer replied, rising to his full stature at the mention of his rank.

"Sir, there's been an accident. Colonel Blucher sent me to inform you."

A chill ran through him. "An accident?"

"Our men went to escort your sister to the colonel for a routine meeting when apparently shots broke out. I'm afraid, sir, that your sister has been killed."

Archer heard the words, but they barely registered. In his years of military life, he'd seen dozens of friends and allies die around him. And he had killed many himself; it was the nature of war. But that was all behind him, or so he had thought.

Andrea . . . dead. That couldn't happen. It wasn't possible. How could she be dead? He'd been away from Thorin when their parents had died. But this time he was here, and he should have been able to protect her. A roar of blood rose in his ears as rage and confusion whipped into a white hot flame in his mind. Andrea dead?

"How?" he said in a low tone rimmed with anger. "Where?"

"I was told that it was in your home, sir. That's all I know. The colonel asked me to escort you to Central Hospital, where she was taken. He will meet you there."

Archer closed his eyes for a moment. Killed in their own home . . . how? . . . why? Though he felt his blood nearly boil with rage, he somehow kept his outer composure. This soldier was not responsible; he was just doing his job. He would save his ire for the others, for whoever had harmed the only family he had left.

"Very well, Sergeant Major. Let's go."

They had taken him to the morgue to identify the body, which took only moments. Her face was so serene, so peaceful, despite the fact that she'd been gunned down. They had asked if Archer wanted any of her personal possessions, and he had only taken one. Now he held it balled in his fist, could feel the metal digging into the calluses of his hand. It felt cool to the touch, just as it had the day he'd received it from Prince Victor. He'd given it to Andrea as a sign that he would always protect her, but when the time came, it couldn't save her life.

He was standing in the empty hallway outside the morgue and turned slowly at the sound of footsteps approaching. It was Colonel Blucher, looking concerned. He came up and put his hand on Archer's shoulder as if to comfort him. Archer looked at Blucher's hand, then into his eyes. Again, the fires of rage began to burn in his brain.

"Archer," Blucher began, "I cannot tell you how sorry I am. This is a tragedy."

Archer wanted to lash out at the man responsible for this. He wanted, in that single moment, to kill Felix Blucher with his bare hands. Somehow the memory of his sister's calm and peaceful face held him in check. There'd been enough killing today.

"Tell me what happened," he demanded.

"My Provost Officer is still taking statements and is just finishing at the scene. According to Leutnant Fisk, the officer in charge, your sister granted my men access to the house and said she had to go get something she wished to bring with her to the fort. Fisk and the others saw her draw a knife, and they reacted to protect themselves."

"What! A knife? Don't tell me that you believe this? How many soldiers did you send on this duty?" The thought that Luther Fisk was responsible twisted Archer's stomach even tighter. He'd disliked him instantly when they'd met. Now Andrea's blood was on his hands.

"Four total, not counting the Leutnant," Blucher replied.

"Colonel, you've been around long enough to know how that sounds. Do you honestly think that my sister drew a knife on five men with guns?"

Blucher just shook his head sadly. "I'm just telling you what's in their initial statement, Archer. That's why I have the Provost looking into the matter."

"I told her you would be sending for her. It wasn't any surprise. If she were as violent as you say, I have plenty of weapons in the house she could have used. This doesn't add up—and you know it."

"You have my assurances that a thorough investigation will be held, Archer. I promise you I'll get to the bottom of this. The local press has picked up on the story. I want the truth as much as you do."

Archer heard the words, but years in the military had taught him that often times the truth was swept under the rug to save careers. "Sir," he spat out, "I want the full truth, the *real* truth. I want the men or women responsible brought to justice. If that is you, then consider this a threat. If not, consider this a warning to those who did this."

"I realize that this must be hard for you," Blucher said, ignoring the threat.

"No, sir, with all due respect, I don't think you have any idea what this is like for me. Andrea was all I had in the world. She was my only family. I trusted you, and now she's dead at the hands of your men. She was all I had left. Now that's been taken away from me, too. Only this remains . . ." He held up the Cameron Star, then stuffed it into his pants pocket.

"I will get to the bottom of this," Blucher said. "You have my word as an officer and a gentleman."

"Is there anything else, Colonel?" Archer asked coldly.

"If you need anything, please contact me."

Archer's eyes narrowed. "Yes, there is something. I want the head of the man who did this." He couldn't even speak Fisk's name

Blucher bowed his head slightly as Archer turned and walked swiftly to the doors leading to the main hall. He found them hard to push open because of the weight of the people standing on the other side. Almost a dozen people were pressed into the hallway, all attempting to get to him.

Voices swam around him, calling his name, tugging at his shirt. One was louder than the others. A young woman with a head-worn holovidcam pushed into his path.

"Leutnant Colonel Christifori, I'm Katie Winson from DBC. We understand that your sister was killed today by Lyran troops. As a former Medal of Honor winner and a leader in the community, I'm wondering if you can tell us how you feel about all this?"

Archer found a vent for his rage. She never saw his fist coming, but he was sure it would make for good rating. He felt her nose break under the impact of his punch, and when she flew back, it plowed a path through the mob of reporters.

He stepped over the reporter's fallen form. "That's how I feel," he said.

The house was dark by the time he arrived. A handful of neighbors were standing out front, but simply moved aside to let him enter. He knew they were there to show respect for his sister, and they'd placed bouquets of flowers along the street out front. He'd stayed in his office until the calls from reporters became overwhelming. Some of his employees cried openly, others sat in quiet numbness at their desks. They'd all known his sister, had worked under her while he had been gone. He gave them all two days off with pay.

On the front door of his house was tacked a notice from the police. He didn't read it in detail, but tore it off and went inside. As the lights came on, he saw that things were out of place. People, the authorities, had been through everything he and Andrea owned under the guise of gathering evidence. He walked down the hall into the room where Andrea had died.

This was the spot. This was where her life ended. A deep silence hung like a pall over everything. He went to the credenza, where one drawer was still half-open. It was the one Andrea used for her personal papers, and he had respected her privacy. Now he was alone in the big empty house, and privacy would be a curse rather than a blessing.

He glanced into the drawer and noticed a hand-written sheet. Lifting it out, he recognized Andrea's writing immediately. Her penmanship was always better than his, and he had taken to printing everything he wrote. He printed as fast as she could write cursive. He remembered how she used to tease him about it.

He unfolded the sheet of paper and scanned the page. It was apparently a draft of something she'd been working on. Words, hers and those of others. She always carried around scraps of paper on which she jotted her thoughts rather than dumping them into a noteputer.

Written across the top was, "A Time for Conviction, by Andrea Christifori." He read on: "Wendell Phillips once wrote that, 'Insurrection of thought always precedes an insurrection of arms.' We, as loyal Lyrans, are entering the gulf between these two acts. Our leader has begun a campaign of widespread oppression of a people she claims to benevolently rule. In reality, the Archon has systematically abused the power entrusted in her against the people of the Federated Suns.

"And why? She has done so in the pursuit of her own power, her own desires, not those of the common man. Stendhal wrote, 'The shepherd always tries to persuade the sheep that their interests and his own are the same.' I contend that the proclamations of unity and the tripe that comes from the palace on Tharkad are nothing more than the act of a shepherd attempting to control her flock.

"I for one will not stand by and be deprived of my basic freedoms, nor support a government built on the rumors of assassinations and violence against the people it alleges to protect. My convictions, and my soul, are not for sale nor should the people of Thorin's be.''

The piece was not complete. There were other notes scribbled along the margins, where she had considered changes. Archer seemed to hear the words as if she were speaking them, whispering them into his ear. He carefully refolded the sheet and slid it into the breast pocket of his jacket. Then he turned and shut off the light, letting the darkness once more take the room where Andrea had died.

He walked out to the stairway to the second floor. Ascending slowly, Archer Christifori was alone with his memories and the sound of his footsteps echoing on the hardwood floors.

6

While at the Battle Academy on Robinson, Arthur [Steiner-Davion] has grown close to the Sandoval family, who almost universally regard the Draconis Combine as the only enemy worth guarding against. Anti-Combine elements in the Draconis March may attempt to use Arthur as a figurehead—and frankly, Arthur is emotional enough to be vulnerable to that kind of manipulation.

—Page 37, intelligence report prepared by Lieutenant General Jerrard Cranston, SLDF Intelligence Command, for Precentor Martial Victor Steiner-Davion ComStar/Commanding General, Star League Defense Force, 1 November 3062

Ecol City, Thorin
Skye Province
Lyran Alliance
12 November 3062

Like Felix Blucher himself, his office in the fort was Spartan except for a few antique paintings he'd carried with him from command to command. They were prints dating back centuries, military images of soldiers of the nineteenth century. He'd collected them because the uniforms and the expressions on the men's faces hearkened back to a simpler, nobler time. A time of heroic deeds when battles were won through bravery and honor.

There was a crisp knock at the door, and Blucher straightened his uniform slightly. That could only be Leutnant Fisk answering the colonel's summons. On the slate gray desktop was the preliminary report of the incident involving Andrea Christifori. Blucher had interviewed the other personnel present at the scene of the shooting and had arrived at his own conclusions about what had occurred.

Fisk entered the room, his posture rigid in the highest tradition of the Lyran military. "Reporting as ordered, sir," he said formally. Blucher was unimpressed.

"Yes, Leutnant. We have some matters to discuss." He opened the file on his desk and scanned the written report. He had read it twice, then read between the lines. He'd been a soldier long enough to know that many times military justice was anything but just. And his interrogations of the soldiers present at the death of Andrea Christifori were disturbing. Blucher slowly closed the file and gave Fisk a long, hard stare.

"So tell me, Fisk, did you really think you could pull it off?"

"Sir?" Fisk stammered.

"Don't insult me by pretending you don't know what I'm talking about. I've spoken with the others present at the shooting. You should be proud of them. For the most part they held to the story you fed them. One of them finally told the truth—you panicked."

"I reacted as I've been trained to, sir. I saw a weapon and sought to protect myself," Fisk countered, but the tightening of his facial muscles gave him away.

"A lone female civilian, three armed men in the room, two outside, full riot gear, and she knew you were coming. And you believe she was insane enough to pull a knife?" Blucher's voice rose in pitch as he spoke. He was furious. "Your lack of judgment is appalling, Leutnant."

"I did what I thought was right."

"And your attempt to cover this up was"—Blucher groped for the word—"pathetic. I'd say unbecoming an officer, but at this point I'm embarrassed that we are in the same organization, let alone the same unit. What were you thinking? Trying to protect your precious family name?"

"What you call a 'cover-up' was done for your benefit," Fisk said.

"And what do you mean by that?"

"We both know there is a rebel element here on Thorin. We've seen the signs and read the intelligence reports. That's why the Fifteenth was posted to garrison this world. I compiled a list of suspected leaders under your orders, and we could have rounded up and detained them after the terrorist attack on our troops at the bar. This time we've got something even better. The death of one of their leaders. It sends a clear message to those who think to rise up against the Archon. The price of resistance is death. The only way to suppress open rebellion is with an iron fist."

His last words echoed sentiments recently expressed by the Archon in a message aimed at keeping her military forces unified and focused under her leadership.

Blucher stared at Fisk for a moment. Then he almost laughed at the sad stupidity of the man.

"You are such a fool, Luther. You spew rhetoric like a trained monkey and haven't a clue what you're really doing. Yes, some rebellions can be suppressed in the manner you describe. But in this case it will only work against you."

"The Archon—"

"The Archon," Blucher cut in, "is a young woman who is a politician at heart. She has not had to live among the people she rules. Lived with them and fought to preserve their freedoms—the very freedoms you are attempting to smother. Her actions are those of desperation, not leadership."

"You're speaking treason?" Fisk asked angrily.

"No," Blucher replied coolly. "I'm being pragmatic. You've just given these people a reason to fight against us. You've killed a well-known figure who was also a woman and defenseless. A woman whose brother is a global celebrity. You've handed those who might rise against us a purpose, a reason, a cause."

"Sir, with a properly worded press release, the loyal citizens could be easily turned against Christifori. If you do nothing, he will remain a threat to the integrity of your command." The concern in Fisk's voice was genuine.

"You're the only one who sees Archer Christifori as an enemy of the state. All you've done is earn yourself a dangerous enemy."

"You keep speaking with such reverence of our dear Leutnant Colonel Christifori. Did it ever occur to you that he may be one of those working against the Archon?"

"I would rule nothing out."

"If you move now, you can eliminate him as a potential threat."

Blucher shook his head once. "No, Leutnant Fisk. If I do as you suggest, I become part of the problem. I refuse to do that."

"Have you no loyalty to the Archon?"

Blucher was on his feet in an instant, and he

pounded on the desk with such force that it seemed to shake the room. "Never question my loyalty! You *were* my aide, but that does not grant you any special rights, especially now. I am totally loyal to the government and to the office of the Archon."

It was hard to believe the boy's insolence. Felix Blucher had been in a cockpit fighting and killing for the realm before Fisk was even born. If not for his father's influence at court, Luther Fisk could never have risen to this rank or posting. How dare someone like him question Blucher's loyalty? There was a time when such officers would have been drummed out of the service. Now they were merely promoted.

In the long silence, Blucher stared directly into Fisk's eyes, which made the young man look away. The line had been drawn between them, invisible yet real. Fisk still stood at attention, and Blucher could see beads of sweat forming on his brow, which pleased him.

"If I may ask, Colonel, what are your intentions?"

"For you? That is simple. You are under arrest and will stand for court martial as soon as possible."

Fisk sagged visibly where he stood. The angry red on his face drained to white. "You can't be serious, sir."

Blucher placed the knuckles of both fists on his desk and leaned toward the younger man. "I am quite serious. Charges have already been drafted and filed with the Provost Marshal. There are two guards standing just outside the door. They will take you to the brig to await trial."

Fisk trembled, just enough for the trained eye to spot. For the first time since they began to talk, Blucher felt some degree of grim satisfaction.

"I will be contacting my father, the Count."

Blucher was only surprised by the fact that Fisk hadn't already done so. Count Nicholas Fisk carried a lot of weight in the royal court, but Blucher wasn't a man to be swayed by the gusts of political wind. He was a soldier in his heart, and he knew his duty when he saw it.

He also wasn't blind to the risks of court-martialing his aide. It was very possible that high command might intervene on behalf of the boy's father. Until that time, there were rules and procedures that must be followed. "I anticipate that your father will send many messages, try to call in many favors. But Odessa is a ways away, and you will find that under my command, justice is swift."

Fisk's voice was bitter. "I wonder whose side you are on . . . sir."

"I was unaware that there were sides," Blucher returned curtly.

"What are you going to do about the rebel activity? What of Leutnant Colonel Christifori?" Fisk's voice betrayed a hint of fear.

Colonel Blucher hit the small control stud on the corner of his desk. The door to his office opened, and a pair of armed guards entered. One of them was holding a pair of wrist-cuffs. He stepped over to Fisk and smoothly pulled the leutnant's hands behind him and slipped on the handcuffs.

"Don't worry about Christifori," Blucher said sarcastically. "If you behave, I promise not to let him get his hands around your throat." Then the guards turned Fisk around and marched him out of the office.

Archer sat in the family room of his now empty house, almost as if the early evening darkness and shadows were old friends come to visit. It had been a long day with much to be done. He'd made arrangements for the funeral, but barely remembered doing so. There had been several visitors to the house, all expressing their sorrow at his loss. Catherine Daniels had come by with dinner, then burst into tears before he could invite her in. He didn't remember the food. He did remember eating, possibly for the first time all day, but that was all.

Hauptmann Katya Chaffee had also come with condolences from the other members of the Thorin Militia and something else he sorely needed—conversation that took his mind off thoughts of loss or grief. She talked instead of what was going on in the unit, its mundane doings and activities of the day. For a brief moment, he was able to forget. But with Katya's departure, Archer was alone again, sitting in the dark, trying to call up memories of better times.

When he heard the knock at the door, he wasn't sure whether he imagined the sound or if it was real. He got up and walked as slowly as an old man to the front foyer, which Andrea had always referred to humorously as "the reception area" or "the lobby." He turned on the external light and opened the door, squinting in the sudden brightness.

Colonel Blucher stood in the doorway, his long coat unbuttoned, his leather dress gloves in one hand. Archer merely nodded. He wasn't on duty now, and he didn't particularly feel like saluting the officer who commanded the man who'd killed his sister.

"Colonel Blucher," he said flatly.

"I hope I didn't disturb you."

Archer shook his head. "No, Colonel I was just attending to some personal business."

"I wanted you to know, before you heard it in the media, that I have formally charged Leutnant Fisk in the death of your sister. He will be court-martialed as soon as possible."

Archer's face didn't change expression. "Someone must answer for this crime."

"He will, Archer. I've gathered ample evidence. The matter will be resolved quickly."

"Very well, Colonel. Is that all?"

Blucher lowered his gaze for a moment, then looked back at Archer. "If there's anything I can do for you, Leutnant Colonel, please let me know."

Archer stared so hard at him that the colonel actually took a step backward.

"Yes, sir," he said. "You can make sure that justice is done."

With that he shut the door and the darkness closed around him again.

The midday sun made him too warm in his black suit, but Archer ignored it. He glanced around at the others gathered with him on the grassy hillside, saw the sorrow on their faces. He couldn't bring himself to look at Andrea's coffin, which was behind him. It was too much to bear. Some cried. Others looked stunned. He knew the feelings. He'd experienced them all in the last few hours. Right now was not about him or his grief. Now was the time to say goodbye.

He thanked his many years of military life, which gave him the stiff spine to keep himself tall when he felt so weak. Among those in the first row of mourners he saw Katya Chaffee, who bowed her head in greeting. Archer drew a long, deep breath, catching the scent of morning dew. In the distance, he heard the chirping of birds, distant, yet with enough music to keep him focused on the present.

"We come today to pay our last respects to Andrea Kendrick Christifori," he said. "We knew her as a friend, employer, comrade, and beloved sister. She spent her life trying to help better the lives of others, whether it was in running our family business or her work in the community."

He let his gaze travel over the gathering, acknowledging them all. "My sister died before her time. It was a wasteful death, one that didn't have to happen. In the last weeks of her life, she spent much time writing, hoping her words would warn the rest of us that our freedoms come at a price. Her death reminds us that human beings can be corrupted by two things; power and fear. She understood this, and hoped to persuade the rest of us that we must stand up against those who abuse their power, regardless of petty mortal titles or positions.

"Let us never forget her," he said, choking back his words slightly, "and let us never forget the message she tried to give us."

As the crowd drifted away a few minutes after the short ceremony, Katya Chaffee approached. She seemed different, almost odd, then Archer realized that he'd always seen her in uniform. Today, dressed in black civilian clothing, she seemed more human, more female than he'd ever noticed before.

She reached out and touched his arm. "Sir, is there anything I can do for you?"

Archer shook his head. "No, I'll be all right. And we're not in uniform, Katya. Call me Archer."

She nodded. "Your sister was loved by a lot of people."

He watched the other mourners as they moved away. "Yes, she had many friends."

"A lot of us in the unit, as well as friends of mine, have been reading her editorials. They were brilliant. She understood so well what's been happening on Tharkad and throughout the Alliance."

Archer rubbed his brow slightly. "Her beliefs, her words, are what got her killed."

"That's what makes them all the more important. Andrea wouldn't want her ideals to die because she did."

"What are you saying, Katya?"

"I'm saying that she wouldn't want her ideas to end here. If we're going to honor her, we should honor the words she was trying to say to us."

Archer nodded. "I found a piece she hadn't yet

finished. They killed her before the final words could be written."

"I only met her once, Archer, when she came to visit you at the post. But I've been reading her editorials, and I think her last words should be heard—and even acted on."

Archer turned around finally, for the first time able to look at Andrea's coffin being lowered into the ground. Now it's up to me, isn't it? he asked her silently. He picked up a handful of dirt and let it drift over the open grave. Rest in peace, Andrea. Your left your work unfinished, but it will be done.

Then he turned back to Katya and led her away, thinking about many things Andrea had said and what would be his next course of action.

7

In a move that today took the whole Capellan March by surprise, the Eighth Federated Commonwealth RCT attacked the First Capellan Dragoons on the key FedCom world of Kathil.

The Dragoons, recently recalled to Kahi from Verlo by the duke, took over from the Eighth RCT, which was being rotated to a new posting. The battle still rages, but it is still unclear what triggered the attack. Reliable sources within the FedCom military report that the Eighth's commander has been outspoken in his opposition to "leaving the Capellan March exposed to enemies—from within and without."

—Local news bulletin broadcast from the city of New Hope, Kathil, Lyran Alliance, 16 November 3062

Ecol City, Thorin
Skye Province
Lyran Alliance
16 November 3062

Felix Blucher stood in front of the cell and stared into the shadows. The command post's brig was dingy, ill lit, and rank with the same sweaty smell of barracks and brigs all across the Inner Sphere. The cell had two bunks, one toilet, a dull gray concrete floor, a small metal sink, and one man: Luther Fisk. Gone was the crisp uniform, replaced several days ago by a faded orange and red prison jumpsuit. Sitting on the edge of the lower bunk, he glared up at Blucher.

The court martial had been little more than a brief meeting of officers. Because of Archer Cristifori's personal involvement with the victim, he had not been one of them. There were three witnesses, and Fisk's defense was a "no contest" plea. That alone made Blucher suspicious, but the matter was settled within the hour. On the charges of manslaughter and misconduct, the colonel himself had meted out the sentence—thirty years.

Felix Blucher was no fool. He knew the boy's powerful family was already working to win his freedom. Yet, with all the turmoil in the Federated Commonwealth these days, it surprised him how quickly a response came down from on high. A priority HPG transmission had arrived from the palace itself, a message that would surely create more problems on Thorin.

Blucher said nothing for a long moment, knowing that the situation was all about to change. Fisk stood up and walked toward the bars of his cell. "Come to gloat, Colonel?" he said with that arrogance Blucher had come to detest.

The colonel crossed his arms and stared at the young officer, hiding his anger behind a mask of calm. "You've been a busy boy, Luther," he said finally.

Fisk's face suddenly lit up. "I take it you've heard from my father, then?"

Blucher just stared at him for a moment. "A message has arrived from the Archon herself. Your father must have paid dearly for your skin. By order of Archon Katrina Steiner, the sentence of your court martial has been commuted. I have been ordered to restore you as my aide de camp as well. You are a free man."

Though Blucher kept his face stony and his tone neutral, everything in him rebelled at speaking those words. He was a loyal military man who understood how important justice was in order to maintain command. Now that had been usurped by the Archon. Worse yet, he knew that the local population wouldn't stand for it. The Archon was buying her political support with favors like this, leaving men like him to solve the messes it created.

Fisk leaned his head against the bars. "I tried to tell you this would happen, Colonel. My father has great influence with the Court."

"Watch your tone with me, Fisk. I'm not impressed by this little stunt of yours. You may have a father who is owed favors, but you are still under my command."

Fisk acted like he hadn't heard. "When will I be released?"

"In a few moments. First, you and I need to have a little talk. You've scored only a partial coup, my friend. Did you believe you could totally escape punishment? Well, not as long as I am in command."

Fisk gave a short laugh. "Colonel, how I obtained my freedom is not important. You claim to read history. Surely you know that the ends justify the means. You have your orders. Release me."

"You don't understand, do you, Fisk? I will obey, but as your commanding officer, I still have a great deal of leverage."

"And?"

"First off, you're free, but you're also busted to Senior Warrant Officer. Secondly, you'll find a list of assignments on your desk, including kitchen patrol, perimeter security, and the like. For someone like you with such a proven track record, this is the best possible posting. Wouldn't you agree, Warrant Officer Fisk?"

The color momentarily drained from Fisk's face. "You can't be serious. KP duty?"

"I'm quite serious," Blucher said, sliding his access key into the lock mechanism on the cell door. It clicked audibly, and Fisk could now open the door and leave the cell whenever he wished. Instead the newly busted Senior Warrant Officer stood stunned, staring at the colonel in disbelief.

"You're free to get back into uniform and start your duties immediately, my dear Fisk."

Fisk seemed to come back to himself, as if he'd suddenly cogitated an idea. "You overestimate your authority, Colonel. If overturning a court-martial was so easy, it should be nothing at all to get the Archon to restore my commission."

"Perhaps," Blucher said, "but I'm betting that your father must have used up his favors getting you free. He can't go back for more so soon. It will make him look like a fool and insult the Archon that her pardon isn't enough. No, I'm willing to bet that dear old daddy will have to wait a while. And even then, there are things I can do to you as your CO that neither you nor he ever thought of."

"He'll just buck me for a transfer," Fisk countered.

"I've been a soldier most of my life, Fisk. Many officers in the Alliance military are close friends of mine, and most owe me favors because I've never stooped to back-office politics. Yes, you might slip my grip, but you'll spend the rest of your life looking over your shoulder to see if I or your other threat is following you."

"My other threat?"

Blucher was grinning like a cat. "You've made a powerful and dangerous enemy out of Archer Christifori. From what I've heard about him, there won't be many places in this galaxy where you can consider yourself safe. In many respects, I pity you, Warrant Officer."

Archer sat at his desk and slid the bills over to one side as a knock came at the door. It opened slightly and Catherine Daniels looked in. "You have visitors, sir."

"Catherine," he said, leaning back in his chair with a sigh, "you've been holding my calls and keeping everyone else at bay. What's so special to suddenly break your track record?"

"It's Miss Chaffee and a Mister Hopkins. They said it was important, and I saw you with Miss Chaffee a few days ago at your sister's service . . ."

"She's a good friend, Catherine."

"You need a friend like that right now, if you ask me," she said protectively. Archer was used to her treating him more like a son than her employer, and even appreciated her concern. Her presence helped fill a gaping void in his life, as did Katya Chaffee's.

"You're meddling again, Catherine," he said in mock reproach.

"Just doing my job."

"Show them in."

The door opened the rest of the way, and she ushered in his two friends. Katya was dressed in fatigues and did not return his smile when he gestured for the two of them to sit down. As Catherine closed the door, Archer reached out and shook hands with the older officer, Sergeant Major Darius Hopkins. The man had the rough, callused hands you'd expect of the Militia's infantry commander.

"Good to see you both," Archer said. "I must admit that this is unexpected."

Despite his relative good humor, both his guests looked grim. Katya's forehead was furrowed with worry, and Hopkins' mouth turned down sullenly under his thick salt and pepper mustache.

"Something's happened. I can see it on your faces."

"Sir, haven't you heard?" asked Katya. "We came over as soon as we heard it on the news."

"Heard what on the news?" He looked quickly back and forth between Hopkins and Katya.

"Leutnant Colonel," Hopkins said, "that bloody Lyran colonel has released Luther Fisk."

The words hit Archer like a blast from an artillery barrage. His mouth hung open, but only for a moment. "That's not possible. He was court martialed and found guilty."

"Blucher said that the Archon herself cut the orders," Katya explained. "Fisk's daddy pulled some strings in the Royal Court to get his boy out of the brig."

Archer listened in stunned disbelief. He'd ordered his calls held. If Blucher had tried to contact him, he wouldn't have gotten through. "This can't be happening."

"It is, lad," said Hopkins.

"That bastard killed my sister. She was defenseless, gunned down in our home. Now he's free?" His mind raced. Where was the justice? If the Archon did this, then damn that bitch to hell. Then it hit him. Andrea had been right about Katrina Steiner all along.

"Blucher tried to put a good spin on it. He says he busted Fisk in rank, but now he's being forced to retain him as his aide," Katya added. "I'm sorry, sir."

Hopkins gave a scornful laugh. "He even went so far as to try and tell us he will respect the rights of the citizens of Thorin and that people should not overreact to this announcement—that he's taking action to make sure Fisk is properly punished. I've been around the block long enough to know that he's fighting a battle he can't win. The Archon has gone too far this time."

Archer nodded. "Blucher promised me justice would be done. I can't believe this is happening."

"I do," Hopkins said. "Katie Steiner is so wrapped up in tossing her power around that she's forgotten she works for us, not the other way around."

Archer rested his chin on his hand in thought. "You're right. This isn't about Blucher. This is about her, the Archon. She's abused her power."

"We came to tell you, sir, that the entire battalion is behind you," Katya said slowly and carefully, "no matter what course of action you take."

Archer looked into her eyes and saw the same anger and frustration he was feeling. He turned to Darius Hopkins, whose weathered face looked determined and bitter.

Hopkins abruptly stood up from his chair. "Sir— Archer . . . I've known you since you were fourteen and joined the militia. Hell, I trained you myself so you'd qualify at NAIS. I chaperoned your dates when your father was busy, and I helped you study for your finals. When you were promoted, I traveled to New Avalon to stand at your side. When you returned from Huntress, I was there to greet you. I'm here for you now, sir, no matter what."

Archer felt weighed down by the burden of what they were hinting at. "What you two are talking about is treason. You know that, don't you?" His voice was barely louder than a whisper.

"Treason is a word used by an oppressor to describe his victims," Katya said. "We're talking about overthrowing a government that no longer represents the best interests of its people. We're talking liberation."

"Either way we'd be placing Thorin in the middle of a potential civil war like we've seen brewing all over the FedCom."

"Innocent lives may be lost, Leutnant Colonel,"

Hopkins said, "but more than that is at risk if we do nothing."

"Don't kid yourself, old man." The nickname was an affectionate one Archer often used when he and Hopkins were alone. "The Fifteenth Arcturan Guards aren't some green unit. They'll come after us with everything they've got—and then some. Our troops are good, but we're only militia."

"Planning will be the key," Hopkins said.

"And hope," Katya added.

Archer looked first Katya, then at Hopkins, and each nodded in turn. He felt a new burst of energy rush through his body, a kind of drive he hadn't known for weeks—no, make that months. Not since he'd left the service of the Star League. As a military man, he'd had purpose—the bold and noble campaign to crush the Smoke Jaguars and force the Clans to end their invasion of the Inner Sphere. Now, Katrina Steiner, always the loudest proponent of peace, was protecting the guilty and letting innocents be slaughtered.

He suddenly felt some of that same old sense of purpose. "If we do this, it won't be for revenge. The mission is simple; we drive the Fifteenth Guards off Thorin. Without them, the Archon can't impose her twisted justice or petty rules. Thorin will be free, and innocent people won't have to fear for their lives."

"Agreed," Hopkins said, and Katya nodded as well.

"We have much to do before we can make any moves. Blucher will be keeping a sharp eye on us for a while. Let him. We will lay our plans in secret while we work to strengthen ourselves for when the time is right."

"How will we know when that is—when it's time to strike?" Katya asked.

"When there's a reason for the population to rally behind us rather than sit on the sidelines in a fight.

If the people of Thorin back us, the Guards will never be able to stop us.''

Archer looked around the room where he'd spent so much time sitting behind a desk over the last few years. Sometimes it had felt more like a prison than an office. Now it wasn't just Luther Fisk. Archer Christifori was free as well.

=8=

The Lyran Alliance Government News Bureau categorically denies reports that open rebellion has broken out on more than a dozen Alliance worlds. According to official spokesperson Valerie Hart, reports of Davion-sparked terrorism are on the rise, but she disputes underground media reports that some worlds are in open rebellion.

—Holoclip from *Newsline*, Donegal Broadcasting Company, Lyran Alliance, 24 November 3062

Ecol City, Thorin
Skye Province
Lyran Alliance
26 November 3062

Senior Warrant Officer Luther Fisk sat in the small, open-topped transport following along as the security team patrolled the street on feet. The driver matched their slow pace, while Fisk closely observed the reactions of the people they passed. Most gave the soldiers barely a glance, sidestepping out of the way as if they were merely other pedestrians. Others gave them icy stares as they stepped aside. One even stopped in place, forcing the trooper to push past him, their shoulders bumping as he did so. The look on that man's face showed pure hatred.

Perimeter security was one of the few duties left to Fisk after being busted in rank. He was still Blucher's aide de camp, but in name only. Worse yet, the old officer's prediction had been accurate. Fisk had sent a message to his father to protest this new indignity, even requesting that the colonel be reassigned elsewhere. The message, sent faster-than-light via the planet's hyperpulse generator, took a few days to reach his father. Another few days later Fisk received his father's response. The count didn't mince words. He said that the family could do nothing more right now and that his son was going to have to learn to fight his own battles for once.

As the vehicle slowly rounded a corner, ignoring the traffic signal, Fisk still fumed over his plight. The only good news was that members of the Arcturan Guards security force seemed to sympathize with his warnings about the threat of an uprising on Thorin. Most of them believed, as did he, that the bombing of The Foolery had been an act of terrorism rather than a so-called tragic accident. In a short few days, he'd rallied most of them to his position, saying out loud things that they'd only thought. Better yet, getting busted to the ranks of the NCOs seemed to have made him "one of the boys" in the eyes of the security troopers.

Ecol City, the capital of Thorin, was relatively small. It had been all but destroyed during the fall of the first Star League, gutted by bombings and street-to-street fighting. The city, like the old fort, had been rebuilt, but had never returned to its former glory. Fisk had seen some of the urban areas on the northern continent during a recent security review and, despite its appearance, Ecol City was one of the more thriving centers on the planet.

He still believed that Thorin was a powder keg of pro-Davionists waiting to erupt. There had been a few small protests, which he'd ordered surrounded by his guards, only to have Blucher order them back to a more discreet distance. He'd had more luck with his proposed plan for securing a five-square-block area around the fort, which Blucher had approved. Under Fisk's command, military security now patrolled the streets hourly, and this one section of the city was, at least in his mind, relatively safe.

As they reached the corner, he asked the driver to stop the vehicle. Then he got out and went to join the troopers. They were standing before the barren lot that was all that was left of The Foolery. He was thinking that years from now, they would say that this was where it all had begun. He savored the moment, knowing that in this place, the fight to save Thorin from the rebels began.

"Did you men know any of the soldiers who died there?" he asked.

Staff Sergeant Brandon Carmichael, a young man with a prematurely receding hairline, stared out across the empty space. "I knew Sergeant Veerson. Good tanker. You should've seen him when we locked horns with the Jade Falcons. After all that, for him to die here—what a damn waste." The other soldier said nothing.

"Our colonel believes that the locals had nothing to do with it," Fisk said. He knew that wasn't the whole truth, but he wanted to test the leanings of Carmichael, as he'd done with a number of the other troopers. He needed a sense of who was truly loyal to the Archon.

"He's been behind a desk too long, then," Carmichael replied. "The explosion wasn't a gas leak or anything else. It was a bombing."

Fisk played it dumb. "You think so? We never found any conclusive evidence in the ruins."

"We should've arrested anyone even suspected of involvement," Carmichael said. "My sister is in the First Alarion Jaegers, and they arrested more than three hundred suspects in a similar action a few months back. You can bet that stopped the locals in their tracks. They knew that if any more of our soldiers were killed or injured . . ." He sliced one finger across his throat in the time-honored sign for death.

Fisk nodded slowly, as though Carmichael was giving him a whole new perspective on things. "Well, I've made similar suggestions to Colonel Blucher. He believes such measures would only provoke the locals."

Carmichael shook his head sadly. "They say that when you make Leutnant, they cut off your testicles and take a scoop out of your head. And when you make Colonel, they give you one of your testicles back."

All three men chuckled at the expression. "What does he think will happen," Carmichael went on, "that a terrorist cell is going to brag to the media about what they did, that they'll challenge him to a duel or something? This isn't like fighting the Clans or the Draconis Combine. This is about maintaining order."

Fisk didn't respond immediately, as though he were working this whole thing out in his mind. When he spoke, his tone was all sweet reasonableness. "Our colonel is a seasoned veteran. I think he's simply waiting for conclusive proof before he acts."

"But all he's done is talk to people. If he's got a list of suspects, we should round those buggers up before someone else gets killed."

Fisk had led Carmichael, like he had others, down the path of his own logic, letting the sergeant believe he'd arrived there on his own. It was almost too easy at times. "Maybe if there was something that could be proven as more than an accident . . . perhaps then the colonel would act."

"He just might," Carmichael said slowly, pondering the idea.

"No one would have to be killed, either. If the colonel understood the magnitude of the real threat to our command integrity, I'm sure he would respond the way we wanted," Fisk said.

"What about Leutnant Colonel Christifori? Word is that after what happened with his sister, he's out to get you."

Fisk shrugged. "A militia commander is hardly a real threat. He's old news. I'm not worried about him at all. And his unit, all they've got is some outdated, battered equipment. Nothing that poses a real threat. Oh, he's an apt trainer, but he's long retired. Besides, I think some of the problems may be tied to him. His sister was definitely working against the interests of the Archon. And what about that Hauptmann Chaffee, his intelligence officer? Her name has been linked with some of the dissident groups. If the colonel moves against any rebel factions, she'll be arrested and most likely so will Christifori."

There was a hint of truth in what he said. Katya Chaffee had been on his original list of suspects. Fisk also knew that as long as Christifori was a free man, he represented a serious threat. If he could be linked in some way to rebel activity, they could lock him up and throw away the key. And for someone who had killed Archer Christifori's only living relative, having him locked away seemed like a very satisfactory end to his career as a hero.

Archer sat at his desk studying the data display, then rubbed his tired eyes. It was late, and the office felt stuffy. The last few days had been hectic as he continued to shuffle papers and keep up appearances as nothing more than a local businessman. He and the others had to meet at night, carefully laying their plans to put everything in place for when the time was right.

Katya Chaffee paced across the office silently, reading some of the reports that her four-person intelligence team had submitted. Her pacing was oddly reassuring, reminding Archer of his sister's presence on the many nights they too had worked late. Katya had taken the precaution of sweeping his home and office for bugs, but thus far the Lyrans didn't seem to be aggressive about listening in.

"I've run level two surveillance on all of our personnel," Katya said. "There are four possible Lyran loyalists in our ranks. One mechanic, one MechWarrior, two infantry." She slid her noteputer in front of him with the names. "They aren't high risk, but how you want to handle them?"

"We do nothing. When the time comes, we cordially escort them to the door, or better yet, send them on TDY. I don't want any harm to come to them. We part ways as comrades."

Archer knew this wasn't going to be the kind of war he'd fought in the past—a straight-up fight against an enemy. For this one, he'd have to change the way he'd been trained to wage war. He had to concentrate more on strategies for the coming fight than the tactical aspects of individual battles.

"We still have maneuvers slated with the Guards," she pointed out.

Archer nodded. "That will be an important exercise. I want a dossier on every one of the Guards, their 'Mechs, their capabilities, fighting styles, the whole shooting match."

"We could always switch to live ammo. It would be a quick little victory."

"And position ourselves and our cause as the aggressors? Slaughter soldiers who have no chance of fighting back? Not my style, Hauptmann. You know that."

"That's why you're in charge," she said, smiling slightly.

"I heard from Lee Fullerton this afternoon," he said, switching to a subject he liked better.

"Isn't he one of your DropShip captains?"

"Right. The *Angelfire*. He's transporting a hold full of expendables for the Lyrans—missiles and autocannon rounds. He has orders to deliver them to the garrison here on Thorin."

"And?"

"Fullerton and my family go way back," Archer said. "My father co-signed his mortgage, helped keep his family afloat during some bad times. I'm not saying that he owes us, but he's more likely to be loyal to me than to the Lyran Alliance."

"You going to deprive the Lyrans of their precious ammunition?"

"Maybe," Archer said. "I've found something of a munitions expert and have him en-route to the nadir point on the *Shiloh*, my other ship. He's carrying a message for Fullerton and will take care of a couple of other tasks."

Christifori Express boasted two DropShips and a JumpShip. They were far from new, but still represented a potent force. DropShips traveled between stars by hitching a ride docked to a JumpShip, which could leap almost instantaneously from one star system to another.

Katya didn't ask what the mission was that Archer had dispatched, but he could tell she was curious. She knew him well enough to sense when to press an issue and when not to. That was why he'd put her in charge of the militia's intelligence.

A light knock at the door startled them both, but it was Catherine Daniels, arriving with a cup of hot coffee in each hand. She smiled maternally.

"Catherine, it's way past work hours," Archer said. "What are you doing here?"

She set one of the cups down on his desk and handed the other to Katya. "I'm here to help you, sir," she said politely, but with a hint that she knew more than she was letting on.

"Catherine—"

She held up a hand to stop him. "Before you say anything, I'm going to remind you that I've worked for your family for decades. Your sister was like a daughter to me. You've been like the son I never had. My mother worked for your grandfather when he ran the business, then your grandmother after he died.

"I think I know what's going on here, and I want to help. You can try and kick me out, but that won't stop me from trying." Archer recognized that determined tone in her voice and knew she'd never take no for an answer.

"There's great risk in what we're doing," he said.

"There always is. The greater the reward, the greater the risk, your sister used to say, God rest her soul. I've changed your diapers in my time, Archer. I think I know that you're going to set things right."

"Well, I'm going to try," he said.

Catherine sat down in a prim fashion and took out her noteputer. "What do you need me to do?"

Archer smiled. There was something right about Catherine joining them, as if she were a thread to his past, a link to his sister, a way to keep his moral compass charged. "Well, I'm willing to bet that the minute we make our move, Felix Blucher will shut down Christifori Express. We've got a lot of employees. I want to shuffle the cash into funds that he can't trace and that we can access if we need them. Further, I want to make provision for everyone to get paid, no matter how long we're shut down. No one else should suffer because of my decision."

"*Our* decision," Katya said, taking a small sip of the hot coffee.

Catherine finished punching in her notes, then looked up at Archer. "Andrea would be proud," she said.

"I hope so," he said softly. "I wasn't there when she needed me the most. I intend to pay that debt, and I don't think it will be much longer before I get the chance."

9

Unconfirmed reports from Nanking indicate that clashes have occurred between the Nanking militia and the First Federated Commonwealth Regimental Combat Team on that world. Thus far there has been no official comment from Tharkad spokespeople, who have previously denied such reports.

—*News at 11*, Channel 13, Opal City, Thorin,
  29 November 3062

Dublin Swamps, Thorin
Skye Province
Lyran Alliance
30 November 3062

The humid swamp air hung like a shroud around Archer's *Penetrator* as it slogged its way through the bog. The going was slow. With each step, the *Penetrator*'s feet plunged into the muck, sinking deep. He fought the foot pedals and the joystick as the machine sluggishly resisted each step. It had been this way for the last two hours, but it was worth it.

The Dublin Swamps, which ran south and west of Ecol, were notorious for their difficulty of navigation and as the breeding ground of insects of phenomenal size. The equatorial swamps were nearly two hundred kilometers in diameter, with island-like hills rising from the shadowy mire. The exercise Colonel Blucher had planned was a simple mobile engagement. Why he had chosen the swamp was beyond Archer, except that once more it offered a level playing field. This was terrain where neither the militia nor the Guards would have an advantage.

Archer's attitude had changed since their last fire exercise. That had been simply training; this time he intended to learn all he could about the enemy he would soon face in real combat. The next time he fought Blucher's forces, it would be to kill them. Piloting a 'Mech somewhere on this mock battlefield was Luther Fisk, Andrea's murderer. She was dead, but Fisk had cheated justice and was still alive. Archer reserved a special hatred for him, though he tried to keep a distinct line between his desire to avenge his sister's death and his disgust at the actions of Katrina Steiner. On days like this, that line seemed much more blurred.

The terrain presented a number of problems. First, his ground armor was far from effective. The militia had some hovertanks, but not many. He'd hoped to get them to one of the high-ground hills, but had been forced to scrap the plan because the bog was too deep. He and Katya had come up with the alternative of sending the ground armor around the northern edge of the swamps to hit the Guards' rear area. His infantry, under Sergeant Major Hopkins, had dug in along some low wooded hills to set up a series of ambushes. They weren't there to wipe out large numbers of the enemy, only to tie them up and slow them down while Archer and the 'Mech forces moved in. At least when they started, that had been the plan.

This was only a battle simulation, a game the battle

computers played with each other, simulating damage from powered-down weapons and dummy rounds of artillery and missile warheads. To Archer, it was more than that. Sim or not, it would reveal important information about the enemy.

The first day's action went as planned, almost. The Thorin Militia put up a good fight, taking out a number of the heavier Arcturan Guard 'Mechs, but it cost them nearly thirty-percent of their infantry. When the sun came up, the Guards had mysteriously pulled back. Archer knew Blucher was no fool, and that the odd silence and absence of his foe meant the enemy was up to something.

There were a handful of options left to him. The first was to stick to plan, a course of action that had often led to disaster in military history. Besides, his strength had always been the ability to adapt on the fly. At the first sign that something had changed, Archer asked himself what he'd do if he were Blucher, and the answer wasn't long in coming. Blucher had not seen Archer's ground armor the day before, but he must have surmised their position and was now intending to wipe them out piecemeal.

Archer had other plans. "Specter One to all Specters, keep moving. We have eight kilometers to go. Watch your flanks and keep your long-range sensors on the prowl." He had halted the flanking run of his ground armor and ordered them to pull back to a high rocky ridge north of the Dublin Swamps. There, they dug in and hunkered down, waiting for the arrival of the 'Mech forces. Archer knew there were times to divide your army and times to concentrate your strength. The key was knowing when. Archer felt in the pit of his stomach that the time had come to concentrate.

Hauptmann Alice Gett's voice came over his neurohelmet earpiece. "Sledgehammer One to Specter One, I've got bad guys at the front door." Her tone told Archer it was more than a mere probe. She didn't sound scared; Gett was far too much a professional soldier for that. No, it sounded like she was speaking through gritted teeth and locked jaw.

"Specter One acknowledges. Can you hold, 'Hammer?"

"Do I have a choice, sir?"

Archer smiled as he stepped up the tempo of his *Penetrator*'s stride as much as possible without toppling over into the marsh growth and muck. "Sledgehammer One to The Brain, show me a tactical feed of the Guards."

He looked at his secondary display and saw the spots of light that indicated Gett's small company of armor positioned at the top of a wooded hill. The Guards were advancing on three sides. Alice Gett's command was almost totally surrounded and was outnumbered three to one. Almost all of the Guard 'Mechs were accounted for. His own BattleMech forces were concentrated in a short line that was closing on the Guard's rear ranks.

"Specters Five through Eight, break to the east. You're the right flank. Everyone else follow straight up the middle. Let's show these solider-boys just how we locals fight."

Archer climbed to some harder ground and broke into a run toward the hillside. Despite the trees and thick vines, he could make out the forms of the distant Arcturan Guards almost two-thirds of the way up the hill. Specter Five was Warren Ashe, known as "One-Eye" because of the artificial eye he'd gotten while fighting the Clans. His force fanned out along the woods to Archer's right.

His heart pounded as he brought the *Penetrator* into a small clearing where he could get a clear shot and a cleaner view up the hillside. As yet, the Guards didn't realize they were about to be hit from behind. Among them Archer picked out a single 'Mech struggling its way meter by meter up the hill. An eighty-ton *Salamander* striped in maroon and brown camo, its back was still turned to him. There was only one *Salamander* in the ranks of the Guards, that of Senior Warrant Officer Luther Fisk.

Archer nudged his joystick to bring the targeting reticle onto the thin rear armor of the *Salamander*. The change of color came with the target lock tone in his ear, and he immediately fired.

His Clan-built extended-range large lasers both hit. The beams had been powered down, but the simulation programs in both computers registered the devastating damage. The paper-thin rear armor on the *Salamander*'s center and right torso was gone. The mock-energy of the blast ripping into the internal structure, the guts, of the BattleMech, stopped Fisk's *Salamander* in its tracks. It seemed to quake as its battle computer registered simulated internal explosions. Archer grinned to himself.

All along the Militia line, his Sledgehammer 'Mechs poured their fire up at the rear of the Fifteenth Guards. Caught between the ground armor at the top of the hill and the surprise force at the bottom, most of the Guards turned and attempted haphazard charges back down the hill. A Guards *Hollander* paused long enough to let go a salvo from its gauss rifle, the dummy slug shredding fictitious armor off Archer's right torso. The computer rocked the 'Mech back to simulate the hit. Sweat ran down his body inside his coolant vest as he fought to compensate from the kinetic force of the impact. A cluster of long-range missiles twisted and snaked near him, firing at their maximum range but missing their mark.

Archer wanted to go after Fisk again, but there was work to do. He spied the heavily modified *Dervish* piloted by Sergeant Kristine Rhelms, Specter Eight. The 'Mech, which had already seen too many decades of action, fired a salvo of LRMs into a Guard *Panther*. The *Panther* vibrated, so riddled with mock missile fire that it crashed backward into the hillside.

In the distance, Archer saw the menacing form of an *Atlas*, Colonel Blucher's 'Mech, slugging it out with two lighter 'Mechs of the Militia. Blucher's powerful *Atlas* waded into them, firing, dodging, then lumbering ahead.

One of his 'Mechs dropped fast, but Archer did not join in. The *Hollander* that had gone for him before was attempting to break through. He brought most of his medium pulse lasers on line and fired. The *Hollander*, an odd-shaped machine with the tube-barrel of its gun jutting out from the right shoulder, was making a run for freedom.

For a moment he forgot that the barrage was a powered-down assault. The green pulses of laser light lit up the space between the two 'Mechs as the *Hollander* caught the fire in its right torso and arm. The wave of heat generated was only slightly less than if he'd fired the weapons for real. His damage display showed that the *Hollander* had lost one arm and its only weapon.

Archer began to head in the direction of the *Atlas*, signaling to his mangled ground armor on top of the hill. "Specter One to Sledgehammers, we got their attention. Hit them from behind now." There was no verbal confirmation, just the visual one as the tanks began to rush down the hill, once again hitting the Guards from behind.

A Militia Savannah Master swept down past a dull green-gray Guard *Vulcan* that was attempting to jump free of the area. Savannah Masters were fast little armored hovercraft that had only cardboard for armor and minimal firepower. In battle, they stung just hard enough to demand attention. As Archer spotted the *Atlas* in the distance, he also noted that the *Vulcan* was pouring fire at the little bug of a hovercraft, but not hitting it.

He locked onto the *Atlas* and was just about to let go against Blucher when his own 'Mech rocked from a massive impact against one side. A glance at his damage display showed that he'd taken nearly thirty-five long-range missile hits all along his right arm, torso, and leg. His armor had held, but the one leg had very little left. Another hit there and he'd be as crippled and worthless as the *Hollander* he'd shredded. With a muttered curse, Archer torso-twisted to face the new foe.

In the distance, he saw the maroon and brown form of Luther Fisk's *Salamander* standing in place, leveling itself to give its missiles a more stable firing platform. Archer brought his reticle onto target as another wave of twenty long-range missiles lanced out at him, simulating hits on his left leg and center torso. It wasn't too bad, but enough to spoil his target lock.

Then it happened. A Militia tank, a distinctive olive green Burke, broke like a charging animal through the brush behind the *Salamander* off to Archer's right. It was Sledgehammer One, Alice Gett. Her turret swung into line as Archer also brought his weapons to bear. The moment seemed to stretch out in slow motion as Fisk's *Salamander* brought its own missiles into a locked and loaded mode.

There was a flash as the Burke's two remaining powered-down particle projection cannons unleashed their simulated fury. Fisk's rear armor was already gone, and Gett would be credited with the kill. Simulating a breach, the *Salamander*'s fusion reactor shut down, and the 'Mech fell onto its side, twisting and rolling into the brush.

Archer ran forward to where Fisk had dropped, scanning the battlefield as he went. Blucher had dispatched two of the three 'Mechs engaging him, but his *Atlas* was so damaged there was little fight left. Two of the damaged Guards had broken free of the line of battle, only to stumble into the remains of Hopkins' infantry. Though hurt themselves, the ground-pounders were holding their own while "One-Eye" and the two remaining 'Mechs in his lance provided assistance.

For all intents and purposes, the fight was over. The Thorin Militia had handed the Fifteenth Arcturan Guards a pounding. This time there was no mistake, no gray area as to who was the winner. It was clear that the Militia had held the field of battle, despite the sudden change in plans.

That only left one matter.

Archer's heart was still pounding in his ears as he moved up to the fallen form of the *Salamander*. Somewhere in the armored cockpit head was Luther Fisk, strapped safely into the command couch, no doubt looking up at the *Penetrator* towering over his helpless form. Archer stopped and gazed down at his enemy, the man who had taken his sister from him—taken his life from him. His eyes narrowed, and he heard a roar in his ears as his blood pressure seemed to peak

Without saying a word, he lifted one of the *Penetrator*'s feet and held it in the air. Keeping the 'Mech's balance was tricky, but he had years of practice. The giant foot hovered over the *Salamander*'s cockpit. He knew that, down below, was Luther Fisk looking up in sheer terror.

It would take so little . . . A slight jostle of the foot pedals and he could smash half of the *Penetrator*'s seventy-five tons through the armor of the fallen *Salamander*. His sister's killer, her assassin, would become no more than a greasy brown-red smear in the mud under his feet. Given the angle of his fall, Fisk could not eject, and climbing out would make him an even more inviting target.

Still with his 'Mech's foot lifted in the air, Archer heard a voice coming over the commline. "Leutnant Colonel Christifori, I have signaled our defeat. The victory goes to you and your Militia." It was Colonel Blucher's almost aristocratic tone of voice. Archer didn't look to see him, but he knew that the colonel was nearby. He was being watched, not just by Blucher, but by everyone in the vicinity.

He said nothing. He simply stood with the foot poised to crush Fisk.

"Archer," Blucher said in a softer tone. "Killing him will not bring your sister back."

Archer stared down at the cockpit below him. He could not see much of it because of the position of the foot. He wondered how Fisk liked it, having the shadow of death hanging over him.

"Don't martyr him, Leutnant Colonel," said Katya Chaffee. "Andrea wouldn't want it. Not this way. There'll be other times, a better way."

Archer stared down for another long moment. Slowly, methodically, he set the *Penetrator*'s raised foot back down on the ground. The *Salamander*'s cockpit opened, and Fisk climbed out. His body was drenched in sweat, and he was almost shaking with fear. He ran to the *Atlas*, which stood a few dozen meters away. Archer reached over and opened his own hatch. The cooler air outside the cockpit made his skin tingle as he made sure his holster and side-arm were in place around his waist.

Blucher was making his way down the handholds of his *Atlas* at the same time Archer was also descending to the ground. Luther Fisk was waiting for him and began babbling away while Archer took long, slow strides to join them.

"Arrest him," Fisk said, stabbing a finger toward Archer. "He was going to kill me."

Archer was stony-faced, giving Fisk no more emotional energy than if he were a fly. Blucher stood like a tree himself, looking at Fisk. "Shut up, Fisk," he said.

"He tried to kill me," Fisk stammered.

"If he wanted to kill you, he could have," Blucher said.

"You have a duty to perform. I want him brought up on charges."

"Do that, Colonel," a deep voice said from Archer's side, "and I think I speak for everyone on Thorin when I say Luther Fisk will never live to see the trial." The voice belonged to Darius Hopkins. He was covered in mud, and his fatigues were torn from the thorny vines.

"Is that a threat?" Blucher demanded

"No," Katya said from Archer's other side. "It's a reality."

Archer turned and saw that many of his Militia force were gathering around. Across from them, the stragglers of the Guards had also started to gather.

Now is not the time, Archer told himself. He would kill Fisk, but not today. Doing so would only ruin important plans. He would turn away from the brink . . . *this time.*

"Colonel, you have my apologies," he said calmly.

"Then that will suffice, Leutnant Colonel."

Fisk was stunned. "You can't just let him walk away. He was going to crush me."

Blucher looked from Fisk to Archer. He was a veteran commander who understood that if this turned into a brawl, it might end up spilling into the streets of Thorin once word got out. That was already happening on other FedCom worlds. "You were mistaken, Fisk. The Leutnant Colonel was simply holding his foot raised to maintain his balance." He reached out and gave Fisk a hard, probably painful squeeze to one shoulder. "And this matter ends *now.*"

Archer turned and walked back toward his 'Mech.

One by one, the other members of the Thorin Militia followed suit. He'd gone only a few steps when he heard Blucher call after him.

Archer turned quickly. Fisk was gone, probably gone to slink off into a corner and sulk. Colonel Blucher stood in his coolant vest and shorts, his combat boots covered with mud from the swamp. "You and your force did an outstanding job today. Good work." As a gesture of honor and respect, he saluted.

Archer stood at attention and returned the salute. "Thank you, sir." Then he turned and continued on toward his 'Mech. When he reached the giant metal foot of his *Penetrator*, the very foot that had almost taken the life of his sister's killer, he leaned wearily against it.

"That was close," Katya Chaffee said softly, coming up beside him.

"Too close." He rubbed his forehead to soothe the headache he felt coming on. "Do you know the sad part of all of this, Katya?"

"No, what?"

"I *like* Blucher. I'll do what I have to, but it may mean killing someone I respect." Without another word, he grabbed the nearest handhold and started the long climb back up to his cockpit.

10

In recent public appearances, young Arthur Steiner-Davion continues to caution our people that the Federated Commonwealth must remain vigilant in its dealings with our old enemy, the Draconis Combine. Many try to tell us Theodore Kurita is no threat to the worlds of the Draconis March while he serves as First Lord of the Star League. But was it not First Lord Theodore who brazenly stole the Lyons Thumb planets not so many months ago? And could such a small bite ever satisfy the appetite of the Dragon?

—Pirate radio broadcast by the anti-Combine political sect The People Unbound, Robinson, Draconis March, 4 December 3062

Ecol City, Thorin
Skye Province
Lyran Alliance
5 December 3062

Colonel Blucher stood at the communications console in the Fifteenth Arcturan Guards command bunker, staring at the editorial enlarged and hovering in virtual space over the holographic display. He had set up several data searches to seek out any media clues that might lead him to those opposing the Archon. It had been his idea and Fisk's duty to implement. If the bombast like this had popular support, then matters were worse than he'd thought.

This editorial was more disturbing than any of the other half-boiled rhetoric they'd turned up. It was the voice of a dead woman, Andrea Christifori. According to the accompanying note, it was her last written commentary on the plight of Thorin. The piece was long, and there was a noticeable change of style from the fourth paragraph down. Blucher realized what must have happened. Andrea Christifori had died before finishing the piece, and someone else had completed it.

None other than Leutnant Colonel Archer Christifori. The editorial was entitled "A Time for Conviction," and Christifori's name was emblazoned under his sister's. That disturbed Blucher almost more than the seditious sentiments expressed in the piece. No member of the Lyran Alliance military would put his name to such a document and go unpunished. However, Blucher wasn't sure he had the authority to discipline Archer until he'd fully mobilized the militia.

"I see you've read it as well, Colonel," came a voice from behind him. Blucher turned to see Luther Fisk standing there and that he'd wasted no time restoring his Leutnant's rank insignia. The latest order had taken some days to come down, but arrive it did. Apparently Fisk's family still had influence to burn. Field Marshal Nondi Steiner had personally counter-signed the order reinstating the young fool to his full rank. The usurpation of Blucher's authority was now complete, but he would never let Fisk see that he knew it.

"Yes, I've read it," Blucher said, shutting off the

holoprojector. "It must bother you, Leutnant, a voice from the dead reaching out from the grave."

Fisk was cocky as ever. "If you had cracked down on Christifori when I suggested, this trash would never have seen the light of day."

Blucher was in no mood for his insolence. "That's enough, Fisk. Remember, you are merely my aide and an officer under my command. The last I checked, freedom of speech had not been revoked."

"Yes, sir," Fisk said, surprisingly meek. He glanced at his chronometer. Then, "We really should be going, sir."

Fisk had stepped up security patrols, per Blucher's orders, and today had arranged for an inspection. He checked the time again. "Your car is waiting, Colonel."

Blucher walked out the door, with Fisk close behind as they left the command bunker. Outside, the normally bright blue Thorin sky was streaked with deep purple clouds edged with wisps of white. A cool breeze blew across the courtyard as the two headed toward a sleek black hovercar flying the flag of the Fifteenth Arcturan Guards. It was Blucher's personal vehicle, and he used it anytime he wanted to get around the city. With the defense perimeter extending outward from the fort to the city streets, a driving tour was in order.

The colonel was some ten meters from the hovercar when it exploded with a blast of light and a sound that went from loud to nothingness. He felt a thunderclap of force hit and hurl him through the air. His lungs exhaled, his eardrums popped, and his eyes were blinded by bright light and twisting colors. He couldn't see, but he landed hard—hard enough that he had to gasp for air. Stunned, not understanding what had just happened, he rolled over on the ground and craned his neck to see his car.

Which no longer existed. In its place was smoke,

black and twisting in the air. Fire dotted the ferro-crete parking area, and several other burning hov-ercars also sent gray and black smoke upward. Where his vehicle had been parked was a small crater gouged out with furious power.

Staggering through the smoke was the form of Lu-ther Fisk. His uniform's right arm was torn in several places. He was shaken, but seemed uninjured.

"Colonel!" he called out, spotting Blucher. "Your leg!"

Blucher didn't know what he was talking about. He didn't feel anything wrong with his leg. Looking down then, he saw a small piece of the frame of the hovercar sticking out the back of his thigh where it had stabbed into him like an arrow. Slick red blood drenched his pants leg. Only when he saw the wound did he feel a pain that rippled through his whole body. Fisk dropped next to him on his knees, staring at the wound.

Training kicked in. "Take off your shirt," Blucher commanded. "Tie it around my thigh. Use it as a tourniquet."

Fisk seemed dazed, but he obeyed. He pulled off his torn and flash-burned shirt and tied it tightly above the wound. Already a fire team was starting to pump foam and water on the nearby fires. One of the Guards medics came over and knelt down next to Fisk, gently pushing him aside. Blucher looked away, toward the blast, as the medic worked on him. It was better than watching. He felt the occasional numb tug and the sharp, stabbing pain of his wound.

Fisk moved into the colonel's field of vision. "I don't believe it," he said. "A bomb."

Blucher's mind was still processing the pain as well as the sudden turn of events. "You're right. Sound an alert to perimeter security."

"Already done, sir," Fisk replied, drawing in a

long breath. As if to confirm, the alert klaxon began to blare in the background.

"This is madness," Blucher panted out, wincing sharply as the medic continued to tend to his wound.

"Rebels. They were trying to kill you, sir."

Blucher could only shake his head in confusion, despite the evidence still burning nearby. "Why me?"

"Kill the head and the body dies," Fisk replied. "To these Davion-lovers, you are the Lyran Alliance on this world."

The medic leaned into Blucher's field of view. "Sir, I've stabilized you, but we're going to have to operate. I'm going to give you a sedative." Before Blucher could say a word, the young medic had jabbed him with a needle. As the medic slid the emergency hypo into his sleeve, Blucher felt the only moments of rest he was likely to get for weeks to come.

Katya stood behind Archer at his desk, the two studying the image on the built-in holoprojector. It showed the small crater where the explosion had occurred and the injured form of Colonel Blucher being carried away from the scene of the blast. The reporter narrating over the images spoke of "Davion terrorists" and "local radicals." Archer jabbed his finger down on the control button and the scene vanished.

"Not good," he said solemnly. It was an understatement and he knew it.

"One thing's for sure, they're going to start cracking down. That's why I came over here as soon as I got the news," Katya said.

Archer frowned. "The media is already spinning this. 'Davion terrorists.' How could they know that? The explosion took place only an hour ago. Already they're trying to whip the population into their camp." Archer wasn't sure what bothered him more, that someone had tried to assassinate the colonel or that the press was exploiting it. In the end, he knew it didn't matter.

"I've checked with all of my anti-government contacts," Katya said. "They all deny responsibility for the bomb. I'm not saying none of them are capable of doing this, only that none of them is claiming credit for it."

Archer rubbed his chin in thought. "It probably doesn't matter who's responsible, Katya. This has given the Steinerists what they've been lacking till now, an irrefutable excuse to crack down. It may force us to accelerate the timing of our plans." The bombing had handed the government a justification for coming down as hard here on Thorin as it had on other troublesome planets.

He, Hopkins, and Katya already had a plan for how to respond to something like this. Now that they had their pretext, the Lyrans would most likely start rounding up suspected terrorists. FedCom Anti-Terrorists Manual, Chapter Three, Archer thought. There would be curfews, restrictions on the media and the right to protest. Even travel would stop. There would probably be raids, perhaps even a few trumped-up charges and an execution or two. The propaganda machine would paint these as actions necessary to safeguard the citizens of Thorin. Resistance would increase, as would the reprisals against both the guilty and the innocent. Brute force would rule, and Thorin would be crushed under the Archon's iron heel.

Archer saw the inevitable unfolding before him, and he felt too weak, too mortal to stop it. He touched the chain around his neck and the Cameron Star that hung from it. Wordlessly he pulled the medal out and sat looking at it in his hand.

He'd worn it only a few times before giving it to Andrea, and she'd died wearing it. Thinking of her and how fearless she was in her convictions, he wondered if he had the strength to press forward, to try and change the course of events. Maybe, maybe not, he decided. He hadn't earned the medal because of some heroic idea about changing history. He was a soldier and had done what he had to do, nothing more, nothing less. On Huntress, reason wouldn't have advised him to take on so many Smoke Jaguars at once, but he'd acted from a soldier's instincts. If he'd hesitated, tried to analyze whether or not he could succeed, the lives of the men and women he'd defended would have been lost instead of saved.

That was all the answer he needed: Do what had to be done.

"Archer, what do you want me to do?"

"Alert your contacts in the city. Things are about to get worse. Tell them not to react, not yet. It's important that we have the support of the people, but acts of violence will only turn them against our cause. Tell your contacts we need to meet, coordinate our efforts. Standing together, we cannot . . . no, *will not* fail."

Felix Blucher stared intently at the list Leutnant Fisk had handed him. The dull gray-green of the hospital walls and the antiseptic smell were almost as irritating as the pain in his leg. Several hours had passed since the explosion, and it looked like Fisk had been right all along. Traces of explosives recovered at the site seemed to be of Davion manufacture. While no group had claimed responsibility for the bombing, a swift reaction was necessary.

He quickly scanned the list of possible suspects drawn up weeks ago after The Foolery bombing. Some of these people may have been responsible for the attack that nearly killed him. A few seconds more and he'd have been close enough to be killed in the explosion. All he'd wanted was to be fair with these people, and they had repaid him with an attempt on his life.

"This is the entire list?" he said, rattling the sheet in his hand

"It is the primary list of suspected radicals, sir," Fisk said. "There is a secondary list. Shall I order them rounded up?"

Blucher looked up sharply at the junior officer. He spoke so casually about revoking the rights of people that it was hard not to be suspicious of his motives. The colonel had seen it before in his long career—young men tasting power for the first time, letting it go to their head. Power was as heady as a drug, and some men would do anything to get more.

"I want you to listen carefully, Leutnant. You will bring these individuals in for routine interrogation only. No physical harm, no cruel treatment. We have no evidence to link them to what happened yet. I just want them questioned. You may hold them only if you have evidence against them."

Fisk was a little surprised. "But Colonel, I thought that after being attacked that you would, well—"

"I told you before, Fisk, I'm a student of history. If you come down too hard on these people, you'll only add fuel to the fire. You've already given them a martyr in Andrea Christifori. Don't make matters worse."

Blucher had intended the Christifori comment as a verbal slap, and Fisk seemed to take it that way. "I understand, sir," he said, lowering his head.

Blucher leaned back against the crisp white pillow and closed his eyes. His young aide could never have guessed how tempted the colonel was to strike back at these terrorists, but that was not his way. Other officers on other worlds might be wrong in their handling of similar situations. Only by remaining calm and in control did Blucher believe he could keep

Thorin safely under the aegis of House Steiner for decades to come.

At the scene of the bombing a security squad patrolled the perimeter of the blast site. Fisk arrived in a hovercar, then climbed out and approached the security cordon with a spring in his stride that he hadn't felt in weeks. He now had just what he needed to act—permission from his commanding officer. He'd been given restrictions, but the old man couldn't be everywhere at once. He couldn't possibly know what happened in every interrogation.

The nearest guard gave him a quick salute, which Fisk returned. The man, Staff Sergeant Brandon Carmichael, handed him a small device that Fisk quickly slipped into his pocket. The plan had been simple yet effective. He worked it out in the wee hours of night with others of like mind—true loyalists of the Archon and the Alliance. The device in his pocket was the remote detonator Carmichael had used to trigger the explosion. Fisk couldn't help smiling, partly because things were going well and partly from the satisfaction at having manipulated Felix Blucher with such ease.

"I take it everything went as planned, Leutnant?" Carmichael said.

"I have been ordered to take some action against the local rebels," Fisk said almost gleefully, avoiding a direct answer.

"Finally." Carmichael gave a mock sigh of relief. "I guess you were right. It just took some prodding."

"Yes," Fisk murmured. "Some prodding . . . but for now, we have work to do, you and I. We've got some suspects to apprehend."

11

"We're not performing mass arrests as some of the media has implied. This is a routine investigation, nothing more."

"Is it true that your investigation has led you to target members of the Thorin Militia?"

"No comment."

—Holoclip from interview with Media Liaison Leutnant Luther Fisk, *Thorin Week in Review*, Donegal Broadcasting Company, 6 December 3062

Ecol City, Thorin
Skye Province
Lyran Alliance
6 December 3062

Leutnant Colonel Archer Christifori's office at the Thorin Militia HQ differed in many ways from his more elegant office at Christifori Express. The only similarity was the way the paperwork was arranged in neat stacks on his desk. Otherwise, there was no question that this room was military in nature. The walls were painted a glossy gray that was scuffed and chipped in places. The windows were frosted-glass coating over thick, slightly discolored armored glass. The painted floor—lifeless gray concrete—was even more battered-looking than the walls. The battleship of a desk was metallic, heavy, and so outdated that the style was starting to become a collector's item. And there was a certain odor, a mix of over three centuries' worth of cigars, perspiration, dust, and must that was oddly familiar.

Archer sat making entries to his noteputer with the same sense of urgency that had kept him, Katya, and Hopkins so busy of late. The sheer logistics of their proposed operations were staggering. Not only did he need a plan for getting his personnel and gear out of Ecol City to one of the three bases they were secretly staging in the countryside, but he also needed one for evacuating and hiding their families. Far too many times in the history of the Inner Sphere innocent family members had been held hostage to force military leaders to capitulate. Though Archer didn't believe Blucher was that kind of man, someone like Fisk was obviously capable of such acts, and worse.

At least one phase of the planning had already been put into motion. Captain Fullerton had brought in the Express DropShip the day before and unloaded the cargo containers intended for the Arcturan Guards—tons of long- and short-range missile ammunition and mines. What no one knew was that Archer's other DropShip, complete with a munitions expert, had been docked with the transport for days, performing some transfers and alterations to the cargo. The Lyran Guards had been so focused on the arrival of the DropShip that they'd paid no attention to the fact that the ship had lifted off and, flying under radar, had disappeared, with no flight plan filed.

There was a rap at his door, a knock of urgency. He encrypted the file he'd been reading and went to the door. It was Katya Chaffee, with an odd look on her face. Beyond her he saw why. She was surrounded by a squad of Arcturan Guards and two officers. One he knew instantly as Luther Fisk, once again wearing his Leutnant insignia and a fresh, cocky expression.

Next to him, in his long black formal overcoat, was Colonel Blucher. He stood leaning slightly, his weight supported on a cane. He betrayed no emotion as Archer gave him a quick salute, which he returned. Then he limped through the office door, brushing past Katya as if she wasn't there. The security squad stood at the ready, their rifles held up, as if they would, on a single word, level them and fire. Blucher motioned with his free hand into Archer's office, and two of the troopers followed him in.

"Good to see you up and around, sir," Archer said.

"Yes," Blucher said abruptly, taking a seat. "Sit down, Archer."

Archer didn't argue. "Problems?"

Blucher nodded. "I must say that I was surprised to see your name added to your sister's editorial. The language was less than supportive of the Archon and her policies."

"Given that Andrea died at the hands of the Alliance military on this world, I thought it fitting that her final thoughts be known."

"Of course," Blucher said, as if the two of them were dueling with swords rather than words. "But that makes what I've come to tell you all the more difficult, though I trust you will receive it with an open mind. There is strong evidence that Davion supporters were involved in this last attack. As you know, I've tried to use my command as a positive force for the people of Thorin. If I overreacted to this latest terrorist bombing, it could result in matters getting even further out of hand."

"That's true," Archer said. He leaned his elbows on the desk and templed his fingers.

"You would also agree, I'm sure, that such an attack on a military installation is intolerable. You know what something like this can do to the morale of the men under your command."

Archer nodded; there was no point to rebut.

"As such I am initiating two courses of action. First, I am formally mobilizing the Thorin Militia, placing you and your unit directly under my command. In the next few days, we will fully integrate the two units within the infrastructure of the Guards."

"Understood, Colonel," Archer said.

"Good. I am also ordering that the suspects in this attack be brought in for formal questioning."

"Sir, this will turn the populace against you. Are you sure you want to go down this path?"

Blucher's eyes narrowed slightly. "The orders came down from High Command. I may not like it, but I have no choice. As it is, I'm still not cracking down as hard as my orders instructed." He adjusted his wounded leg slightly. "It's not my intent to make matters worse here on Thorin, only to maintain order."

"I understand, sir," Archer said, and that was the hard part, he *did* understand. But being a good solider simply wasn't enough any more since Andrea died. The time had come to be a good leader. Everything was changing.

"Your name is on the list, Archer, but I think it would be inappropriate at this time to question a man of your stature in the community. It was only because of that editorial that your name came up at all, and by your own account, they are your sister's words, not yours."

Archer nodded, knowing Blucher was testing the waters of his loyalty.

"Also on the list is your intelligence officer, Hauptmann Chaffee. She has been seen associating with several Davion loyalists on Thorin. We may learn something by questioning her."

"I have known Katya Chaffee for several years, Colonel. You have my word that she is no terrorist." Not yet anyway . . .

Blucher rose to his feet, leaning heavily on his cane. "Be that as it may, we will escort her to the fort. It's just a formality. In the meantime, I will set in motion the plans to integrate the Militia into the Arcturan Guards—just for the duration of this unpleasantness."

Blucher walked laboriously to the door and opened it. Outside, the security detail was putting the handcuffs on Katya. Archer's and Katya's eyes locked for a second, and he saw that she was scared. Katya had been a MechWarrior once, but had been so severely injured in battle that she no longer qualified to fight. She'd been injured protecting these people, Archer thought angrily, the very people now handcuffing her.

Darius Hopkins had come over to see what was going on, but Archer shook his head very slightly when it looked like he might say or do something. Other members of the Thorin Militia were also starting to gather around. The temptation was there. With Blucher outnumbered and surrounded, Archer could simply bark an order and turn the tables instantly.

He didn't because the time still wasn't right. For his plan to work, they needed to have the people with them. Blucher's crackdown would eventually win the rebellion more popular support, but he doubted that alone would be enough.

Blucher gave Archer a quick salute and he, Fisk, and the troopers led Katya across the 'Mech bay and outside. Archer motioned for Hopkins to join him as he returned to his office.

Hopkins reached him in two quick strides. "Sir,

just give the word and we'll hit these bastards with everything we've got."

Archer put his hand on his old friend's shoulder. "She's not the only one they're bringing in. This whole thing is right out of the Lyran Alliance manual on civilian control. Blucher's ordered a dragnet to pull in anyone who's even vaguely associated with someone who knows something about that blast. He told me that my name is even on the list."

"You don't think he suspects, do you, sir?"

Archer shook his head. "No. He's fishing, hoping to provoke an overreaction and make his enemy tip his hand. I know the game. Hell, I was trained the same way."

"What about the Hauptmann?"

"She'll be fine. Katya will never talk, and I think he's too honorable to use drugs on her. For the moment, we've got other problems. Blucher is mobilizing the unit, which means we've got to call up everyone to active duty. He intends to integrate our commands."

Hopkins' bushy eyebrows furrowed at the words. "If they combine our command structures, we'll never be able to carry out our plans."

"I know," Archer said. "But the time just isn't right yet, Darius. That doesn't mean I'm going to sit by and do nothing. We'll start getting the families of our people to safe locations the way we planned. Tell them we'll be making our move soon and that they'll have to be ready on short notice.

"We'll also start moving some of the electronics gear to Base Camp One. Use your personal truck for that. They'll be expecting us to move the gear with the militia's Prime Movers, so we have to fool them. Also, I want you to pull Katya's operation files and intelligence dossiers on the MechWarriors we've fought in the Guards. Let's get this information circulating. Purge her noteputer and smash the storage chips—just in case Fisk and his friends decide to do more than ask her a few questions.

"And the three Lyran loyalists in our ranks will soon get orders to carry out an intelligence survey on the southern continent." These were the Thorin Militia members that Katya and Hopkins had pinpointed as potential risks because of their strong support for the Archon, despite her recent despotism. Temporary assignment half a world away should keep them from interfering in Archer's plans.

"That ought to keep them out of our hair," Hopkins said. "Sir, why not just have us break out now? The troops are ready. Damn, I thought they were going to jump those security folks when they showed up and took Katya. Worse yet, Fisk was there, and you know how the unit feels about him after all that's happened."

"We don't move until I'm sure we've got the support of the local population. Otherwise, Blucher and his cronies will simply paint us as terrorists."

Archer knew Hopkins wanted to ask when they would act, but didn't. Even if he had, Archer didn't know yet. The only thing he was sure of was that fate would present him with an opportunity and that he'd have to be ready to seize his chance.

"Understood, sir," Hopkins said. "There is the matter of Leutnant Sherwood, sir."

Strategy often required the ability to see beyond the next rising of the sun. First Leutnant Thomas Sherwood was just that. His sister was a crewmember on one of Archer's DropShips, and his family were long-time friends of the Christifiris. Archer had personally sponsored Thomas for admission to the NAIS College of Military Science, where he'd earned his degree. He'd retired from the military after the defeat of the Smoke Jaguars and, like Archer, took his place in the Thorin Militia.

When Archer had proposed his plan to Katya and

Hopkins, they'd suggested Sherwood as the most likely candidate. Archer agreed, and they codenamed him Prince John. The risks were considerable, but Archer believed Sherwood was up to it. If it worked, his people might be able to take on the Fifteenth Arcturan Guards and stand a chance of surviving.

"Colonel Blucher will need a liaison to help merge the Militia with the Guards. Let's give it to Leutnant Sherwood. That will get him some contacts among the Lyran officers and some face-time with Colonel Blucher."

"Yes, sir," Hopkins said.

"And Sergeant Major," Archer added.

"Sir?"

"Keep your eyes open and your head down." It was the exact same lesson Darius Hopkins had taught Archer years ago, preparing him for a life of service in the Federated Commonwealth. Those days now seemed like a whole other lifetime, but Hopkins gave him a knowing wink and went off into the 'Mech bay with his orders.

The plan had been put in motion . . .

12

As we reported last hour, the breaking story is
that there has been an attack or an explosion on
the planet Robinson and that the Draconis Combine
is responsible. Details are sketchy at this time, but
the initial report indicated that Arthur Steiner-Davion, younger brother of the Archon, might have
been wounded in the incident, which occurred as
he was speaking before an anti-Combine rally on
Robinson. Wait—I was just handed this release. Oh
my god—

—*Media at the Minute* news flash, Thorin, Donegal
  Broadcasting Company, 5 December 3062

Ecol City, Thorin
Skye Province
Lyran Alliance
8 December 3062

Archer moved along East Catulpa Street as he had
so many other times in his life. The call from Katya
had been brief, but at least he knew she wasn't being
mistreated. For now, both she and his secrets were
safe. But once he and his people acted, they would

have to get Katya out, lest the Lyrans use more "persuasive" means to break her down. She said they'd told her she was being transferred to another facility later that day. Apparently the city jail was jammed with those Fisk and Blucher considered to be potential subversives.

Suddenly he noticed more and more people on the streets, which were usually almost empty at this hour of the day. He saw them beginning to huddle in small groups, all talking excitedly, and some even shouting. On their faces were anger, fear, and confusion. Something was wrong. Dead wrong.

Archer walked over to one of the groups and tapped one of the women on the shoulder. "What's going on?" he asked.

"Haven't you heard? It's all over the newscasts."

Archer shook his head, but his heart sank. Another terrorist attack?

"Prince Victor Davion has declared that the Archon was responsible for their brother Arthur's death on Robinson. He claims to have evidence that she is trying to frame the Combine for the hit. He has called on all loyal troops to rally to him to depose his sister."

Archer seemed to freeze in time and space, and the woman gave him a squeeze on the arm as if to jostle him back to reality. It didn't work.

Archer had heard the news of young Arthur's death on the news a day or so ago, and it was sobering. He had no idea what proof Victor Davion had of Katrina's complicity, but Archer didn't doubt he had it. Davion couldn't make such a claim without the evidence to back it up. The grim truth hit home. Katrina Steiner had finally gone too far, and this time she'd lit the fuse on a full-fledged civil war.

In the distance he saw two young men in a shoving match. All around him people were talking about what all this meant. Some were saying it couldn't possibly be true. Others argued that if it was, Katrina Steiner wasn't fit to hold power.

Victor Davion had lost his throne while away, but had become the head of the Com Guards, which would have given him ample power if he'd wished to use it for himself. He hadn't done so until now. Having declared his intention of removing his sister from power, there would be no turning back.

As he stood on Catulpa Street only a block from his office, it hit Archer that he was standing in a moment in history. All around him a distinct point in time was occurring that would change his life forever. He began to walk again, very fast, almost running. Everyone would remember this day, would remember where he or she was when they heard the news. The moment he'd been waiting for had finally arrived. This was something the public could rally behind, at least enough of them to sustain a guerrilla effort. Now was the time to make his move. Now or never.

It took a few congested minutes to reach his office at Christifori Express. He closed the door behind him even as Catherine rushed to get him coffee and to pick up his coat, which he'd casually discarded. Once behind his desk, he activated the built-in comm system. He called up the discreet channel directly to Darius Hopkins' personal communicator. It took only a moment for the Sergeant Major to respond with the formally curt, "Hopkins."

"Specter One here," Archer said, only now taking a seat.

"We're clear." That meant it was safe to talk.

"The Eagle is aloft," Archer said slowly and carefully.

"Roger that, Specter One. The Eagle is aloft." It was the code phrase they'd come up with just in case the Lyrans were tapping communications. "We'll be ready for you in twenty."

Archer activated his noteputer and punched in his authorization code. Catherine Daniels came in with his cup of coffee, but he shook his head.

"Catherine," he said, putting the noteputer down for a moment, "you've heard the news?"

She nodded gravely. "Yes, sir."

"Good. I want you to contact all Express employees. We'll be shutting down indefinitely. I've arranged for the electronic transfer of funds into their accounts until the money runs out, but that won't be for months. I've also prepared a statement and stored it in your personal directory. Please pull it up and distribute it. If anyone asks, you had no idea that this was coming . . . no one did. These actions are my own, not those of Christifori Express."

"Yes, sir," she said, sounding almost military. "Jack and I will be joining you and the others tonight. I'm sure several of the others will want to come, too."

"Keep it limited to the two of you for now. No point in risking everyone's neck."

The comm system on his desk flashed and beeped, indicating an incoming message. Glancing down, he saw that the protocol tag on the message was from the command post of the Fifteenth Arcturan Guards at the other end of Ecol City.

Archer looked at Catherine as the system beeped for his attention. "It's Blucher. Chances are he's calling to order me to activate the Militia to help put down any trouble." He didn't answer the call, but simply stood watching the small blinking green light.

"Sir?" Catherine asked. "Aren't you going to answer?"

Archer smiled. It was the first true full smile he'd allowed himself since Andrea died, and it felt wonderful, as if it empowered him with life and energy. Reaching into the top drawer of his desk, he took out an envelope that was already addressed. Then he took something from his pants pocket and put it in the envelope. "This is my answer to Colonel Blucher. I don't ask for many personal favors, Catherine, but will you deliver this to him in person?"

She smiled back and took the envelope, holding it close to her chest. "With pleasure, sir."

"Thank you for everything so far. Take your time in getting over to the fort. I need about an hour. And when you're done there, I'll have an info disk for the media." He dug out a silvery data disk and slid it into the recorder system.

"It's begun, hasn't it?" she said almost sadly.

"Yes. Starting wars is easy, ending them is what takes the real skill." Archer sat down, ready to record his message to his people.

Shortly after he arrived at the Militia base, Archer went straight to the 'Mech bay, becoming energized even more by the bustle of activity. He'd donned his combat jumpsuit. It was faded from years of use, but offered him a sense of comfort few other things could. Crates were being loaded onto transports, BattleMechs were being prepped, and everywhere he looked, his troops gave him broad smiles, thumbs up, and nods of support. He'd have liked to let himself get caught up in the moment, but he understood the gravity of what was happening. Civil war was the worst kind. Brother against brother. Friend against friend. Parent against child. The enthusiasm around him was infectious, but Archer knew that some of these good people would die at the hands of those they would be fighting to save.

Darius Hopkins was directing traffic in the center of the 'Mech bay as Archer approached. They saluted each other quickly, then Archer cut to the chase. "How much time?"

"Ten more minutes," Hopkins said, at the same time handing off a list to an infantryman who'd been waiting for orders. "Good thing we started moving some of the stuff earlier or this would be stalled already."

"It's all in the planning," Archer said, sweeping his eyes around the bay. "Any sign of the Arcturan Guards?"

"Our comm team has been monitoring their transmissions. Nothing yet. They've been caught off guard as much as any of us. We've received several priority messages for you from Colonel Blucher. He finally spoke with Hauptmann Snider as your acting second in the command. Orders are to report to the Guards base and bring all equipment."

"Good. Since it looks like we're packing up to obey the orders, Blucher will suspect nothing. Have you contacted the remaining families?" That was an important part of the plan. As with his people at Christifori Express, Archer didn't want to leave behind any innocents who might give Fisk and Blucher leverage against him or other members of his command.

"Only a few hadn't yet moved their families into hiding."

"Good work, Sergeant Major," Archer said.

"Speaking of 'the plan,' it calls for a diversion so we can break out of the city before the Guards have a chance to react. You never specified what that diversion was."

"Is my 'Mech ready?" Archer asked, thumbing at his *Penetrator* behind him.

"It was the first one on-line. You're good to go," Hopkins replied. "Now, then, what was that diversion we were talking about?"

Archer smiled. "If my 'Mech is ready, then the diversion is ready. I head out in five minutes. You and the others follow five minutes after that. Use the pre-planned routes out of the city. Separate to lance level, move fast, get to the bases, and hunker down."

Spreading the militia out over the city as they left would be risky, but it would create the illusion that they were everywhere at once, the illusion that Archer had more troops than he actually did. In the coming days and weeks, the Thorin Militia would need the people's total confidence in them. Winning that started with small acts . . . which started today.

"You mind telling me what you have in mind?" Hopkins pressed.

Archer smiled. "I'd tell you, but you'd only disapprove."

Muttering something to himself, Hopkins turned back to his work. "That's what I'm worried about," Archer was sure he heard him say.

Demonstrations had erupted throughout Ecol City. Some were small, people spontaneously taking to the streets, chanting that the Archon should step down. Katrina supporters came out, too, counter-protesting. There was no pattern to it, no organization, just sheer chaos. While some major streets were empty, others were packed with a roar of demonstrators, each side attempting to out-yell those opposing their point of view. Rioting hadn't yet broken out, but it was only a matter of time.

The police headquarters and jail were in the same four-story building near the center of the city. Around it were special barriers against dangers such as crowds or car bombs getting close enough to do damage. The protests were minimal in this part of town, and there were enough police to keep the two sides from going at each other's throats. Tension was in the air, however, and the late morning clouds cloaked the city in gray shadow.

Archer piloted his *Penetrator* to the edge of the protective perimeter around the police HQ, deliberately crushing two of the concrete barriers as if to say that the building's defenses were no match for the sheer destructive power of a BattleMech. He targeted the satellite dishes and antenna on the roof and sprayed them with his pulse lasers. Emerald bursts of raw energy hit the towers and dishes, making them explode, crash, melt, and burst upon impact. Sparks flew as the larger tower fell.

About a dozen police—probably all that remained in the building—rushed out the front door. They wore riot gear and had their weapons drawn, a mix of rifles, tear gas projectors, and pistols, which they aimed up at his cockpit. It made Archer think of the old, old saying about not bringing a knife to a gunfight. Even using their rocket launchers, the police would be no match for his *Penetrator* if he let go with all of his firepower. None of them fired as they stood there on the steps of the building, but none of them lowered their weapons either.

He activated the external speaker system in the 'Mech's armored shoulder. "Bring out Chief Dunning," he said, then also opened the external microphone system.

A large man, muscular and fit, stepped forward. He carried a hand-megaphone and seemed unafraid of the towering weapon of death. "This is Chief Dunning."

"Mike, it's me, Archer."

There was a pause. Archer and Dunning had been schoolmates and good friends before he'd left Thorin to begin his military career at the NAIS. They still met for lunch maybe once a month, but it looked like Archer would be missing the next few.

"Arch," came back the chief's voice. "What in the name of hell are you doing? You've fried my communications system."

"Sorry I can't tell you more, Mike, but I have to ask you to release the prisoners you're holding for Blucher."

Again a long pause. Chief Dunning lowered his

microphone for a second as he winced at the request. "You're putting me in a real crappy situation, Arch. Why not come down here, and we can talk it over."

Archer checked his cockpit chronometer. "Sorry, Mike, not enough time. My beef isn't with you but with the Steiner government. Release those prisoners, and I'll leave the city. If you don't release them, I'll have to blast a few well-placed holes in the walls so they can get out. I don't want to hurt any of your troops, but those prisoners must be freed."

"Arch," his old friend said, "I can't tell you how many laws you're breaking."

Time was wasting, time Archer didn't have. He'd taken out the primary communications grid, but that wasn't the only way the police could communicate. By now word would have reached the Arcturan Guards post that a Militia BattleMech was attacking police headquarters. They would scramble to get here.

Archer targeted an oak tree some thirty meters from the chief and let go with one of his pulse lasers. The bright green bursts hit the tree, causing the moisture in it to boil instantly. The oak exploded, sending wisps of fire and smoke drifting into the air. Three of the police ran, but Dunning didn't even blink at the demonstration.

"Mike, let them out now or I start making doors of my own for them."

"Blucher's going to have my hide."

"You can always join us," Archer said half-jokingly.

Dunning put down the megaphone and turned to say something to one of the men nearest him. The man then ran into the building. "Hold your fire, Archer. They're coming out."

It took five minutes, but the prisoners were finally led into the open. The police fanned away. Most of the prisoners looked up at his 'Mech with awe, some with broad smiles. One stepped forward and waved. It was Katya Chaffee.

Without hesitation, she started to climb the handholds to his cockpit. He popped the door just in time for her to slip into the cramped confines of his *Penetrator*. Once he saw that no more prisoners were coming out, he activated the external microphone one more time.

"Chief, let them go."

Dunning waved to his men and they lowered their weapons.

"You prisoners," Archer said, "a new day has started here on Thorin and throughout the Alliance. You were arrested without cause. Now I'm setting you free."

He shut off the microphone and the freed prisoners scattered and raced off in different directions into the surrounding streets. Some of the police tried to follow them, but it was an impossible task. Archer throttled up his 'Mech and started to move away.

"I take it the situation has changed?" Katya said, settling into the folding jump seat behind him.

"Katya," he said, maneuvering around a building and starting down a relatively empty street, "that is an understatement."

Colonel Blucher looked up as Luther Fisk entered the tactical operations room of the base. He returned Fisk's salute, then turned back to the holographic display of Ecol City coming into view on the big command and control table. Centuries before, sand tables had been used to test operational deployments. Now holographic, computer-driven projections provided the same information.

The room was deliberately dark, illuminated only by thin reflective lighting where various personnel worked furiously at the wall of communications monitors. The brightest light came from the holo-image of the city. Blucher looked over at Fisk and could see that he was actually enjoying all this. It was what he'd wanted all along, but that was because he hadn't a clue what war was really like, especially a civil war.

"What's the word on that BattleMech that was seen near city hall?"

Fisk shrugged slightly. "Information is sketchy. With situations like this, it's hard to get good intelligence, sir. Per your orders I've sent two lances out to flank the area. Our communications are down in the area and I've ordered them to find out what's caused it."

Blucher nodded. Situations like this were fluid. Tactical data was getting harder to sort out, and that was no fault of Fisk's. Matters had escalated in a matter of hours with Victor Davion's accusation that the Archon was involved with her brother's death. He knew that a formal response from Tharkad would be forthcoming, and he didn't doubt that it would consist of denials and counterattacks on Prince Victor. Katrina Steiner would never step down as Archon. He was as sure of that as he was of his own name. She would fight to the last breath—the last breath of soldiers like him—to hold onto her power. He respected that in her, thinking how much she was like her grandmother.

He knew that the cry in the streets was for Katrina to step down, that she'd forfeited her right to rule, but Blucher had sworn allegiance to the Archon, an oath he considered almost sacred. It was the foundation of his sense of honor and integrity. His personal opinions did not weigh in the balance. When the shooting stopped, he wanted his honor to be intact.

"What is the word on the Militia? Have they arrived yet?"

"That's the problem," Fisk said. "When I checked with the troopers I posted to monitor their base, they said Christifori's people had mobilized and had, in fact, left twenty minutes ago."

Blucher raised his eyebrows in surprise. "They should be here by now."

"Yes, sir. They should. Apparently this wasn't their destination."

"And I'm only getting this information now?"

"Sir, the streets are congested with all the confusion. I thought they might have gotten bottled up in traffic."

Blucher was not pleased. "Don't try and think for me, Fisk. I don't need my data filtered."

A sergeant approached and saluted, then handed the colonel an envelope. "This was delivered by a woman to the front gate. She said it was for you, sir."

Blucher nodded and tugged at the flap until it ripped. Inside was a single sheet of paper and two metallic objects. The paper was a commission to the Thorin Militia for one Leutnant Colonel Archer Christifori. It had been neatly torn in half. Then he dumped the two small objects in the envelope into his left hand. They were Christifori's rank insignia.

Blucher said nothing. He dropped the torn sheets to the floor and held out the rank insignia to Fisk. "I believe you should take these."

"That traitor," Fisk said bitterly.

Blucher shook his head. "He's no traitor, Fisk. He's a patriot, at least in his own mind. Now he's our enemy. An enemy that you created. I hope you're up to the task, because if not, he'll kill us both."

BOOK TWO

Rebellion's Brew

The area from Leesburg Pike to the Melissa Steiner Freeway should be avoided at this time due to the presence of unruly demonstrators in the streets. Colonel Blucher of the Fifteenth Arcturan Guards has temporarily declared martial law. Citizens are under a strict curfew and are ordered off the streets.

In the midst of all this, a disk was delivered to our station from Archer Christifori of the Thorin Militia, a well known and popular figure on Thorin. Network management is permitting me to play this . . . and again this is a Donegal Broadcast exclusive . . .

> *"People of Thorin. Based on the recent actions of the Archon in suppressing the rights of Davion nationals and her brother's claim that she was responsible for the assassination of her younger brother, I am resigning as the head of the Thorin Militia. The Militia is no more. It is now an army of liberation; liberation from the oppressive rule of Archon Katherine Steiner.*
>
> *"I am not here to kill innocents, but the Archon, in her haste to seize and maintain power, has shown she is not fit to rule. I will not rest until Thorin is*

*free of her iron heel and she is removed from power.
If that can be done peacefully, so be it. If not, then
whatever happens will be on her head.*

*"I ask for your support as a native son of this
world and a man loyal to the memory of Melissa
Steiner Davion, who gave her life in the service of
our people. Resist peacefully any way you can. We
will fight with and for you. Let no one stand in our
way."*

—Holoclip from *News at Five*, Ecol City, Donegal Broadcasting Company, 8 December 3062

13

This is the Muphrid Emergency Broadcast System. This is not a test. Under orders of Kommandant Constance McCoy, the citizens of MacArthur and Ridgeway are ordered to remain in their homes until further notice. Rioting has broken out in both cities, and the Arcturan Guards and the Muphrid Militia have been mobilized to restore order. Anyone in violation of the curfew will be prosecuted and punished. Your cooperation is required until the end of this emergency.

—Muphrid EBS, Skye Province, Lyran Alliance,
   10 December 3062

Remington Forest, Thorin
Skye Province
Lyran Alliance
12 December 3062

Many of Archer's troops had no idea that the place he'd chosen for their secret base was an historic site, the ruins of the ancient University of Thorin. In the three hundred years since its destruction, Remington Forest had almost totally overgrown the site. Massive oaks grew where there had once been roadways and paths. Thick vines and wild undergrowth carpeted the ruins of large, crumbling buildings. Small animals scurried among the lush vegetation, and birds swooped overhead.

The University of Thorin had been a shimmering gem in the crown of the First Lord before the fall of the old Star League. The greatest of the League's liberal arts colleges, it had been ransacked, burned, and bombed during the Amaris coup, then abandoned. There had been talk of rebuilding, but the total collapse of the Star League intervened. As the years passed, the place was forgotten by the Inner Sphere, including most of Thorin.

Archer was one of the few still aware of its existence, which was the main reason he had chosen it as his primary base of operations. The other was that the remains of the great granite buildings, though crumbling with age, still offered some degree of protection for BattleMechs and vehicles. An old field house, missing most of its roof, had been converted into a makeshift 'Mech bay. A dormitory, whose lower floors had flooded and were a mire, still had rooms in the middle level that were serviceable enough for makeshift quarters.

Most of his force was present, if not all of their 'Mechs. Archer thought it would be unwise to have his whole force concentrated in one place, in case Blucher discovered their position. In addition to the MechWarriors present, there were others who had rallied to his cause. Some were family members of Militia troops. Others were employees of Christifori Express who had, under the guidance of Catherine Daniels, been channeled to this location.

It felt more like a family gathering than an army, but these were the people who would help Archer liberate Thorin. The odds were stacked against them, but Archer didn't care. If he was worried about the odds, he'd never have started this in the first place. This wasn't about winning or losing. It was about avenging his sister's death. Her fate had been a symptom of a greater problem, one he now stood ready to confront.

Climbing up on the moss-grown remains of a stone pillar, he stood tall over the small gathering, and all eyes turned to him.

"I want to thank you for being here, for taking the risks you have," he began. "The Fifteenth Arcturan Guards are probably already looking for us, and it's been a long day just to get everyone here and settled.

"If you're here, you're here to fight for the freedoms we all cherish. I don't care if you're Davion or Steiner in your loyalties. If you're here, you're fighting because the current Archon has shown herself unfit to rule. She manipulated events to deny her brother and sister their birthrights, and now we've learned that she arranged for the murder of another brother in her quest for power. I don't know about you, but that isn't the kind of person I can swear to obey and protect.

"Maybe some of you are thinking I'm going to march the Militia into the city and challenge Colonel Blucher to fight it out for control of the world. Well, I'm not. The truth is he's got more resources than we do. The odds simply aren't even. So we're going to fight them on our own terms. Not mindless bloodshed, but surgical strikes. I'm not out to kill fellow soldiers who are simply doing their duty, but we can make this a world they would rather not defend at all. That's the goal.

"One more thing—we're no longer tied to the Lyran Alliance military structure. New rankings will be assigned you. For now I've decided to use the ranks of the old Federated Suns. That should make our position perfectly clear. Don't worry, none of you got busted. Just don't expect a big boost in your paycheck." A ripple of laughter ran through the gathering.

And that was it. Archer had no more to say, so he jumped down from the shattered pillar to the sound of applause muffled somewhat by the thick canopy of trees. Several people came toward him, including Darius Hopkins and another familiar face. Archer motioned for the two men to come closer.

"Sergeant Major Darius Hopkins, meet Captain Lee Fullerton," he said. The two shook hands, while Archer could see them mentally trying to size each other up.

"Darius, Lee is the captain of the *Angelfire*, one of my DropShips."

Recognition dawned on Darius' face. "You're responsible for those crates of missiles I saw in the storage bunker?"

Lee Fullerton smiled and rested his hands on either side of his large stomach. "Let's just say that I transported all the *crates* I was scheduled to deliver to the Lyrans. What was in them, or how well those munitions perform, well, that's a matter that's best left to Archer here."

"Is the ship secure?" Archer asked.

"Settled in the bottom of Lake Sprague about fifty kilometers north of here. With all of that iron at the bottom of the lake, their satellites would have to be trained right on it to see it."

Archer smiled and shook the captain's hand. "Thanks for your help, Lee," he said. Then he turned to Darius. "Speaking of satellites, it's a safe bet Colonel Blucher is looking for us right now. How are we set?"

Hopkins stroked his bushy mustache and looked up as if he wondered if the Lyrans were peering back down at him. "All our gear is covered from visual observation. The satellites have heat scanning, but the forest will provide a lot of deflection—that and we're also using the superstructure of the buildings as a means of masking ourselves. The 'Mechs are the real problem. As you know, BattleMech fusion reactors can show up on a concentrated neutrino scan from low orbit—even from a satellite, so I've draped all the 'Mechs with a tarp interwoven with a suppression unit. That should mask about eighty percent of the emissions, meaning that unless they scanned a specific 'Mech for a whole hour, they wouldn't be able to confirm whether it was there or not."

"We did the same thing during the latter part of the Clan invasion," Archer said.

"I didn't claim it was an original idea, just one that works," Hopkins said. "I hope you've selected some initial targets to get us going."

Archer understood the urge to start the fight. "I thought I'd take care of some organizational issues first. We need to work in tandem with any other rebel factions, keep them united. I've already sent some inquiries out via HPG and the Express ships to some business contacts on Muphrid, asking them to keep us posted on the local situation and what the Guards are up to there."

"Muphrid?" Lee Fullerton was surprised. "I thought we were only taking on Thorin."

"We are," Archer said, "but Muphrid is where the rest of the Arcturan Guards are garrisoned, and they'd be the easiest reinforcements for Blucher to throw at us. I want to make sure things stay heated up for him on Muphrid, so that he can't afford to keep those forces here."

Hopkins said, "I also made sure that our three Katrina loyalists were kept in the dark. They've been sent to the southern continent on special assignment to search out a new training area. I imagine they're just learning the news of us about now."

"Good work," Archer said. "And Prince John?"

"No word, but then again, I didn't expect any. Besides, intelligence is Chaffee's bailiwick. I'm just a ground-pounder with an attitude."

Hearing her name, Katya came over too, noteputer tucked under one arm. "Problems?"

Archer shook his head. "Just talking. I think we can count on a few hours of peace and quiet to get established. By now, Blucher is realizing that finding us isn't going to be easy. If he reacts the way I think he will, he'll deploy lances on patrol to hunt us down."

Hopkins tipped his head and smiled slightly. "Most would say that's the time to strike."

Archer grinned back. It was a lesson the older man had explained to him when he'd first decided to pursue a career in the military, and he hadn't forgotten it over the years. "You know I won't fall into that trap."

"But it makes sense, sir," Fullerton said.

"The MechWarriors and troopers he sends out now are going to be on edge, with all their senses cranked up. Besides, it's what the Guards will be expecting us to do. They'll be poised to respond if we so much as pop our heads up."

Katya nodded agreement. "We wait a few days. Let Blucher's troops patrol and start to get sloppy. Let the tension ease a little. Let them get a little comfortable with the duty. They'll be more susceptible to making mistakes."

Hopkins excused himself and took off toward the temporary 'Mech bay, handing out orders all along the way. Archer watched him go and drew in a long breath of air.

Katya rested one hand on his shoulder. "Everything's going to be fine. Everything's going according to plan."

Archer turned to her. "Everything may be going according to plan right now, Katya, but no plan ever survives contact with the enemy," he said.

*   *   *

The image of Thorin spun in the air over the holographic display table as if it were solid mass. Several officers worked around the display, feeding in data from various computer sources or key-coding it by hand. Still others were busy along the far wall, monitoring communications, feeding pertinent data to the several intelligence officers in the other room. Felix Blucher stared at the slowly spinning globe of light and color in front of him and pondered his predicament.

He had spent the morning calming the nerves of the Thorin Planetary Ruling Council, the whole time thinking that politicians were definitely a group who deserved to die for a cause. With the Duke away at the Royal Court, his advisors were champing at the proverbial bit. Blucher had reassured them and listened to their pleas, but, for the most part, had promised them nothing.

He glanced over to one of the comm officers. "Did you get my message off to the garrison at Muphrid?"

The officer gave him confirmation of the transmission in the form of a data burst on the screen. Not wanting to repeat the mistake he'd made on Thorin, the colonel had sent word for the Muphrid Militia to be absorbed immediately into the Guard. Those who didn't wish to cooperate would be detained indefinitely and their gear confiscated. There had been some violent protests, but the locals were no match for BattleMechs.

He sidestepped awkwardly to the next terminal where satellite recon was being coordinated. The pain from his leg injury was a constant reminder of the attempt on his life.

"We've been able to track some of the Militia movements up to when they began to leave the city. Since then we've been unable to pinpoint them, sir."

The young woman's voice did not betray her nervousness, but Blucher could sense it.

"Keep looking. They'll have to emerge at some point."

Then he saw Leutnant Fisk in the light coming from the holographic display of Thorin. "Sir, our troops have successfully suppressed the demonstrations and riots. For the most part, Ecol City is quiet, and the other urban areas report the same."

"Have you deployed patrols in search of the Militia?"

"Yes, sir," Fisk said crisply. "We'll find them."

Blucher allowed himself a light chuckle. "That's highly unlikely, Leutnant."

"Sir?"

"We're not going to find Archer Christifori until he wants us to, and then on his terms."

"Why do you say that, sir?" Fisk sounded unconvinced.

"Simple. If he wanted to engage us, what better time than when the streets were filled with chaos? He didn't. That must mean he plans to use a more guerrilla-style war against us."

"We'll crush him, sir," Fisk said with real enthusiasm. Several other comm personnel turned and gave reassuring nods, everyone confident that they were up to the task.

"This isn't the kind of war we were trained to wage. We're going to have to rethink our approach, change our tactics," Blucher said. He knew that overconfidence couldn't stop an incoming missile.

"Our decisive movements and show of force in putting down the riots are already paying off, though, sir," said Fisk. "One of the Militia members, a Leutnant Sherwood, has come over to us. You remember him. He liaised on some of the preliminary merger plans with the Militia. Apparently Christifori didn't trust him and sent him off on some pointless duty to keep him ignorant of what the rest of the Militia was up to."

Perhaps something was going right for once, Blucher thought. "This Sherwood, does he have any information that might be of use?"

"The only thing he knew for sure is that Archer sent three other soldiers on a mission to the southern continent to locate new bases of operations, allegedly for training purposes. I think we can surmise that Christifori was planning on setting up bases in the south."

"I want orders put out to find those troopers. If we can locate and interrogate them, they may be able to tell us more about Christifori's plans."

"The orders have already been cut, sir," Fisk said confidently. "And I'd recommend that you meet with Leutnant Sherwood. I'm sure we can get something out of him."

"All right," Blucher said, leaning on his cane to take the weight off his injured leg. He was going to need all the help he could get.

"How would you describe Victor Davion's call for troops to rally to his so-called cause, Andy?"

"One word, Phil—desperate."

"You think he's going out on a limb?"

"First of all, this so-called evidence could have been doctored. Let's face it, he's most likely just trying to secure a little kingdom for himself. If it takes killing a few thousand innocents to do that, well, we all know Victor's reputation."

—Holoclip from *Issues and Counter-Issues*, Donegal Broadcasting Company, Lyran Alliance, 12 December 3062

Village of Louisa, Thorin
Skye Province
Lyran Alliance
15 December 3062

The coastal village of Louisa was a small factory town almost three hundred-fifty kilometers northwest of Ecol City. The town's two factories produced steel and processed circuit boards, and everyone in Louisa either worked in one of the factories or was simply passing through on their way to a nicer place. A thin haze rose from the chip-manufacturing plant and drifted into the nearby forests and hills, giving visitors a whiff of the place ten kilometers before they got there.

Once they had, Archer and Katya didn't have to look far to find The Bagpiper, the local tavern where their meet was set. If the air outside had a distinctive smell, the one inside the bar could have come from any of dozens of similar places Archer had known in his travels across the Inner Sphere and beyond. The yellowed lights, the buzz of conversation, the aroma of stale ale, whiskey, sweat, and smoke were so familiar they were almost comforting.

The bartender seemed to know why they were here. He whispered something to Katya and indicated an unmarked door in the back of the dimly lit bar. Archer's eyes stung from the pipe and cigar smoke as he and Katya made their way to the door. It opened into a room where five men and one woman were huddled around a worn table. All of them looked up as Archer and Katya entered and shut the door behind them. The small room was more brightly lit than the bar.

Arranging this meeting had taken several days and some degree of risk. For security, Archer had brought only a pistol—a pistol and a lance of BattleMechs hidden outside of town, sitting in low-power mode just in case the Arcturan Guards showed up. He wasn't too worried, though. He and Katya had taken precautions to make sure no one trailed them here. Still, it paid to be careful.

They pulled up two empty chairs. No one said anything for a full minute as they looked from one to another, sizing each other up.

Katya broke the silence. "I want to thank you all for coming tonight."

One of the men smiled nervously and extended

his hand to Archer. "I'm Martin Fox out of New Poughkeepsie." Archer gave him a firm handshake. Looking to the next person, a young and muscular Hispanic man, he got a confident nod.

"Las Volk," the young man said. "So you're the war hero."

Archer raised his eyebrows and shrugged. "That was a while ago."

"Yes, it was," a man to his right said caustically. His face was gaunt, with a devilish goatee and a sneer for an expression.

"And you are?"

"King." The man leaned back in his chair and crossed his arms. "Rufus King."

"Don't let the passage of time fool you, Rufus," Archer said. "I can still take care of my own."

"So we saw the other day," the only other woman in the room said. She wore a black leather jacket and jeans. "Joey-Lynn Fraser's the name. I'm out of Opal City and leader of the White Tigers."

Archer knew something of the gang. The White Tigers had started as a local criminal gang, then had somehow evolved into an anti-Katrina organization. If rumors were true, they had already killed almost a dozen Katrina supporters.

Archer sat back in his chair. "Well, so much for introductions. You all know why we're here. Things have come to a head, and it looks like Thorin's headed for a civil war."

"No thanks to your heroics in the capital," King commented dryly.

"As I recall, Rufus, you weren't so cocky or arrogant when he came and broke us out of jail," Katya told him. King just sat there, arms still crossed, and gave her a dark glare.

"Listen," Archer said, "we can hang separately or hang together. Frankly, for us to be successful against the Lyrans, we need to start coordinating our efforts and operations. This meeting is a start."

"What exactly have you got in mind?" asked Las Volk.

"Right now, Thorin has resistance movements. We need to change that to Thorin having an organized resistance movement. Simply put, we need some basic structure, some rules of operation, sharing of logistics and intelligence, and defensive planning. Even more important, we've got to have a strategy for dealing with the Arcturan Guards or any other units the Alliance may throw at us."

"Do you think they'll pull in reinforcements?" Fraser asked as she stood, turned her chair backward, and re-seated herself, straddling the narrow chair back.

"They wouldn't dare," King said.

"Actually, I don't think they have the resources, at least not yet. The Guards are already stationed on Muphrid and here. Most of the other Lyran units are spread fairly thin except those posted along the Jade Falcon border. We're not the only world where protests and outright rebellion are breaking out. I don't know how quickly they could respond."

Martin Fox shifted nervously in his seat, beads of sweat forming on his wide forehead. "All right, so let's talk about strategy, like you said."

Archer looked at Katya, then back at the group. "Our goal should be simple: to drive the Alliance presence off Thorin. To do that, we need to make sure our strategy achieves several objectives. One, we need the support of the local population. That means we can't afford any terrorist attacks that kill civilians."

"What about the civilians who are supporting the Lyrans?" King asked. Something in his voice told Archer he had some particular individuals in mind, including how he wanted to deal with them. Something also told him it was far from pleasant.

"We're here to liberate these people, not hurt them. Secondly, we need to make Thorin a place acutely uncomfortable for the Arcturan Guards. These men and women are soldiers and, for the most part, just following orders. Killing them only gives them more motive to fight back. I ought to know . . . I was just like them once. We need to find ways to make them paranoid, fearful, and stressed, but we won't kill unless we absolutely have no choice."

"You've got all that firepower with your Militia, why not simply waste them? One big battle and boom, no more Lyrans," Volk said, widening his hands in the air to simulate an explosion.

Archer shook his head. "It's tempting, but you've got to remember that the Fifteenth isn't some green unit. They're front-line troops with better classes of 'Mechs than we have, as well as a bigger stockpile of expendables. I'm not ruling out a straight-up fight with them, just not right now. They'd have the upper hand, and if we lost, all of Thorin would be lost. The key is to wear them down to the point that we can be assured of victory."

"Why spare the soldiers?" Joey-Lynn asked. "We can kill them easy enough. Little ambushes, some bombings, whittle them down slowly."

"Killing them will only harden their resolve. Look at what happened with the bombing attack that wounded Blucher. That backfired all over us and led to a crackdown on 'suspected terrorists.' Some of you were arrested, right? We have to avoid handing Blucher anything he can use against the local population."

The mention of the bombing seemed to stir Fox. "We were talking about that before you two arrived. None of us ran that one. That leaves you."

Archer was surprised. "I assumed that one of you

did it." He looked to Katya, who only shrugged. One by one the others shook their heads. Rufus King stroked his goatee and smiled a yellow-toothed grin. "I guess someone hates the Lyrans as much as we do, and we simply haven't found him yet."

"Or," Katya said, "it wasn't someone from Thorin at all."

"Meaning?" Volk asked.

"Perhaps it was somebody within their ranks. Someone who wanted to escalate the situation."

Archer waved his hand to cut off the conversation. "Enough speculation. For now, we'll just say it's a mystery. We need to move on. I've taken the liberty of having Katya prepare some kits for you. They detail our code words, how we communicate with each other, and so on. We'll work in a cell system, so that no one can totally expose or damage the entire operation. Your point of contact to me is through Katya. She'll handle your supply requests as well as operational assignments."

Katya handed out the kits, which consisted of data disks and a few sheets of hardcopy.

Rufus sat up straight. "You're giving us assignments?"

Archer nodded. He'd anticipated some resistance. "Overall, we need to change how we're working. No more independent actions. If you want to undertake an operation, request it. Otherwise, we'll plan the initiatives, and you folks will handle the tactics and execution. If we don't keep to a plan, we risk being defeated piecemeal or being played off against each other. Unified, we stand a damn good chance of winning. If we don't work together, I doubt we'll ever be able to defeat the Guards."

"Any ideas for the near future?" Joey-Lynn asked, seeming intrigued with the direction Archer was attempting to lead them.

"As a matter of fact, I have several. First, we need

to inflict a little damage to some of Blucher's patrols, just enough to keep them on their toes. Then I think we should run an exercise among ourselves. It'll be our first test of working together, and there's a role for each of your organizations."

Martin Fox laid his kit down on the table. "Okay, let's have it."

"First a little ambush, with your help, Martin. Then, we play with the HPG in Ecol City."

"The ambush I understand. But you hit an HPG and ComStar will be all over us like flies on stink," King said.

"I know. We're not going to hit the HPG, just the power feeds from the city power supply. It doesn't violate the terms of the planetary agreement with ComStar, but effectively shuts down the HPG for several days. I'm also counting on some slack, given that Victor Davion is in command of the Com Guards."

"No offense, Christifori, but so what?" Volk said, looking puzzled. "What good is hitting an HPG?"

"Blucher is a military commander with two worlds under his jurisdiction at this time. Cut off communications with other worlds for a while and it sends a ripple of fear into them. They may assume that we're coordinating our efforts against them on Muphrid. Or that we're planning to hit them here and prevent them from calling in reinforcements. Either way, Blucher's got troops deployed, rolled out, and pressed into long, tense hours of duty. Nothing happens, but they feel the strain. Best yet, it gets us some press coverage and draws attention to our cause. Coupled with the ambush Katya has come up with, we stay in the good graces of the local population and inflict some paranoia on the Arcturan Guards." He could see that the idea appealed to everyone except Rufus King.

Who spoke up immediately: "So, aside from these

little irritating missions, you expect us to take orders from you?"

"I'd reword it, but that's the gist of it. You'll gather intelligence, too, filtering it through Katya. But in the end, from your perspective, yes, you'll be taking orders from me."

"So who put you in charge? You think just because you were a weekend warrior that we're automatically going to fall in line? Every one of us at this table has our own following. You have no proof that if we work alone, we won't be successful."

Archer drew a quiet breath. He let his eyes meet those of the others one by one as he spoke. "You don't have to follow me, that's true. I'm not going to force myself on you. Why should I? I'm the only party at this table who fields a battalion of troops.

"The truth of the matter is that this has nothing to do with me being commander of the Thorin Militia. What matters is that I'm the only one here who's served in the FedCom military. I know how the Guards have been trained, which lets me predict pretty accurately how they might react. I know where they're weak, and I know how to exploit it. Add to that, I'm the only one of you other than Katya who's ever seen real combat. Finally, I've got experience dealing with Blucher.

"If you don't want me to head this up, show me someone who's better qualified, and I'll be happy to submit to him or her."

After only a brief silence, each of the rebel leaders nodded or verbally agreed. The last to capitulate was King, though Archer didn't think he could ever totally trust the man's commitment. After another hour of discussion, he and Katya left in a small hover transport, taking a lonely road through the night woods.

"What do you think?" she asked as she maneuvered the hovercar down the narrow lane.

"They're rough, amateurs. And we're going to have to keep a sharp eye on King."

"Do you think we can make it work?"

Archer smiled. "You forget, Katya, we don't have a choice." And neither did they.

15

Open warfare has broken out between Davionist and Steiner forces, mostly on worlds where troops from both sides are already stationed together. Fighting is confirmed on Kathil, New Aragon, Coventry, Nanking, Kikuyu, Demeter, Algol, Benet III, Brockway, Bromhead, Ft. Louden, Rasalgethi, and Thorin. Meanwhile, the Archon has broadcast this message to her people: "My brother claims I am unfit for the throne, yet how much more innocent blood will he spill trying to remove me from it? Is this the vaunted way of the warrior? Does this serve the people he claims he wants to save? My forces will fight if provoked, but the only thing *I* want for my people is peace."

—Reported by *Word from the Underground*,
  pirate broadcast, Thorin, 10 December 3062

Gauley River Valley, Thorin
Skye Province
Lyran Alliance
23 December 3062

Some forty kilometers due north of Ecol City was Lake Gauley, a massive reservoir built centuries ago to provide the capital city's freshwater supply. With the Gauley River dammed, the reservoir supplied more than enough water for the city. During the spring and late summer, the water was drained to maintain the dam's integrity.

At the base of the dam were five massive drains. The nearby control room could open the flow to as much as 48,000 cubic feet of water per second, changing the Gauley River from a quiet fishing stream to a raging torrent of class V and VI rapids. Some of the locals liked to go whitewater rafting when the floodgates were opened, but most of the time the area was deserted.

This was the river's quiet season, and the steep rock formations that loomed on either side made it a perfect highway for moving BattleMechs away from prying eyes. Archer had planned it that way. Using the few access roads down to the shallow waters of the river, he could move north and south above the city, pop up on the roadways, strike out at the Fifteenth Guards, and retreat to a place where their sensors would be hindered.

About a dozen kilometers west of the river was a major thoroughfare running along the mountain ridges back to Ecol City, linking the capital with another industrial city, Kendal. The Arcturan Guards had been using the road to patrol between the two cities; it was the only major roadway linking them. They were searching for signs of Archer and his people. Today, they would find them.

Archer stopped his *Penetrator* on a flat rock ledge high above the east bank of the river. From here, he had a perfect downward-angled firing position onto the trail up the western bank. He gazed at the river, which was no more than a meter deep and moving slowly, and remembered the excitement of rafting down it when the floodgates were opened. That was years ago, a lifetime ago. Andrea had been along, too, with some of her friends. He'd been an awkward young man at the time, trying to impress girls. It hadn't worked, but to this day the trip was a fond memory.

Time for new memories, he told himself as he switched to his command frequency and ordered his light lance of 'Mechs to move forward. "Timing is everything, people," he said.

In the role of bait was Kane Livernois in his *Stealth*, recently repainted in forest greens and browns. Kane was still not entirely confident in his position as a lance leader, but Archer saw his potential. If nothing else, this operation would tell whether he had the stuff to command under actual battle conditions.

"Remember, once I give the signal, you must be clear of the zone," he said. "Get their attention and draw them here as quick as you can."

"Copy that, Specter One," Kane replied as he splashed through the shallow river and up the winding dirt trail. Following behind the camouflaged *Stealth* was a battle-worn *Battle Hawk*, a long-ago captured and refit *Panther*, and a *Javelin*. Archer watched them proceed up the trail, stirring up dust as they disappeared into the dense growth of trees and vegetation. His short-range sensors, interfered with by the iron deposits in the rocks, lost track of them sooner than expected.

As the other lance under his command moved into their pre-arranged positions, Archer looked around at the vivid green of the trees and at the way the mid-afternoon sun sparkled on the water. He felt relaxed, if only for a moment. He hadn't really felt that way since Andrea died. Every moment since then had been focused on some problem, some goal, some decision. Now he was oddly at peace.

A voice in Archer's earpiece broke his reverie. It was Martin Fox. "Specter One, this is Pit Bull. We have secured the dog house."

Archer let loose a long sigh, saying farewell to his moment of peace. "Understood. Any difficulties, Pit Bull?"

"No. As a matter of fact it looks like we've got some people here who'd be happy to join us."

"That's good, but we'll still need to tie them up when this is over. I don't want the Lyrans to turn on them or their families."

"I understand," came back the distant voice.

"Heads up, Pit Bull," Archer said. "Wait for my signal."

They didn't have long to wait, only a couple of hours. It began with a crackle in Archer's earpiece, followed by the voice of Kane Livernois. "Specter Nine to Specter One," he said, panting for air.

"Go, Kane," Archer said, wrapping his hands around his joysticks.

"I found the Guards, sir." In the background was a slight ripple of static. Archer recognized it immediately. It was the sound of a PPC discharging near a 'Mech cockpit.

"Reel them in."

"I don't think that'll be a problem. I will be in visual in just a minute," Kane said. "I have two lances coming in. Specter Ten has taken some damage."

Archer checked his long-range sensors and got a flicker of the approaching mass of death and destruction. The winding, narrow mountain trail would work somewhat to their advantage, preventing the Guards from forming a combat line or flanking. It would be a long-running battle between their lead 'Mech and Livernois' rear guard.

"Specter One to Two, Three, and Four. Stand by to throttle up. Stick to the plan. We're here for cover fire as they approach. Hold your fire until I give the word—no exceptions."

Switching to short-range sensors, Archer saw the snaking line of 'Mechs almost in visual range. The match would be even, except for the surprise he had waiting. He'd been expecting only a lance of Guards, but the patrol consisted of eight 'Mechs instead of four. Blucher must be running his patrols close together.

Looking up, he saw his lance of 'Mechs come around the trail in a sluggish run, crimson laser beams lancing at their rear as they descended toward the river bed. Smoke trailed from Harry "Hawkeye" Hogan's *Battle Hawk*, and the legs and arms of Subaltern Grath's *Panther* were now charred black and its left side almost stripped of armor.

The Arcturan Guards came into view, moving in single file led by a gray and green *Nightsky*, blasting with its large pulse laser at Hogan's *Battle Hawk*. The emerald bursts of light missed wide, exploding the rocks that lined the trail into clouds of gray dust. Archer knew that his command lance could hit them from where they were, but he held their fire. Hidden in the rocks, they'd remain concealed until exactly the right moment—unless they were spotted visually or scanned directly,

"Specter One to Pit Bull," he said slowly, as Hogan torso-twisted and fired back at the advancing Guards. He sent a short-range missile duo past the *Nightsky* and into the *Cicada* that was second in line, ripping its armor above the left knee.

"Go ahead, sir," came back Martin Fox's voice.

"Pull the plug."

"Copy that, Specter."

Livernois paused his *Stealth* in the middle of the riverbed and turned, unleashing his short-range missiles, both the six- and two-packs. They snaked up and into a dark green *Blackjack*, pitting frontal armor plates upon impact, gouging small holes. Kane activated his jump jets and leaped away as soon as the missiles found their mark, rising up to Archer's level but further downstream.

The *Nightsky* moved to the water's edge and opened up on Corporal Jillian Shantea's *Javelin*. The pair of medium pulse lasers hit both legs of the smaller 'Mech, shredding armor as they ate away the protective plating. The *Javelin* seemed to vibrate under the impacts, but Jillian managed to keep her balance and start up the trail on Archer's side of the river. His field of vision was obscured as Subaltern Grath's *Panther*, its most recent wounds still billowing white smoke, rose on its jump jets to a small ledge just below Archer's position.

The Guards must have detected them. One lance remained just above the river's edge, while the rest were in a line of battle in the middle of the shallow river. Steam rose around the feet of the *Blackjack* as it loosed its large lasers at Kane's *Stealth*, venting heat into the cool water.

Archer checked the chronometer on his cockpit display and leveled his weapons at a stout *Flashman*, one of the 'Mechs on the higher ground just above the river's edge.

"All Specters," he said, "concentrate your fire on the high ground and brace yourselves."

His target fired at Grath's *Panther* just a millisecond before Archer got a weapons lock. The *Flashman*, a deadly in-fighter armed with more lasers than a platoon of armor, had triggered its three large lasers and three of its mediums. True to its name, the 'Mech lit up the air with brilliant cherry red streaks. Grath's *Panther* twisted, contorted, and fell in a wash of laser light. A burst of autocannon rounds from one of Archer's people missed its mark, blasting the rocks around the feet of a Lyran *War Dog* that was blasting back.

Archer fired his own large lasers, the scarlet beams gouging deeply into the right leg of the *Flashman*, slicing off armor with a popping sound that echoed in the tight confines of the ravine. Suddenly there came a roar, a sound somewhere between that of launched missiles and a summer thunderstorm. Faint at first, it grew louder, more dominant, consuming. For a full five seconds, there was no shooting, no fighting as every MechWarrior listened to the growing sound.

Almost six meters high, the wall of water came, a huge, frothing wave of destruction. Somewhere several kilometers upstream, Martin Fox and his Pit Bull team, had opened the floodgates on the dam. In an instant the shallow stream became a raging torrent— a solid slab of water roaring like an animal.

The Arcturan Guards only had two seconds of reaction time as the river rushed at them. The leading 'Mechs attempted to break and run, but the river curved sharply only a half a kilometer downstream and the uneven rocks prevented a flat-out run. Not that it would have helped. The *Flashman* and the 'Mechs on the bank tried to retreat back up the same trail that had brought them down.

"Keep firing!" Archer commanded and fired his second target interlock circuit at the *Flashman*, as its pilot attempted to save himself from the wild onslaught of the river. Most of Archer's laserfire missed, but enough hit to add to the confusion. Then a lone BattleMech, the *Nightsky*, climbed up from the churning white waters onto a flat rock and then rose upward on its jump jets. It wavered drunkenly in the air, then crash-landed on the shore, with its legs in the river and the rest of its bulk battered on the rough rocks. The rushing water had consumed its three comrades trying to flee downstream.

One Arcturan BattleMech, a *Hatchetman*, was still standing on the trail. The pilot fired his autocannon, hitting Archer's *Penetrator* in the chest and exploding off several tons of protective armor. The *Penetrator* reeled under the assault, but Archer fought back and kept the 'Mech upright. He was about to change targets when he saw that most of the Specters on his bank had returned fire. As if on cue, the *Hatchetman* was hit with no less than five different barrages. It collapsed in a cloud of black and gray smoke as the *Flashman* and a nimble *Dervish* beat a hasty retreat past the fallen 'Mech, leaving it for dead.

The *Nightsky* rose slowly to its feet, fired its jets again, and managed a listing landing on the trail just beyond the flames and smoke of the *Hatchetman* burning like a bonfire. Someone from Archer's side of the river fired a large laser that hit the *Nightsky* just as it was turning to flee, splaying armor plating wildly as it gouged deep. The Guard BattleMech tottered, obviously suffering from internal damage that was most likely a gyro from the way it wobbled and fought for balance. Its footing crumbled to nothing on the rocky trail, then the 'Mech slid down the jagged rocks along the raging river, ripping off armor plating with each grinding meter it fell.

Then, suddenly, it was over. Three of the Guards had managed to flee the scene. The rest were either damaged by fire or missing in the river. The churning white water continued to break over the rocks, heedless of the damage it had done. Archer saw the green and yellow form of the Guard *Cicada* just before the bend in the waterway, pressed by the crushing force of the river against a massive boulder, unable to move. The others were either underwater or attempting to breach the surface somewhere downstream.

"Commence rescue and recovery operations," Archer ordered. "Pit Bull, tie up our friends, give them our thanks, put the plug back in, and get out of there."

Colonel Blucher came up to the blackened remains of Senior Warrant Officer Mary Jane Grand's *Hatch-*

etman lying on the trail. Smoke still rose from the impact area that had once been a BattleMech. The 'Mech's arm, severed at the shoulder, lay nearby, the trademark hatchet still in its hand. The sickly sweet smell of burned coolant and myomer bundling filled the air. Below him, the level of the torrential river was beginning to drop. He had sent troops to the control center, and they had rescued the two workers tied up there.

This wasn't good. He had lost five BattleMechs, counting the destroyed *Hatchetman*. And from their scans of the river from this point downstream, it was obvious Christifori hadn't left the Guard 'Mechs behind. There were signs of one 'Mech destroyed on the other side of the river, but it too had been removed—salvaged for parts. Christifori had captured Blucher's 'Mechs along with their MechWarriors.

Blucher ordered his aerospace fighters and another company of BattleMechs into the area to try and spot the rebels, but they came up empty-handed. He looked down at the river and crossed his arms. He knew that Archer Christifori was every bit the MechWarrior and commander that he was. Thorin was also Christifori's home planet. He knew the place inside out, and the locals loved him. He was also fighting for a cause, and that alone made an enemy dangerous and somewhat unpredictable. Worse yet, this loss would do nothing for the morale of Blucher's own troops.

The mistake he'd made today was letting himself be drawn into a fight on Christifori's terms, but this was only the beginning. He would eventually pinpoint the rebel base of operations and bring the full might of his battalion against them. Looking down at the remains of the *Hatchetman* on the ground, he vowed silently not to make the same mistake again. Sooner or later, he silently promised Christifori, we will fight on my terms.

*   *   *

When Archer and his force returned to the base, it set off a tumult of rejoicing. His command lance would patrol the area, just in case the Guards had somehow picked up their trail. He doubted they had, but his infantry and that lance would be more than enough to hold them at bay until reinforcements arrived.

Everyone was waving their hats, their hands, and anything else they could grab as his small force entered what had been the university's main plaza centuries ago. The Prime Movers coming in behind his *Penetrator* carried the recovered salvage, including what was left of Grath's *Panther*. Grath had suffered a bad flash burn and was being rushed to the makeshift field hospital. Archer brought his 'Mech to a halt, shut down the fusion reactor under his command console, and popped open the hatch to climb down to the ground.

When he got there, Katya and several others rushed toward him, giving him quick salutes and joyous smiles.

"Any sign of the Arcturan Guards?" he asked her.

"Our remote cameras in the river valley show them still there, doing post-battle damage assessments and scouring the area trying to find us," she said, checking her noteputer. "The infantry teams we placed in the mountains did a good job of obscuring our trail visually. Pit Bull and his people got out as well."

"And the gun-camera footage?" he asked, unhooking the coolant vest. He was drenched in sweat, and the cool forest air sent a shiver through his body.

"I'll have the techs pull it and combine it with some of the camera footage we got from remote feeds. We'll smuggle it into Ecol City sometime in the morning, and by tomorrow everyone on the planet will know what we've done."

"I want you to get a compressed copy of the footage sent to some of my contacts on Muphrid as well. If nothing else, it will be a blow to their morale. Who knows, we might be able to give Blucher a hot-foot somewhere other than Thorin."

"On it," she said. "What about the next phase of the operation?"

"If the Guards follow standard procedure, they'll be scouring the area near the river for the next day or so, trying to locate us. Blucher will be forced to pull 'Mechs off their normal patrol routes to help out. That should make it easier for Joey-Lynn to get her team in position to do their job."

"Ecol City isn't her home turf," Katya reminded him, expressing a concern that had already come up several times.

"But she's got the street savvy to pull this off. Send them word in the next hour that they should proceed at their discretion as soon as my message goes off to Muphrid." Fraser would give Blucher something else to worry about.

Las Volk and his people had been working with Fox to come up with a way around the satellite problems too. All Archer had to do was keep the Guards from finding his force.

Katya finished making her notes and then folded down the noteputer's cover. "And, sir, I think congratulations are in order."

"Yes, they are, but not to me," he said. "Send a message of thanks to the Pit Bull team, and make sure we let all our people know it was a job well done."

"What about you, Archer? You're the commander." A slight blush colored Katya's cheeks.

He shook his head twice. "I'm just a man with brass on my shoulders. Those people did all of the work." He looked all around him, then took in the whole busy scene with the sweep of one arm. Even in the midst of the rejoicing, both MechWarriors and technicians were already beginning the task of repairing and rebuilding the damaged BattleMechs.

16

As we have been reporting for the last few days, it appears that war is once again about to ignite inside the Federated Commonwealth. Initial dispatches on the death of Arthur Steiner-Davion reported he was killed by Combine assassins, which set off a series of deep raids by Federated Commonwealth regiments along the Combine border. Precentor Martial Victor Steiner-Davion quickly refuted Combine involvement and declared he had proof his sister Katrina was responsible. He called on all loyal forces to rally to him, and it appears they have. The Archon refers to the clashes erupting on many FedCom worlds as "minor domestic incidents." This reporter, however, has obtained exclusive footage smuggled out of Nanking, showing exactly how serious the conflict has become. Take note, however, that this footage may contain scenes too violent for younger viewers.

—Reported by Dwight Lansing, chief correspondent for
  the holovid newsmagazine *The Real Deal*,
  Free Worlds League, 20 December 3062

Ecol City, Thorin
Skye Province
Lyran Alliance
26 December 3062

"What is the estimate to repair the damage?" Blucher asked as he adjusted the holographic table control to make the command room a little brighter. The place had become something of a prison to him, and his patience was stretched thin. Christifori wasn't giving him a chance to do what he did best—a fair fight on an open field of combat. The debacle at the river had been an ambush. Worse yet, it had forced him to weaken security in the city.

And he'd paid a high price for it. Three separate car bombings had disabled the power substations that fed the planetary HPG, effectively cutting Thorin off from the rest of the Inner Sphere. Without the HPG, there was no way to send or receive messages from other worlds, which meant he hadn't a clue what was happening in the rest of the Lyran Alliance. It also made it impossible to contact his other two battalions on Muphrid.

Much had happened in the last few days, and the situation had become more volatile. Civil disturbances had escalated to uprisings now that Victor Davion had declared his intention to depose the Archon. Blucher had to admire the man as a warrior, but he was more Davion than Steiner in the colonel's eyes. Despite the terrible accusations, Katrina Steiner was the Archon, not Victor. Blucher believed his duty bound him to oppose any efforts by Victor to bring down the Archon.

"We can be back up to speed in two, possibly three more days," Leutnant Fisk replied carefully.

Blucher knew that was too long. A lot could happen in three days. His opening moves on Muphrid had been more decisive than on Thorin. He'd done away with the planetary militia, absorbing it into the Guards. His acting commander on the planet, Kommandant Constance McCoy, had done quick work on her own initiative to make sure the media put the right spin on it.

He hadn't been so lucky. Somehow Christifori had gotten edited footage of the ambush into the hands of the media only an hour after Blucher had held a press conference denying the incident. The result was that he'd thoroughly blown his own credibility with the local population. Worse yet, Christifori seemed to be viewed as a hero for fighting the Alliance military with minimal bloodshed.

"And what of your interrogation of the captured terrorist?" During one attack on a substation, Blucher's troops had managed to apprehend a suspected terrorist. A gang member, no less. Were these the kind of people the rebels wanted fighting for their cause?

"We got some names, including the name of his cell leader, a Joey-Lynn Fraser. Both of them are from Opal City, which is a few hours away. They came to Ecol just to pull off the operation."

"Were you able to get the location of Christifori's base?"

"No, sir. He didn't know it. We used drugs during the interrogation to confirm the information he gave us, but we still got no further details. The rebels are organized by cells, and you know how tough those are to break. We did get four other names, and I've contacted the local police in Opal, but so far none of the terrorists have been located. We did locate the family of one of them, though."

"You took them into custody?" Blucher asked.

"It seemed prudent. It may help us flush out at least one of them," Fisk said.

Blucher rubbed at his brow. "I'd hoped to avoid taking such actions, but they're leaving us no choice."

Another officer came over and handed Blucher a report. He took the sheet and scanned it, then looked up at the officer. "Leutnant Sherwood, you served with Christifori. Can you tell us anything that might be of help?"

The sandy-haired officer shook his head. "I wasn't privy to his detailed operational planning, but I do know this—Archer Christifori does very little in life that isn't planned or calculated. If he knocked out our HPG, he did it for a reason, if only to drive us up the wall with paranoia."

"My thoughts exactly," Fisk said.

"We've been at a full stage of alert and have pulled our troops back into the city because of the attacks, but so far we've seen no more action on his part," Blucher said slowly, thinking out loud. "Which means either we're overlooking something or we're doing what he wants us to do. He knows how we're trained to react, and till now, we've played into his hands. I want you to start patrolling again, tight patterns. Let's go looking for him."

"Is that wise?" Fisk asked.

Blucher ignored the question and turned again to Sherwood. "Your thoughts, Leutnant?"

"Well, sir, Christifori's been in the military his whole life. If you play by the book, he'll counter you every time. He knows the book. Hell, he was there when it was written."

Blucher found himself smiling for the first time in days. "Good. Get the patrols out. Forget the HPG problems and what might be happening in the rest of the Inner Sphere. We've got a rebellion right here on Thorin and we're going to put it down." His words were firm, but a part of him hoped that the rest of the Fifteenth Arcturan Guards on Muphrid weren't also hip deep in rebel troops.

Archer stood at the opening flap of the tent that served as his field headquarters and looked out at the ancient courtyard. His muscles ached, but the cool, crisp air was refreshing. Somewhere above him, he heard the flutter of a large bird's wings and the soft cooing of another. The activity around him had the same unhurried feel—the chance phrase, the occasional chuckle. For a moment, it felt more like being in the midst of a pastoral scene than a military base.

Darius Hopkins came over as Archer stood stretching his arms and shoulders. "What's our status, Darius?" he asked.

"I wish we'd fully salvaged more of that *Nightsky*," Hopkins grumbled.

"What about the gear we did recover?"

"The *Cicada* is functional, for a *Cicada*. The *War Dog* suffered mostly armor damage, and we've got the *Blackjack* operational, with some minor modifications. I scrapped the rest, including Corporal Shantea's *Jenner*. Along with what we salvaged from the remains of that *Hatchetman* and Grath's *Panther*, I'd say we're ahead of the game."

Archer nodded approvingly. "I've checked around. One of Las Volk's people used to be a MechWarrior. Let's give him the *Cicada*."

"Good idea," Hopkins said, wiping his hands on a rag he pulled from his back pocket. "Speaking of extras, we've sent the MechWarriors we captured to the southern continent." Hopkins had come up with a plan to smuggle them by boat to the southern farmlands, where they'd be detained on a farm owned by Catherine Daniels' family.

Both men turned to look as a hovertruck came into the open courtyard, its rear section laden with supplies under a plexitarp covering. Katya climbed out of the passenger seat and walked over to them.

"I take it your supply run went well, Haupt—Captain?" Archer couldn't help stumbling over the new rank structure. It was taking some time getting used to it.

"No problems, but our contacts in the city report that Blucher has ordered out the patrols again." She sounded worried.

Archer was a little surprised—and impressed. Felix Blucher wasn't the kind of soldier known for rolling with the punches. "That's a change. Maybe our colonel is learning to adapt."

Katya nodded. "It looks like he's trying to seize the initiative. He's no fool, this Lyran colonel. He's going to try and turn the tables on us."

"How do we stand on Operation Little John?"

"Volk's and King's people are ready with the diversion and for crowd control if things get out of hand. Our teams have been well-briefed on the plan, and they've been training for it."

Archer was pleased with the report, but the flurry of activity around the hovertruck made him turn to look again. Six technicians were pulling out a massive container that filled most of the truck bed. "I don't remember anything that big on the supply list," he said.

"It wasn't on the list, sir," Katya said with a smile. "It came in on a cargo ship and was waiting at the spaceport. Whoever sent it did a pretty good job of paying off the local customs inspectors. I'm not sure how the transport captain got it past Blucher's security people. They're keeping things seriously wrapped up over there. The shipper contacted some of the locals who knew some people who contacted me. I checked over the cargo three times to make sure it wasn't some kind of trap. The paperwork came with this letter addressed to you."

She handed him an envelope, which was addressed to Archer Christifori with the rank of colonel. He took out a small data disk and borrowed Katya's noteputer to play it. He turned away slightly for privacy as it rolled. The message took a full minute to play.

He felt a warm stinging at the corners of his eyes as he listened to the words. It wasn't sadness, but the reawakening of a fond memory. He glanced over at Hopkins and Katya and smiled. He raised the noteputer and turned up the volume so that they could hear the replay of the message.

The image flickered for a moment, then resolved to show a man looking proud and regal in a crisp dress uniform. His face was worn beyond his years, and there was a sorrow in his eyes that Archer understood. His voice, even through the small speaker in the noteputer, rang in the forest air.

"Archer, I have received news of your sister's death and wish to extend my most sincere regrets. I too have recently lost a beloved sibling and know the sadness you must be feeling. In many respects, we have the same person to blame, indirectly, for our losses.

"As your former commanding officer, I wish there was more I could do to help, but other matters are also pressing. Besides, I'd say you have the situation on Thorin well in hand.

"Please accept these items as gifts. I trust you'll put them to good use.

"As a rebel, you'd be held to the whims of Katrina's laws and minions. I can't allow that. The punishment for terrorists can be death. However, I am granting you a commission in the Armed Forces of the Federated Suns at the rank of colonel. Your regimental designation is officially Archer's Avengers, the First Thorin Regiment. As the CO, you can grant your people full commissions and enrollment. That way, if apprehended, you will be entitled to protection as military prisoners under the Ares Conventions rather than being treated as terrorists. I'm not placing you under my command because you haven't asked for it, but this might give you a little extra peace of mind. I hope you'll accept it.

"I know you hadn't planned to resume your life as a warrior, but these are dark times and there seems no way out but to fight. I will aid you in any way I can in the future, and I'm sure you will do the same for me."

Then the image faded and was replaced by the flaming sun and sword symbol of the Federated Suns.

There was a long silence before Darius Hopkins spoke. "I don't bloody believe it. Prince Victor Steiner-Davion himself."

Archer returned the noteputer to Katya. "He always had a flare for the dramatic. Now tell us what was in the box, Katya."

"Pop-up mines, some pretty sophisticated sensor gear, some shaped charges, a few portable electronic countermeasures units, and some security bypass stuff that'll take a while to figure out."

Archer whistled. "All useful gear. Get it stowed. We've still got work to do on Operation Little John. I'd say we also have to figure out a way to inform the rest of the troops that they just signed up with the AFFS."

17

Reports are only now filtering out of Robinson concerning unauthorized strikes against the Draconis Combine in retaliation for the death of Arthur Steiner-Davion. Said to be spearheading the operation are the First Robinson Rangers, who have apparently attacked and taken the world of Proserpina, with the help of the Eighth Crucis Lancers RCT and the Robinson Academy Training Battalion. There are still unconfirmed reports that the Combine worlds of Al Na'ir, An Ting, and Marduk have also been hit.

—Reported by *Word from the Underground*,
pirate broadcast, Thorin, 26 December 3062

Ecol City, Thorin
Skye Province
Lyran Alliance
28 December 3062

The Second Bank of Thorin was located some eight blocks from the Star League fort the Arcturan Guards were using as their command base. The nondescript brick structure was well over a century old and was situated on a street corner. Undistinguished though it might be, for Archer and his people, the bank had one unique, outstanding feature.

It was the bank closest to the fort.

While some would argue that an army travels on its stomach, the truth is that it survives on its payroll. Soldiers, like everyone who worked for someone else, looked forward to payday. For the Lyran Alliance troops on Thorin, enjoying the things money could buy was part of their reward for having to live inside the pressure cooker the rebels had created for them.

The economy, legal and otherwise, benefited too. Many MechWarriors and troopers went directly to local businesses to spend their hard-earned money. On payday, the local bars were packed, shops of all kinds were busy attending to the soldiers, and in general the local economy got a boost from the influx of money.

Today would be a little different.

In order to actually get their hands on the cash, the Guardsmen needed access to a cash disbursement device, but such conveniences were rare in the run-down neighborhood around the fort. And so the troopers headed straight for the nearest bank—in this case, the Second Bank of Thorin. They would draw on their funds and hit the town.

Blucher's patrols had marked a cordon around the bank, the surrounding businesses, and the fort. It was risky when his people were away from the safety of the garrison, but he couldn't very well keep them penned up.

On almost every street corner stood a pair of infantry, equipped with heavy gear and carrying bulky weapons. At the edges of the area were a handful of armored vehicles, light tanks, and APCs, a military presence that should have been more than enough to ward off any attacks by the rebels.

Archer and Katya had put a lot of thought into

planning Operation Little John—everything from crowd control to the necessary neutralization of the ground forces. Even the name was chosen carefully, right out of the legend of Robin Hood. They'd left little to chance.

Right now Archer was sitting under the murky waters of the Gauley River, which were all he could see through the *Penetrator*'s viewport. He had decided it was the best way to get his 'Mech into position in the city without being seen. Navigating the river's shadowy depths had proven tricky, but he'd managed. He was confident that, like him, Katya and the others were also in position. Now it was simply a matter of execution.

Colonel Blucher usually about a third of his troops out on leave in his safe zone. From there they would be able to get their cash, frequent the local businesses, and return to the fort safely. Then another group would be allowed into the city. It was a tight procedure. One that Archer now planned to shatter.

Seeing only by the illuminated digital displays in his cockpit, he checked his short-range sensors and the chronometer. If all was going as planned, the first phase was underway. He had held back his meager aerospace fighter elements at a hidden airstrip until now. Several fighters should also be on station in orbit around Thorin. Their targets were Blucher's orbital intelligence satellites. Their loss would prevent him from tracking what was going on. All Archer had to do now was wait . . .

Katya Chaffee, dressed like any other moderately poor civilian, moved down the street carrying her grocery bags. She shambled along, taking note of the soldiers on the corner. One of them had just verified her ID, which indicated that she did indeed live in the neighborhood. Thank god for Las Volk's people, who knew some of the best forgers on Thorin.

She turned the corner onto Euclid Avenue, and saw the tank stationed there, a sixty-ton Demon painted in green-splotched camouflage. It blocked one side of the street along the sidewalk. The top hatch was open and its commander hung half in and half out, watching the crowd with a disinterested stare unless a young lady walked into his field of vision.

Katya made her way slowly down the walk, giving the vehicle only an occasional glance as she neared it. The commander threw her a look, but all he saw was a middle-aged woman laden with groceries, no threat to his powerful tank. He was more focused on his fellow Alliance soldiers just up the street. Katya turned around and saw them too. They were heading straight for the bank. Some laughed together, others casually jogged up the steps. They had no idea what was coming.

A few steps past the commander's field of vision, Katya reached into one of her bags and slapped a small device onto the rear of the Demon as she passed. Its signal would be broadcast for kilometers.

Las Volk, wearing an Ecol City maintenance jumpsuit and hardhat, also passed two of the security force as he and one of his people approached a sewer manhole. He stopped to light the butt of a cigarette and stood casually puffing on it for a few moments. Then he used his lift pole to pop open the manhole cover while his companion marked the area with safety tape and two cones.

Suddenly a solider came up alongside them, his weapon raised. "What are you doing?" he demanded.

"Maintenance on the sewage line. Flow is slow," Volk replied, lighting another cigarette and then fumbling around the back of his oxygen tank to pull a scrap of dirty paper from his pocket. "Here's my work order."

The soldier looked at it, then at Volk, who wiped his nose with the sleeve of his jumpsuit. The infantryman went over to their tool kits and kicked them slightly. He heard the rattle of tools and felt the considerable weight.

"Sewage flow?" he queried, wrinkling his nose and upper lip at the same time.

"Yup," Volk replied with a grin. "Somebody's gotta fix it."

"Better you than me, pal," the trooper said, handing back the work order. Then he turned and briskly walked away.

From atop the bank building, Sergeant Major Hopkins and a platoon of infantry huddled near the air-handling units to keep from being seen from the other rooftops. His was one of the few teams in the operation dressed in their uniforms instead of civilian garb. They were a good six stories above street level, and from the small surveillance cameras Hopkins had mounted and was monitoring, the Guardsmen were just entering the bank. Then he glanced across the roof and saw that the rappelling gear was in place. He checked his chronometer.

From orbit over Thorin Leftenant Francine Culver picked up the signal coming from Ecol City on her long-range sensors. The target was painted. She switched the bombing scope of her *Lucifer* and armed her Arrow IV bomb-missiles. Another target lit up as well, and she signaled her wingman, Andrew Hackley, who hovered nearby in his *Chippewa*. "Drew, call the ball."

"I'll take the bravo signal, you take the alpha," she heard him say over her headset.

"Remember the colonel's orders. Two passes, no

more, no less, then we bug out low under radar and head for the secondary base."

"This should be about as easy as those satellites we popped," Hackley said, sounding supremely confident. This would be his first taste of real combat, which Culver knew would take care of that smug arrogance in a matter of seconds. She grinned briefly, then set her mind back to business.

"Let's do it," she said and peeled her fighter into a steep dive toward the blue and white ball of Thorin below her.

Archer rounded the corner in his *Penetrator* and swept the area with his short-range sensors. He picked up a Rommel, a Puma, a Demon, and a pair of Zephyrs. While none of the tanks were in his line of sight, he knew that he was also showing up on their sensors by now. That was fine. It was his job to be bait, to get their attention. He lifted his feet off the foot pedals and throttled to a dead stop. Here I am boys, he thought, now what are you going to do about it?

According to his sensors, the Guards armored forces were trying to signal the fort, but that wasn't going to work. Fox's people had hidden jamming gear between their current posting and the fort, which cut off communications. The Zephyrs were attempting to move on parallel streets, closing on his position. The Rommel moved only slightly on the street he was on, but was obscured by signs and trees on the corner. It was out there, though, that much Archer's sensors told him. Only the Puma and the Demon held their ground. He checked his chronometer one more time, then his long-range sensors on the secondary display. There they were, the two fighters, dropping straight on Ecol City.

"Bingo!" he said. "Specter One to all forces. Execute!"

*   *   *

The air on the street suddenly became charged as if there were an electrical burst nearby. The Puma, an ugly monstrosity with three semi-turrets, traveled about eight meters, positioning itself to provide cover for the Rommel in the middle of the street. Las Volk watched from inside the manhole whose cover he'd popped open only a few moments earlier.

"Hand me the charges," he said to his man in the sewer. He took the charges in the canvas satchel and crawled the rest of the way out of the hole.

He sprinted low to the Puma, which was only a dozen meters away. The infantry on the street paid him not the slightest attention. Everyone else was also in motion, panic setting in as the Lyrans began to respond to the unseen enemy. Volk moved next to the Puma and attached a charge to the top of the rear hatch. It was a shaped explosive designed for just such close-quarters combat. He pulled the timer chord and sprinted for the sewer.

There followed a massive blast that rocked the upper armor of the awkwardly shaped tank. The explosion was so strong that Volk flew right over the open manhole and landed hard on the ground. His companion inside the hole was also tossed back hard, but he recoiled and brought his pistol up and ready, firing at a pair of infantry moving away from him. One dropped quickly. The other, startled by the shot from his rear, swung around the corner. The missed shot kicked up a burst of dust from the brick wall where the slug had ended its flight.

Volk crawled on hands and knees to the manhole and lowered himself in feet first. He could see a thick, oily-black snake of smoke rising from the hatch of the Puma where he'd planted the shaped charge. The tank was still operational, but its crew would be shaken up. A roar from above made him look up. He saw the sleek shape of an aerospace fighter, thundering down between the tall buildings along the street, firing its . . .

". . . bombs away," howled Leftenant Culver as she let go with half of her Arrow IVs. The missiles snaked and twisted in their flight, her weapons lock fed to her by the signal coming off the lock-enhancer planted on the Demon. The tank attempted to move, but could not. Only one of the bombs failed to hit its mark; the rest buried themselves in the front and the right flank of the Demon. In the midst of those blasts, Hackley was also firing down into the turret and front armor of the tank.

Culver pulled back on the joystick, and her *Lucifer* bucked hard, pulling up at a steep angle. She felt her weight increase in the cockpit seat as she fought back the g-forces straining at her. Rising above the tops of the buildings, she set a long, sweeping arc out over Ecol City.

"I got mine, Drew. How'd you do?"

"That Rommel's backside is belching fire, and she's not moving," he answered. "I'm sweeping out wide for another pass."

"Just one more," she said. "Colonel Christifori is going to be expecting us for dinner."

"I just want to thank the ground-pounders who painted those targets for us. It sure is sweet to see everything hit the mark."

"Now!" Sergeant Major Hopkins said as his team rappelled down the front of the bank. Just coming out the doorway were over two dozen Guards personnel staring at the firefight two blocks down. The instant Hopkins and the others hit the ferrocrete, they leveled their Rorynex assault rifles at the troopers' backs.

"Surrender now or die," Hopkins barked. The stunned soldiers turned and found themselves facing a platoon of heavily armed and armored infantry. Most, he noted with satisfaction, stood with their mouths agape, hardly knowing what was happening. His infantry moved in quickly, removing the officers' sidearms and making sure none of the soldiers had any other weapons.

"I'm Kommandant Derkson. What's the meaning of this?" one of them finally managed to demand.

"The meaning is that you're our prisoners. Now, then, Kommandant, if you please, I believe you've got quite a bit of your paycheck in your pockets. All of you, hand over your money now or you'll be shot."

"This is a robbery?" Kommandant Derkson stammered.

"In a way," Hopkins said, giving him a toothy grin. "Have you ever read the story of Robin Hood?"

Archer rounded the corner only half a block from the flanking Zephyr. Low and sleek, the Zephyr hovertank was moving along slowly, holding at less than a half-meter above its skirting. The Guardsman driver opened up with his short-range missiles and medium lasers as soon as he saw Archer's 'Mech. The SRMs ate up a massive chunk of the *Penetrator's* chest, and the 'Mech rocked under the simultaneous impacts. One of the tank's lasers missed totally, but the other two slammed into his legs.

He checked his damage display and saw that the armor had held, which was good news. He nimbly adjusted his joystick and dropped his targeting reticle locked onto the front of the Zephyr. He hit the thumb TIC trigger and listened as the two extended-range large lasers made a whining cycle sound during their discharge.

The bright crimson beams of energy stabbed into the Zephyr's turret. White smoke and melted globs of plating spewed off, and the hovercraft came to a dead stop. As the ripple of heat spiked momentarily in his cockpit, Archer walked the gawky *Penetrator* back slowly to the cover of the building. His sensors told him that the Zephyr was accelerating, apparently intending to cross his field of fire. It looked like the tanker was going to try and rake him with his turret as he passed.

Archer side-stepped the *Penetrator* across the street, giving himself a wider field of fire. That should throw the Zephyr off. The fast-moving hovercraft fired where he thought Archer should have been, realizing only at the last second that he was no longer there.

Archer didn't make the same mistake. While his large lasers recharged, he triggered six of his medium pulse lasers. Their emerald bursts of light pockmarked the tank's side armor, burning little holes all along the left side and its skirt. Two found their marks on the turret, which was already blackened from his previous hit. There was a small explosion, and the turret rocked back, hanging half on and half off the Zephyr.

The Guard vehicle listed hard from the blast, spinning sideways on its path down the street, and a millisecond later passed out of Archer's field of vision. Without its turret, it didn't have much chance of staying in the fight. His short-range sensors confirmed that. The hovercraft was breaking quickly for the fort. Archer found himself wishing he could praise the driver for being smart enough to know when to retreat. It was only one more reminder that the Guards were a top-notch unit.

Off in the distance he saw his two aerospace fighters pull up from their second pass, banking off and away from Ecol City. "Specter One to The Brain," he said. "Sit rep."

"The Zephyrs are bugging out," Katya returned. "Our infantry and Volk's people toasted the Puma.

Hopkins has secured the targets. Scratch one Rommel and a Demon."

"Good. I'm coming in. Have the others prepare for bug-out and let's start working the crowds and the media."

Archer stopped his *Penetrator* in front of the bank and looked down at the crowd that had gathered. Now that the firing had stopped, many people had emerged to see who had attacked, and why.

He activated his external speaker, so that everyone within a city block could hear him. "Sergeant Major, have you got the money?"

"Yes, sir, every bloody L-bill," Hopkins said over his wrist comm.

"Come on up," Archer said. With a satchel over one arm, Hopkins began to climb the hand-holds to the top of the *Penetrator* while Archer began to speak.

"People of Thorin, this is Archer Christifori. We didn't come here today to hurt any of you, only the oppressors who have come to our world. This money is their blood money, funds they are paid to keep us under their heels. They don't deserve the money, but we believe you do."

As if on cue, Darius Hopkins opened the bag and swung it wide. Lyran L-bills, many bearing the face of Katrina Steiner or her martyred mother, drifted into the air. The people reached up, both to the falling money and to the *Penetrator* looming over them.

Archer savored the moment, allowed himself a moment to relish the cheering, crying, and applause, then ordered his teams to depart and disperse. Things had gone well, but he was also a soldier who knew when it was time to go. There was no point in pressing it. Not with an enemy like Colonel Felix Blucher out there, an enemy who would be looking for revenge . . . especially after today.

18

As a result of the recent rebel attack in down-
town Ecol, Colonel Felix Blucher, commander of the
Fifteenth Arcturan Guards, announced this morning
that eight suspected terrorists have been apprehended and taken into custody. No evidence
against these individuals has been made public.

—From *The Thorin Exponent*, byline Beth Ann
  Sorantinno, Ecol City, 29 December 3062

Ecol City, Thorin
Skye Province
Lyran Alliance
29 December 3062

The force of the explosion was so strong that it
tossed Felix Blucher backward nearly five meters
across the command post courtyard. His eardrums
popped, and he rolled over twice before banging to
a stop against a fence. His injured leg throbbed, still
hurting from the last time an explosion had thrown
him through the air. It was, for a millisecond, as if
he were trapped in a nightmare, but the muffled
sounds and the smells told Blucher that this wasn't
a memory or a dream, but a hellish slice of reality.

Lifting his head off the ground, he saw the front gate of the fort in a shambles. Smoke from the exterior wall rose like a funeral pyre into the sky, and flames lapped in through the gate. Personnel were moving about, and it dawned on him that this time he wasn't the target of the attack. After patting himself to make sure nothing was broken or bleeding, he quickly called Fisk over his wrist comm.

"There's been an explosion at the front gate," he said. Off in the distance on the other side of the fort's massive walls, he heard another blast, this one muffled, sympathetic.

"Full alert!" he commanded.

Leutnants Fisk and Sherwood came running over moments later, taking hold of Blucher on either side to help him to a standing position. He gently pushed them away and pointed to the gate, where firefighters and infantry had arrived. Sirens blared along the outside wall, and as his hearing returned to normal, he could hear shouts in the distance.

"What happened?" he demanded.

"It looks like our APCs were hit by a bomb. It must have been a car or truck filled with explosives," Sherwood said, following Blucher's gaze toward the frantic activity around the main gate.

"What about our people?"

Fisk shook his head. "Most of a city block came down on top of them, sir." For once he'd lost his cockiness, and Blucher didn't need to hear more. Any blast that could breach the main gate would have crushed the armored personnel carriers like disposable cups. He'd arrested some troublemakers, and this was the rebels' response.

"Deploy more patrols. Tighten the satellite sweeps of the city. I want our fighters in the air, running recon," he said. The orders flowed from his tongue almost without thought. "I never thought Christifori would stoop to something so vicious, but I'm going to make damn sure he doesn't do it again."

Archer stared at the field holographic projector, watching images of the carnage of an entire city block in flames. He rubbed his chin thoughtfully as Katya came over to watch too. The tape rolled while a reporter's voiceover recounted the death toll of both Guardsmen and civilian alike.

"Who did this, Katya?"

"I finally managed to contact all our cells, but it wasn't easy. The Lyrans have seriously stepped up surveillance ever since Blucher started arresting people. But the word on the street is that this is the work of Rufus King."

"King," Blucher said with disgust, still staring at the street in flames and the rescue workers pulling the maimed and dead from the rubble. It was King's cell that Blucher's arrests had crippled, and King had only barely escaped the dragnet Blucher had tightened around their activities. "And we didn't know this was coming?"

Katya dropped her head in shame. "No, sir."

"King," he repeated, wondering what to do with this man who had defied him. "It's my fault. I should've seen that he never intended to stay in line. I sensed it from the night we first met him."

"No, Colonel. I should have had him tailed. The blame is mine."

"The part that worries me is that this gives Blucher more reason to crack down."

"If he does, it will only drive more people to our cause."

"You're probably right, but that won't happen overnight. In the meantime innocent people are going to suffer. That's the sad part of all this. So far, we've been waging a monkey war. We've been an irritant. We've won battles but avoided bloodbaths. We've robbed from the rich and given to the poor. We've chipped away at the morale of our enemies. But this changes everything. Blucher's going to come after us for real now, and we'd better figure out a way to deal with it."

The message came through to Colonel Blucher's desk comm unit, which immediately prompted him for his command cipher. This was no typical communication, but one bearing the protocol of the Office of the Archon—a personal message from Katrina Steiner.

Rubbing his sore arm, he spoke the cipher phrase that would open the file. "Victory has a thousand fathers, but defeat is an orphan," he said. The words triggered the file-lock, revealing the image of Katrina Steiner sitting behind her desk, the iron fist of the Lyran Alliance draped behind her.

"This must have cost a fortune to transmit on the priority circuit," he muttered, sitting back to watch. Katrina Steiner was wearing a deep blue dress that shimmered on the screen.

"This message is to all regimental commanders in the Lyran Alliance Armed Forces," she said. "It is classified and not for distribution or discussion under the terms of the Sedition Act." She paused and looked directly out from the screen as though into the eyes of each of her commanders.

"As most of you are aware, my brother Victor has recently made false accusations linking me with the death of my brother." Her voice caught, wavered, as if Victor's treachery tore at her heart. "His words have spawned disturbances on worlds throughout the Federated Commonwealth, and many people had to be arrested. Davion terrorists, sponsored by Victor, have also struck at many of our commands. Large numbers of our troops have been killed or injured by these terrorist activities. Some commanders have abandoned their honor and their duty as defenders of the realm and have gone over to my wayward brother. You and your commands have been true to our House through the death of my mother, my brother's war games, and now his new call for war. I tell you now that I am with you, if not physically, in spirit. You are the best of all that is Lyran.

"To protect the integrity of our realm, I now declare martial law throughout the Federated Commonwealth. Individual commanders will use their own discretion in executing these orders.

"Davion forces calling themselves members of the Armed Forces of the Federated Suns have attacked several planets. To prevent the further spread of seditious propaganda, I am limiting the flow of information via HPG. No communications between worlds by any non-military office will be permitted. This may have economic repercussions in the short term, but it is necessary to cripple coordination by our enemies.

"From this point forward, a state of war exists between the Lyran Alliance and the Federated Suns led by my misguided brother. However, we will not make this declaration public as it would only galvanize his efforts to unite rebel elements. But have no doubt, we are already at war. All garrison commanders should consider our enemies to be outright terrorists and should use the harshest measures in dealing with them. The fate of House Steiner and the Alliance depends on your ability to crush these traitors. I will fully support your actions and decisions as those of loyal protectors of the realm."

Her imaged faded as she stopped speaking, melding into the great fist that symbolized the Lyran Alliance. Blucher contemplated the image for a moment, then cut off the communication. He had no need to replay it. He understood the implications of the message and thought the Archon's strategy crafty. She was giving her commanders a free hand in maintaining order and suppressing rebellion, but had left room to indemnify herself if the outcome was not to her liking.

He slumped back in his leather chair, which squeaked slightly under his weight. The situation on Thorin was getting worse, and he'd gotten similar reports from Muphrid, where his garrison had lost nearly a company's worth of MechWarriors. It was true he'd made some headway, had crushed one rebel cell, but that was just a start. Until now Archer Christifori hadn't stooped to murder, but the bombing had revealed him as an enemy without honor. So many had died in that explosion.

With his troops being slaughtered while defenseless, what choice had he but to comply with the Archon's orders as he saw fit? He'd immediately order the establishment of detention camps, though he would not countenance torture or other mistreatment. Yet, he knew that camps and arrests wouldn't be enough to stop Christifori.

From this point forward, he must take and hold the initiative, but he wasn't sure how. He rubbed his chin in thought, then began to see the glimmering of an idea. It might be cost him some materiel and men, but in the end, it would let him finally flush out his prey.

Reaching for his comm system, he switched on the coding to access the surveillance satellite system orbiting Thorin. He had a plan, one that would remove Archer Christifori and his rebels from the picture once and for all.

19

The actions of Leutnant Colonel Christifori and his fellow militiamen should be considered nothing short of reckless. If I had to make the call, Jerry, I'd say that this so-called rebellion will fizzle in a week, two at most.

—*Thorin Week in Review*, commentary by Katie Winson, Donegal Broadcasting Company, 1 January 3063

Village of Louisa, Thorin
Skye Province
Lyran Alliance
2 January 3063

The Bagpiper was empty save for the bartender, two shabbily dressed locals, and Archer and Katya. When Rufus King and two of his people entered the bar, only Archer and Katya took notice. King sauntered over to the booth where they sat in darkness along the back wall. He dropped into the seat across from them.

"I thought we weren't going to have these little face-to-face sessions," he said as his thugs also pushed into the tight confines of the booth, their rear ends squeaking on the synthleather seating. His tone was as snide and arrogant as the last time they'd met.

"We weren't," Archer said in a low voice that couldn't be overheard. "That was before the incident at the Guards base."

"I have no idea what you're talking about," King said innocently, then gave a slight chuckle as if very pleased with himself. It made Archer want to smash the words into his face. Only a fool laughed at the deaths of other people, even enemies.

Katya wasn't amused either. "We have our sources, King. We know all about that truck loaded with explosives."

That got him angry. "Don't wave your moral superiority at me, missy. Just because hero-boy here"— he stabbed a finger at Archer—"isn't willing to do some real damage to the Lyrans, doesn't mean I'm not. I didn't have any choice but to take matters into my own hands. Blucher captured nearly everyone in my cell, while I barely escaped. Well, now he knows what happens when you tangle with Rufus King."

Archer was just as angry. With great effort, he maintained a calm and cool exterior. "I established our rules of engagement. You broke them. This is serious, King."

"If you don't approve of what I did, well, then it's time for me to break with you and your little army and strike out on my own."

"More than a dozen innocent civilians were killed in that bombing of yours. We're not waging war to turn the population against us. Worse yet, you've given Blucher a good reason to harass other innocent people. He's already started setting up detention camps."

King stroked his dark goatee and smiled a yellow grin. The seat squeaked under him as he shifted. "You fail to mention that we killed over thirty of their infantry, not to mention the other two dozen who are still hospitalized. My action neutralized a full company of their infantry. That's more than you've done, Christifori, and you're the one who's got the BattleMechs."

Archer raised one eyebrow, his only show of emotion. "How many innocents must pay the price for your actions, King? Over three hundred have been arrested already, and more are being picked up every day. You just don't seem to get that innocent people were killed in your bombing. You're reckless."

"Well, Colonel Christifori, it sounds to me like we're going to have a little parting of our ways." King nodded to his companions that it was time to go. They slid out of the booth and stood waiting for King to do the same. "You run your war your way. I'll fight it my way. In the end, we'll both win." He stood up and gave the same self-satisfied laugh.

King turned and had gone several steps toward the door as Archer and Katya also slid out of the booth. "King," Archer said, loud enough for everyone in The Bagpiper to hear, "I'm afraid it's not going to be that easy."

King and his bodyguards turned around, and the two guards pulled out their slugthrowers and aimed them in the general direction of Archer and Katya.

"Sorry, Colonel. I have my own plans," King said.

A loud snap and a clicking sound came from behind King. Neither Archer nor Katya moved, but the sound of rounds being chambered, of hammers being cocked, had the desired effect. With fearful looks, they looked over their shoulders and saw the bartender with a shotgun leveled at them. The other two "locals" had submachineguns raised. Katya stepped forward and took the weapons from King's thugs.

"I appreciate the fact that you have plans," Archer said, "but as you can see, so do I."

"What are you going to do to me?" King asked.

Archer let his anger rush away. "Make sure you don't ruin any more innocent lives."

Opal City was a medium-size industrial town some two hundred-fifty kilometers west of Ecol City. Like Ecol, it had been bombed out during the fall of the original Star League and eventually rebuilt. Its factories produced mostly commercial products and chemicals. Opal manufactured no weapons, but the materials they shipped out were among the strategic military assets of the Lyran Alliance. It was also the turf of the White Tigers, the hoverbike gang led by Joey-Lynn Fraser.

Under Blucher's new orders, the Arcturan Guards were forced to patrol all the way to Opal, a duty none of them relished. The White Tigers had continually sniped at the infantry until Blucher replaced them with tanks. When the tanks were fire-bombed, he replaced them with BattleMechs. Since then, the White Tigers had given his men a wide berth.

Tonight would be different.

Two BattleMechs were on patrol, but Joey-Lynn and Darius Hopkins had a surprise waiting for them. Three of her hoverbikers and one of the militia's tiny Savannah Master hovercraft would act as the bait. The bikers, led by Joey-Lynn, would fire on the patrol 'Mechs with shoulder-launched rockets and the Master's laser. That would divert the attention of the 'Mechs while Hopkins and three platoons of militia infantry came in to finish the job.

From his position among the branches of a huge oak, Hopkins saw a flare of light and activity several kilometers away through his night-vision binoculars. He knew what it was: the discharge of short-range missiles and a laser beam stabbing into the night air. He lowered the binoculars and signaled to the rest of his troops. Several of them were also in the trees, armed with grapple rods that would let them latch onto and scale a moving 'Mech. Across the road was a hastily dug line of breastworks that offered no obstacle to a BattleMech, but would provide the infantry some degree of protection. The rest of Hopkins' people were concealed in a slip-trench along the roadsides. In the middle of the road, connected to the detonator in his hands, was a little surprise that had taken hours to prepare.

"I sure hope the engineer boys knew what they were doing," Hopkins muttered to himself, glancing over at the camouflaged earth-moving equipment in a nearby patch of woods.

He heard the high-pitched hum of the hoverbikes first. They slowed every so often, as if to give the 'Mechs time to catch up. The Savannah Master came next, the whirring sound of its laser charging and the crack of its firing audible about the same time that it appeared. Swerving back and forth, the laser stabbed back down the road at a pair of Battle-Mechs—a *Gallowglas* and a *Lancelot*. The laser wasn't doing much except harass the 'Mechs. The *Lancelot* fired its own lasers at the tiny hovercraft, but the vehicle's speed and tight-turning arcs made it hard to hit. One crimson lance hit a tree, which splintered in two, shaking the ground and the tree where Hopkins was crouched.

Both 'Mechs ran forward as the hoverbikes raced through a small gap in the breastworks, barely visible in the darkness. Positioned safely to the rear of the infantry, Joey-Lynn and her comrade now turned to face their pursuers. Hopkins, from his perch among the tree limbs, watched in awe as the 'Mechs passed. Even after all of his years of military service, the majesty of the war machines made armor and infantry pale in comparison.

The *Gallowglas* was in the lead, slowing almost to a stop in front of the breastworks. The *Lancelot* was somewhat further behind, and it stopped just as the

Savannah Master lifted up and over the infantry in the ditch alongside the road. Hopkins watched transfixed. The 'Mechs were directly over the trap. He opened the safety switch on the detonator and pressed his thumb on the trigger.

It was a pit four meters deep—the width of the road—and ten meters long. A false surface was held up by dozens of specially cut metallic supports. The surface had been reinforced but had numerous breakaway joints that were covered with small explosive implants. The militia's combat engineers had outdone themselves in that the pit hadn't collapsed when the *Gallowglas* first stepped on it.

The explosive bolts sheared the breakaway surface, and suddenly the "road" under the pair of Guard 'Mechs disappeared in a puff of smoke, dust, and confusion. The *Gallowglas* MechWarrior was good. Just as the blast occurred, she tried to step forward onto the breastworks. But with one foot lifted high and the other dropping down four meters, it was hopeless. The *Gallowglas* fell backward, hitting so hard that Hopkins' tree quaked again and the grinding of armor plates filled the air.

The *Lancelot*'s MechWarrior never had a chance to respond. As the larger 'Mech fell past him, he fell forward too. The 'Mech turned slightly as it went, then plunged face-down into the pit in front of the breastworks. Hopkins was about to signal the infantry into action, but there was no need. They were already swarming all over the 'Mechs, lashing satchel charges to critical joints on the fallen machines. Other troopers stood on the breastworks and aimed their shoulder-launched SRMs at the 'Mech cockpits only a few meters way. Had the pilots tried to make a break for it, they would have met an odious death.

Hopkins took out his comm unit and opened a broadband channel the Guards were likely to hear. "Power down your BattleMechs and surrender now, and you'll live. You both have enough explosives tied to you to leave your 'Mechs nothing but charred ruins."

"Who is you?" came back a female voice as the *Gallowglas* pilot tried to extricate herself from the pit, rocking the 'Mech enough for the infantry on top of her to jump clear.

"Sergeant Major Darius Hopkins of Archer's Avengers," he said. "You have three seconds to comply."

"Crudstunk!" she spat back. From below he heard the pop and hiss as the hatches of both 'Mechs cycled open. The MechWarriors emerged, their hands on their heads but looking scornful. Hopkins slid down the tree and stood on the edge of the pit as his troopers went to work to remove the explosive charges.

"Good work, men," he said, then turned to the two MechWarriors in their shorts and coolant vests. "Welcome to Archer's Avengers. Consider yourself prisoners of war."

Blucher stared at the man that hung hog-tied from the line run across the security post. He was alive, but only semi-conscious. His mouth was taped shut, but he kept trying to speak and even managed to communicate his distress. He squirmed about like a fish caught on a line, hanging only a half-meter above the ferrocrete beyond the fort's wall.

"How did this happen?" the colonel asked a nearby sergeant as two troopers went to cut the man down.

"Two of our men were on patrol and were stungassed from behind. They were disarmed, but not harmed. When they came to, they found this guy tied here and carrying an envelope addressed to you. We secured the area and contacted you."

Blucher took the envelope and tore it open. He unfolded the single sheet of paper and read it in the dimness of the perimeter lights while moths fluttered around them in the darkness. He recognized the handwriting, which he'd seen twice before, as Archer Christifori's.

"Colonel Blucher," it began. "This man I've left you is Rufus King, the one responsible for the terrorist bombing of your troops. Neither I nor any of my people sanctioned his actions, nor were we aware of his plan. He operated solely on his own. What information he has about our operation is no longer useful to you.

"I deliver him to you with my promise that we will wage an honorable war. Not conventional—but honorable. I am fighting to remove you, as a symbol of the Archon's presence, off the planet Thorin, not to kill people wantonly. Do with King as you must, but I assure you that detention camps will no longer be needed. You have the man who spilled your people's blood. You and I will settle our dispute like true soldiers.

"Signed, Colonel Archer Christifori, Archer's Avengers."

Blucher folded the sheet carefully and slid it into his pocket. "I'm sure you sent that to the media as well, Archer," he said softly, "but it won't be that easy."

"Sir?" asked the sergeant.

"Nothing," Blucher answered curtly. "Cut that thing down and put it in the brig." He gestured to Rufus King's form still hanging in the air like a fly trapped in a web. "There is much to do before dawn."

20

King's attorney, Raul Frost, had no comment on leaving the courthouse, but did file a motion for change of venue, claiming that the publicity around the case precluded King getting a fair trial in Ecol City.

—From *Newstalk at 6:30*, Ecol City, Thorin,
   4 January 3063

Ecol City, Thorin
Skye Province
Lyran Alliance
6 January 3063

Blucher's key command staff stood around the holographic display, which showed a scene of long, rolling hills capped with tall trees. Silently and thoughtfully, the officers studied the terrain, with its narrow dirt paths and lanes that could hardly be called roads.

Blucher, still limping slightly, moved around the table toward the control panel. "Our intelligence has paid off. Knowing that Christifori's people are salvaging our BattleMechs, we were able to lay a trap.

As everyone here knows, all of our heavy gear is fitted with homing devices. We know that his technicians would disable these first, then salvage the equipment. This time we concealed a second set of devices, ones with timed signals set to trigger many hours later. Thanks to our satellite system, we have identified what looks like their key base of operations." He pointed to the forested scene on the holographic display table.

Felix Blucher felt better than he had for a while. Finally, he would engage the so-called Archer's Avengers in stand-up combat on equal terms. They were good, he'd give them that. They'd held their own against his veterans, but only by fighting as guerrillas rather than honorable warriors. And they only fought when they could choose the time, location, and conditions. This wasn't the kind of war Blucher's people were trained for. Nor did they have the advantage of knowing every rock, tree, and stream on Thorin and how to use them against an enemy.

None of that mattered, really. Blucher knew that the fate of the Lyran state depended on him and other commanders fighting to uphold the Archon and the rule of law. The stakes were high, but if Christifori could be captured or killed, the wind would be knocked out of the revolt on Thorin.

"The rebels are apparently using the old university grounds as their base of operations," he said. "Our engineers have pulled up maps of the site and report that many of the structures are still standing. Don't let all of these trees fool you. You may very well find yourself in an urban combat environment when we storm their command post."

He pointed his baton at the holographic display and pressed a small button on the baton. An arrow appeared in bright red along the only trail that led up to the rebel base. "The plan requires a three-pronged assault. Kommandant Derkson, you will take your mixed company up the main trail, which is where their defenses will likely be heaviest. You are a diversion, however. Your job is to draw the enemy down from their base in the hills and into the area along the roadway."

Blucher waved the baton over the table while pressing another of its small control studs. This time the bright red arrow that appeared in the air stabbed downward at the ancient ruins. "Our aerospace fighters will strike at their main base. We will firebomb the area to clear the foliage and incapacitate their command and control centers from the air."

A press on a third control stud showed another set of arrows along the flanks of Kommandant Derkson's force. "Our remaining forces under Hauptmanns Keiver and Gotteb will progress on opposite sides of the road and strike at the rebel base from the flanks. The heavy forest will hinder your movement, so the flank teams will deploy earlier than Derkson. Once the enemy takes the bait, you smash whatever is left of their command and control capabilities and hit them from the rear."

He looked over at Keiver and Gotteb, who were listening intently. Keiver was a dark-haired man with a face so heavily scarred he looked much older than his years. Gotteb had cropped blonde hair and a lightning-bolt tattoo near her right ear that shimmered in the holographic light. Both were obviously primed for a fight, a real fight, not the tricks and skirmishing and terrorist acts the Guards had endured till now.

Leutnant Sherwood was also present. "Colonel, sir, how do we make sure Christifori can't escape?"

Blucher smiled thinly. "Good question, Leutnant. Now that we know where he keeps the bulk of his BattleMech and ground armor forces, our surveillance satellites are making concentrated scans of the area. If he tries to break out, we'll be able to dog his every step."

"When do we move out?" asked Leutnant Karter Moody, one of the few remaining members of his armored company.

"Operations commence tomorrow afternoon. I already have our satellites concentrating to confirm enemy numbers and locations. Make no mistake about one thing, though. We've lost some good people—and some good friends—in this revolt. We will no longer tolerate their rebellion. Our loyalty is to House Steiner and its Archon, regardless of the prattle from the media or Victor Davion. Keep focused, get your people ready. If we win here, the war on Thorin is over."

The officers gathered around the holodisplay nodded and murmured approval. Blucher adjusted his stance to take weight off his throbbing thigh and watched their faces. They understood as well as he that this was a fight they *had* to win. With the losses the Guards had taken thus far, they could never sustain a presence on Thorin with what they had left.

"We're screwed," Darius Hopkins said as Katya concluded her briefing.

"You could be a little more optimistic," Archer said.

"We're *really* screwed, sir." Hopkins scowled and his bushy eyebrows drew even closer together.

"Prince John took serious risks getting this information to us. Now we've got to decide what to do with it."

"We could evacuate," Katya said, "but that would tip off the Lyrans that we'd planted a mole in their midst. We'd have to pull Prince John out."

"Not acceptable. He's too useful." Archer wasn't ready to give up the precious intelligence Prince John was supplying them. It was one of the things that gave him the edge against a powerful enemy. He looked down at the field map spread out in the dingy old room he'd turned into a temporary command bunker. Night was beginning to descend over the forest, and the bunker's yellow lights cast eerie shadows as the group huddled around the map.

"Sir," said Katya, "we have two lances of ground armor at this base. The rest are about fifty kilometers away. We also have about half a company of infantry and most of our BattleMechs here—twelve of them, including the new arrivals. Aerospace elements are still at our hidden aerodrome. The Lyrans have nearly twenty BattleMechs and two lances of ground armor, plus a full lance of aerospace fighters."

"We're outnumbered," said Captain Alice Gett.

Archer frowned. "We've always been outnumbered. That's never been the issue." He had deliberately kept a lance of his own 'Mechs and some additional ground armor and his infantry away from the primary base. Even if this base fell, there would still be enough Avengers remaining to hurt the Lyrans. He had to hand it to Blucher, though. He'd found their command base and immediately come up with plan to destroy it. He was a formidable enemy, and it looked like he was finally pulling out the stops. The rebels would lose no matter how the fight turned out. They could never again use this base now that the Lyrans knew its location. That hurt—period.

"We could pull in our reserves, concentrate for one big battle, take them out now," Hopkins said.

Lanky Captain Paul Snider spoke up next. "Some of our MechWarriors are still raw in the saddle. We've salvaged some decent 'Mechs, but the newbies are still learning how to pilot them. This isn't going to be the ideal of baptism under fire."

Archer studied the map in long, silent thought. The others seemed to know to let him be, but the silence hung ominously in the air. Archer considered and discarded a number of possibilities, then a new thought hit him. There just might be a way to turn Blucher's plan against him, but it was a stretch.

"All right, people. Here's what I want you to do. Immediately begin preparations to withdraw. Load up all gear, expendables, and non-combat personnel. But we don't move, not yet. Just get everything ready to go." He spoke with all the confidence he could muster, hoping the others would take heart from his calm.

"You have a plan?" Katya asked.

"I think so, Katya. We've got about a dozen and a half vibrabombs. We can use them and the pop-up mines to cover the right flank and the main road. Both our infantry platoons will meet the Guards' primary diversion just as Blucher planned it, with just enough ground armor to show the Guards what they want to see."

He traced a line over the paper map. "Their right flank will be slowed by the forest and the mines. Our remaining armor will be there, too, enough to bog them down for a long time. Meanwhile our 'Mechs move around their right flank and hit them hard. Then, our noncoms and techs bug out on the southern trail before the Guards fighters start their runs. We take out their right flank and push it straight into their diversionary force. Then we retreat before their left flank can come at us. We rig the entire base with explosives, booby-traps, and the like. When they rush up here to destroy our command and control center, they walk into a trap rigged to explode around them."

"What about the satellites? When we move out, they'll have us pinned down all the way to our other bases," Katya said.

"That's where you come in, Captain." He looked at her and crossed his arms. "Martin Fox and his people have been sizing up the satellite system for a while now. The satellites aren't the weak link; they're easy to replace. It's the relay stations. Rather than use our aerospace elements to defend this location, we'll bomb one of the relay stations on the southern continent. Katya and Martin's people will sabotage the other one. Blow it to smithereens."

"What about their field satellite relays?"

Archer shrugged. "That would take more time and trouble than it's worth."

Darius Hopkins scratched the back of his head and studied the map. "It might just work," he said. "But we'll have to use up most of our explosives doing it." He looked around the room. "Damn pity, too. This was a great base."

"Say what you will about Blucher, he's technically won this battle just by forcing us to leave here," Archer said. "What we need to do now is make sure his victory isn't complete, that it doesn't turn into a slaughter. We've got to hit him hard, hit him where he's weak, and then get out."

"Where will our new HQ be, Colonel?" Snider asked.

"In my cockpit," Archer said. "This isn't the final battle, but if we do it right, the Lyrans are going to be so busy licking their wounds they'll be bottled up for some time to come."

21

"Mr. Drannigan, as a former consultant to a number of Free Worlds governments on tactical military operations, what are your thoughts on the infighting in the Federated Commonwealth right now?"

"What we're seeing, Dwight, is a series of independent actions on a number of different worlds. Regiments and militias taking sides, squaring off, and fighting guerrilla-style wars. It's like what happened on the streets of Solaris magnified ten thousand fold."

"Well, we know how that fight turned out. If the Solaris analogy holds, any predictions on this big-scale Steiner-Davion war?"

"I don't claim to have a crystal ball, Dwight, but let's face it, Katrina Steiner is mighty popular with her people. She's a hard act for anybody to follow."

—Chief correspondent Dwight Lansing interviewing military strategist Reinhold Drannigan, on the holovid newsmagazine *The Real Deal*, Free Worlds League, 2 January 3063

The platoon of Guards infantry moved rapidly from
one clump of trees to another, seeking whatever
cover and protection they might offer. A Zephyr hovertank snaked along behind them, its turret tracking
slowly. Kommandant Derkson piloted his towering
Quickdraw near the center of the formation. They
were not alone. From behind a thick copse of hicko-
ries, a *JagerMech* piloted by Sergeant Malloy emerged,
its weapon arms mimicking the action of the Zephyr.
Off in the distance, Derkson watched as the fifty-ton
Chaparral moved along the far-left flank, its treads
churning up dust. A bird-like *Hoplite* followed briskly
behind the Zephyr, but more to the side than forward. The wooded trail marked the center of their
formation, but only the *Hoplite* and the hovertank
traveled along the main trail.

"CWO Niles, keep your men moving alongside the
trail," Derkson said into his neurohelmet mike. "We
should be hitting their perimeter any minute now."

The sound of a distant, muffled explosion startled
him. Turning his *Quickdraw,* he saw a puff of smoke
rising from where the infantry had been advancing.
He glanced down at his short-range sensors. They
showed magnetic anomalies moving at the edge of
his sensor range, just ahead on the trail.

"Contact," he barked. "Malloy, advance and prepare to lay down a pattern of suppression fire." Then he called his infantry commander. "Niles, status."

"Sir," came a coughing voice over the commline. "We hit some mines—pop-ups. I've got four men down."

Mines? Advancing was a mistake if they were walking into a minefield, anti-personnel or otherwise. Derkson watched as the ground suddenly exploded under Malloy's *JagerMech*. Dirt clods flew up, and smoke wrapped around the 'Mech like the legs of a lover. The *JagerMech* twisted and dropped to its knees, but the smoke momentarily kept Derkson from seeing much more.

"Pull back twenty meters and assume a defensive position," he ordered as a barrage of short-range missiles raced past him toward the Zephyr. They plowed into its left side, mauling the armor plating in a horrific ripple of yellow and orange explosions. A rebel SRM carrier had moved forward just enough to do the damage, just enough to be inviting.

Derkson opened the command frequency. "Colonel Blucher," he said, "we've hit a mine field at coordinates zero-three-five, Alpha, Zulu, two one. We are engaging the enemy."

He targeted his long-range missiles on the SRM carrier, then deftly wiggled his targeting reticle on the short-range missile launcher until it glimmered bright red.

"Here's some payback for screwing up my payroll," he muttered, jabbing his forefinger on the TIC trigger. The *Quickdraw* lurched slightly as the barrage of missiles shot from their tubes and streaked up the shallow hillside.

Katya Chaffee studied the building at the top of the hill and shook her head. They needed more time. The sat relay station consisted of several antennae and a huge dish for the downloading of data from the Lyran satellites orbiting Thorin. It wasn't a particularly formidable target, and she guessed that only a handful of staff manned the operations booth. The problem was Blucher's thoroughness in protecting the facility from exactly the kind of attack she was attempting. Two rows of sandbags surrounded the station, with a slip trench between them. Sensors mounted on metallic rods dotted the cleared terrain for a full hundred and fifty meters around the station, ready to trigger an alarm if anyone tried to sneak through.

Ad hoc bunkers of sandbags were piled around the defense perimeter, and the nasty barrels of machine guns poked out from them. Even if only a squad or two were present, that would be more than enough to hold Katya's team at bay.

Martin Fox, one-time systems technician turned freedom fighter, came up alongside. "I checked the perimeter, Captain. We couldn't find a gap anywhere in their lines."

"Damn," she cursed softly, then drew a long, deep breath. "Looks like we'll have to do this the hard way."

Martin wiped the sweat from his brow. "Are you sure?"

"No," she said, giving him a rueful grin. "But what choice do we have?"

Archer sat in the cockpit of his *Penetrator* as the lance of Lyran aerospace fighters streaked in on the university ruins from the south. In a perfect "V" formation, they unleashed their missiles—all inferno-tipped rounds—on the forest and the ancient campus. The inferno missiles were the nastiest kind of anti-Mech weapon. They didn't so much explode as spray a napalm-like substance everywhere. Against a 'Mech, they could overheat the machine to the point of shutdown.

The effect of the missile barrage was immediate. Trees ignited, turning into flaming umbrellas. Three of the ancient buildings also burst into flames, making the peaceful forest scene look more like a contemporary city ablaze.

From his position near the edge of the base, Archer watched the fighters pull up and bank away to make another run. The roar of their powerful fusion engines shook the *Penetrator* slightly as they passed overhead. Hopkins had managed to evacuate the non-combat personnel a few minutes before the Arcturan Guards arrived. They were four kilometers away by now, crossing Freeman's Ford out of the combat zone, along with the spare parts and everything else that could be loaded.

The whole site blazed bright reds and yellows, belching an enormous cloud of smoke into the air. Archer didn't waste any more time watching. He checked his long-range sensors, then opened his neurohelmet commline. "Icepick One, sit rep."

"We've got them hemmed in up on the road," Darius Hopkins answered. "We've been shooting some, then pulling back out of their range, then shooting some more. The mines have them skittish."

"Good," Archer said, maneuvering his *Penetrator* toward the trail. "Sledgehammer, move some of your folks in to support Ice Pick. The rest of you, prepare to advance on the left flank." Almost by reflex he began the charge cycle on his lasers.

Leftenant Culver brought her *Lucifer* to an altitude about fifty meters above the ground, just over the treetops. To her right, Andrew Hackley's *Chippewa* also rose higher. As they cruised across the plateau that dominated Thorin's southern continent, they kept close to the ground so that only the most sophisticated Doppler tracking stations would pick them up, and most of those were concentrated on the northern continent.

"I'm painting some light rain over the target site," Culver said, intently watching her long-range sensors.

"Confirm. Time to call the strafe order, sir. I'll cover your six o'clock."

Culver smiled. "Go ahead, hot shot. Hit that station with everything you've got."

The *Chippewa* was essentially a big flying wing with enough missiles and other weaponry to level a city block. It banked slowly and took the lead in front of Culver's smaller *Lucifer*. Far off in the distance, a lone building in a clearing came into view—the southern satellite relay station. Just then, the clouds parted, and the station was bathed in sunshine. You couldn't get a clearer target.

"I'm just about locked on," Hackley said, sounding a little less cocky this time.

"Fire and break to the left. I'll be behind you and to the right." She cut her speed slightly to put some distance between them. Before her, like a massive bird of prey, the *Chippewa* leveled off its flight path and began its run.

"I've got incoming fire!" Hackley yelled frantically.

"Stay on target, hot shot. Fire when ready," she said, keeping her voice as calm as humanly possible.

A gauss rifle slug from an *Atlas* slammed with such force into the right lower leg of Archer's *Penetrator* that the 'Mech almost fell forward under the impact. Fighting the controls and the wave of heat that rose in his cockpit, he somehow managed to keep himself upright, but the damage display told the tale. The gauss slug had sheared off a lot of armor plating. Archer silently damned the *Atlas* to hell.

The *Stalker* in front of him posed an even bigger threat, while the *Atlas* hovered just out of range. He had just reached the point where Hopkins and his troops had dug in along the road and stalled the advance of the Guards. As Archer and his command lance passed, they all fired at once to create the illusion that there was more there than vibrabombs, infantry, and a few lances of armor.

He rushed forward, hoping to plow through the enemy's right flank, but the Guards were putting up more resistance than anticipated. Archer guessed that Blucher must have pulled his center forces over to this side. The man was damn good, Archer thought. Otherwise he wouldn't be at the bloody damn front door to the base. The Guards had already crossed the mine field and weathered the damage, and were now furiously pouring fire into Archer's Avengers. Laser light ripped through the small clusters of trees the 'Mechs and tanks were using for cover, and autocannon bursts plowed up patches of earth, leaving huge craters everywhere. The Avengers had been forced back slightly, but now it was time to turn the tables.

"Specter One to all units, concentrate your firepower on the lead *Stalker* for two salvos, then go to independent fire," he barked ·as he swung his extended-range large lasers to bear on the gray-green *Stalker*. The Guard MechWarrior plowed his boxy 'Mech through a stand of trees, knocking them aside like weeds. Both of Archer's lasers hit the *Stalker*'s left torso, furrowing deep gouges of burning destruction.

Specter Two seemed to appear out of thin air off to Archer's left. The brown- and green-painted *Watchman* landed in a clearing, its leg-mounted jump jets searing the grass as the giant feet sank slightly into the ground. Subaltern Wally George, the *Watchman*'s pilot, immediately let go with his large laser, followed by the mediums. Sergeant Val Kemp's *Crab* fired his lasers as well. The large lasers hit the boxy right weapons pod that served as the *Stalker*'s left arm, and another LRM salvo dug in deep where Archer's shots had hit a second earlier. That was probably Specter Seven, Corporal Tanner's *Whitworth*, which he saw cutting to his rear on the secondary display.

As his cockpit heat slowly dropped, Archer unleashed his medium pulse lasers. Once more the cockpit got hotter than a sauna as the emerald bursts stabbed at the *Stalker*, which reeled from the hits. Almost in slow motion, the 'Mech turned, and Archer saw the missile hatches pop open for its deadly array of long- and short-range missiles. His earpiece whined out the missile lock warning as thirty-two warheads of various sizes streaked toward him from their launch tubes. He activated his anti-missile system and hunched his 'Mech's back slightly to brace for the impacts meant to destroy his *Penetrator*.

The smoke rounds had virtually blanketed the satellite relay station as Katya waited to make her move. Then Martin Fox and his people began shooting from the edge of the woods surrounding the station. Their small-arms fire pattered and spat at the bunkers to her far right, and she could see the forms of troopers scuttling into the fire zone. The station wasn't heavily defended, but its position was well entrenched, giving the Guards the upper hand.

The firefight seemed to change in tempo as Fox's team targeted the bunker with their man-pack PPCs. The man-made lightning cracked outward and tore into the sandbagged bunkers, exploding their defenses with a thunderous roar. The defenders beat a retreat to their second line of defense.

Katya looked over at her three comrades. "We move on my signal," she said. They nodded but didn't look so sure of themselves. She raised her hand and waited as the second wave of mortar rounds hit. These were smoke rounds as well, the necessary cover she and her team, the real threat to the base, were going to need.

Katya dropped her hand, and the quad of soldiers rushed forward. On their backs were shoulder-launched short-range missile tubes. Though mainly used for anti-'Mech operations, today they would serve another purpose. Martin Fox and his "commandos" would tie down the defenders, while her team took out the satellite dish and antenna. The trick was to get close enough to do it, somewhere in between the two trench lines of the perimeter.

Streaking through the smoke with her team, she half-expected to hit machine gun fire, but none came. Then all of them tried to clear the trench, but only one of her troopers made it in a single leap. Katya's stomach and ribs ached from plowing into the side of it. With a furious effort, she managed to crawl out on her hands and knees. Her heart was pounding, her ears filled with the sounds of the fighting. The enemy hadn't seen them coming. At least not yet. In a few seconds, it wouldn't make any difference anyway.

Bringing up the rear, she raced forward to join the others at the inner trench. Now they were in range. Crouched down low, she spoke as softly as the situation would allow. "Standard rounds to start. Follow with the infernos."

Two of the troopers stood and fired first. Their disposable short-range missile launchers fired standard explosive rounds at the base of the massive dish and the upright antenna. Plumes of yellow flames and smoke rose up from the explosions. Katya stood up to fire her own launcher, this one filled with inflammable inferno rounds. Now that the station's equipment was damaged, the infernos would burn it to the ground.

She triggered the rubber launch stud under the SRM launcher's rear eyesight and felt a tug as it discharged its payload. Suddenly, the ground around her seemed to disappear. She heard a roar in her ears, and panic gripped her as she flew to the left, thrown bodily into the air. Sounds, screams—her own—filled her ears as she slammed into the ground.

An explosion . . . Her mind came to grips with the thought as she saw the severed arm of one of her troopers land on the ground only two meters in front of her. Her fingers, then her toes went numb. Noises became echoes, and her vision seemed to drift into a tunnel. She wanted to scream, to call out for help, but the tunnel in her mind got smaller and smaller. The sounds echoed into nothing as she slipped into oblivion.

Looking down and back, Leftenant Francine Culver saw the devastation their strike had created. The satellite relay station wasn't just in flames; it was exploding from the rupture of its back-up fusion reactor. The huge dish collapsed inward on the blast, devoured in a matter of seconds by fire and white-hot death.

"Wow," came the voice of Andrew Hackley as he, too, observed the carnage. "Cool." His *Chippewa* still streamed white wisps of smoke from the impact of the air-defense missiles that had slammed into him, but they'd only charred some plates of armor.

"I think we can call that target pasted," she said, sending the code signal to Specter One. "I figured it'd be tougher than that."

She opened her commline. "Specter One, we're done a little early here. Any other targets?" All she got back was more static and the distant sounds of battle over the command frequency.

The *Penetrator*'s anti-missile system ate up four of the missiles heading toward Archer, but the others continued to rush in. He pushed back into his seat and turned his head to brace for the explosions, but none came. There was an odd and distinct thud as the missiles hit but didn't go off. They were followed a millisecond later by the splattered debris from the missiles his defense system had shredded apart.

No explosions. He smiled slightly, content that his plan had paid off. When the *Angelfire* had arrived with munitions for the Arcturan Guards, he'd sent a trusted comrade to disarm and disable the warheads it was to deliver. These must have been mixed in with the Guards' ammo and were now being used. They fired fine, even read as armed to the battle computers, but their disabled warheads were worthless. Archer listed his *Penetrator* forward and stabbed the thumb trigger to fire his large lasers at the badly mauled *Stalker*.

"Their missiles are duds," he called to the rest of his command. "Let's get 'em!"

The *Stalker* MechWarrior must have realized the error as Archer's undamaged 'Mech fired its large lasers. One penetrated the cockpit, destroying almost all its armor and even caving in the egress hatch. The other shot hit the center torso, digging into the same place where Val's *Crab* had poured its large laser fire.

The commline hissed in his ear for a moment as a voice came on-line. "Specter One, we're done a little early here. Any other targets?" It was Leftenant Culver.

That was good news. One of the two satellite relay stations was gone. He almost decided to bring his aerofighters in to join the battle, then had another thought. "Good work. Now go and hit their command bunker in the fort."

"Sir?"

Archer sidestepped a wave of autocannon rounds that stitched into the trees near him, all failing to explode but unleashing a devastating amount of kinetic damage as they struck trees and rocks with savage impact. "You heard me right. Just a few passes, concentrate on their command bunker. You probably won't do much, but it might distract Blucher's attention."

"Roger that, Specter one."

The Guards *Stalker* listed under the barrage and turned to break off the attack, but the Avengers kept on coming. Maxwell Grath, now piloting the captured *Gallowglas*, made the killing shot. An azure bolt of raw power from his PPC slammed into the *Stalker*'s torso, gutting internal structure and sending arcs of blue-white energy spreading out like a spider web in the 'Mech's center. It seemed to freeze in place as white ozone smoke drifted from the hole in its chest. Then it toppled to one side, smashing into some trees.

From Archer's side of the battle line, missiles, autocannon rounds, and lasers stabbed with renewed fury as the *Stalker* dropped. He saw a newer-model *Cobra* appear and fire its long-range missiles into the captured Avenger *Cicada*. Most of the warheads hit, but only two exploded, giving the *Cicada*'s green MechWarrior a new lease on life. Archer and Grath both fired at the new target, mauling the *Cobra* with enough laser and PPC fire to send it crashing backward to the ground.

The mighty *Atlas* piloted by Colonel Blucher stood on a small rise, firing its weapons at long range, peppering several different targets. A *Hollander* also attempted to turn and fire, only to find itself under a barrage of large and medium laserfire from Wally George's *Watchman*. Wally's 'Mech had taken several hits, and a slick, blood-like flow of green coolant spewed from the 'Mech's torso. Most of his shots hit the *Hollander*'s legs, stripping them down to nothing but exposed myomer muscles steaming with heat as the 'Mech staggered back.

"All units, advance," Archer commanded. "They're

falling back." Then he saw the Guards aerospace fighters bank off again, swinging into the distance past where they'd bombed his base into ruins. He knew instantly what they were doing. The Lyrans had spotted his support forces at the river.

Martin Fox watched as the enemy mortar rounds came closer to his position. He was a systems analyst, not a warrior. The time had come to get out of here. He peered through the smoke and saw the immobile bodies of Katya Chaffee's team lying at the edge of a crater. They'd done it, pulled it off, but at what cost?

"We're outta here," he called over his comm. "Fall back to the getaway vehicles."

One of his team came running up, pointing to where Chaffee and the others had fallen. A burst of gunfire traced after him as he came forward. "What about them?" the man shouted.

Martin waved him on. "It's too late for them. We did our job, and now we've got to get out of here. I'll signal the colonel as soon as we're clear."

Archer's fears were misplaced. The pair of *Lucifers* and the *Stuka* had swung out as if they'd spotted the Avenger convoy several kilometers away, but then banked around to line up for a strafing run on his battle line. His relief turned to fear as they dove in on Rhelm's *Dervish* and Livernois's *Stealth*, both of which attempted to run. One of the *Lucifer's* missiles went wide of target, but the other two found their mark. The LRMs hit the *Dervish*, ripping armor from its thin rear torso and arms. Then the *Lucifer's* large lasers sliced into its right arm, severing it at the elbow. The destroyed limb dropped into the underbrush like a child's toy.

Livernois's *Stealth* bore the brunt of the *Stuka's* fire. Missiles erupted around it everywhere at once, enveloping the BattleMech in a cloud of black smoke

tinged with orange explosions. Large lasers stabbed
and slashed into the cloud, seeking out the *Stealth*.
Judging by the armor plating that flew from the
smoke, the lasers had found it. Archer watched as
Kane Livernois did the one thing no one expected.
Firing his jump jets, he launched backward, just in
time to get out of the way.

Archer expected the aerofighters to swing around
for another run, but instead they banked away and
abandoned the field of battle. He understood. They
must have picked up Culver closing on their base.
She'd be long gone by the time they arrived, but it
got their attention as he'd hoped it would. Again he
had to grudgingly hand it to Blucher. He was using
his assets well.

Archer swept the field and saw the Guards starting
to fall back. One of them, the *Hollander*, hit a vibra-
bomb that had been missed during the initial push
and went down once and for all. He also spied Blucher's *Atlas* in the distance, almost out of his field of
vision among the trees. His target lock was weak,
but he fired anyway, ignoring the ripple of heat that
swept through the cockpit. One of his extended-range
Clan weapons hit the left arm of the *Atlas*, while the
other went wide. The huge 'Mech's armor was pitted
and scarred, but for a moment it seemed that Blucher
turned to face him across the battlefield. Time
seemed to slow down as Archer watched the skull-
like cockpit of the *Atlas* in the distance.

Then Blucher and the remaining Arcturan Guards
fell back, firing as they went.

"Hold your fire and let them go," Archer commanded as he saw Livernois's *Stealth* emerge from
hiding. Most of its armor was destroyed, and myomer muscle strands snapped and dragged behind it
like enormous untied shoelaces.

Archer's tactical short-range scan showed his force
battered but still operational. The Guards had been

hurt, too, and were retreating toward the road back to Ecol City. Archer's Avengers had held the field of combat. Pursuit was tempting, but Archer knew his force was weary. If he pressed too hard, it might simply hand the Lyrans what they wanted—a total victory rather than the stalemate they'd conceded.

"All right, people, let's salvage what we can and make for our rendezvous points. Assignments and bases will be designated there. Get the recovery teams in here ASAP."

They'd bought themselves some time and they'd better use it. Losing their base of operations was still a major loss in Archer's mind, no matter who held the field at the end of the fight.

As he turned his *Penetrator* to go find Hopkins, he wondered how Katya had fared and prayed she'd made it out okay.

═══ **22** ═══

"Today we're here at the Melissa Spaceport, talking with a DropShip trader captain recently arrived from Fort Louden. What can you tell us about the actual situation there, Captain Downer? The official word coming down is that there's no civil war—only some 'isolated, minor incidents' that the Archon has totally under control."

"Well, we didn't stray too far from the spaceport after we heard that the military was patrolling the streets enforcing a stringent curfew. They say the commander of the Fifth Alliance Guards RCT cracked down hard when the looting started."

—From *Ecol News in Brief*, Channel 38, 6 January 3063

Command Post Epsilon
Remington Forest, Thorin
Skye Province
Lyran Alliance
8 January 3063

"**W**as she dead?" Archer demanded as Martin Fox wiped the sweat from his face.

Fox took a small step back as if trying to dodge

the colonel's wrath. "We couldn't be sure. They were either dead or wounded."

"Damnation and hellfire," Archer cursed, turning away from Fox. It had been some fifteen hours since the battle. The Avengers had been reduced by nearly a third—a full company of 'Mechs and armor either wounded, destroyed, or gravely in need of repair.

And now he had to deal with the loss of Katya Chaffee, which went far beyond being a loss to the unit. She was the backbone of his intelligence operations, but also so much more. Since Andrea's death, Katya had become his main sounding board and one of the small circle of people whose counsel he valued.

And now she was gone.

Archer knew that he couldn't really blame Fox and regretted how sharply he'd spoken. He gently laid one hand on Fox's shoulder. "I'm sorry, Martin. It's been a hell of a day. A lot of good people are dead or injured. You and your team did a great job. You've crippled the enemy's ability to track us. That's no small feat."

Archer then turned to Darius Hopkins. "How bad is it?"

"Losing Katya could hurt us. She knows the location of some of our bases."

"You're assuming she's still alive," Archer said.

"I have to. And you should too. If Blucher's got her, he might pry information on our operations out of her."

Archer sighed deeply. "Then we evacuate the bases whose locations she knew. Minimize any advantage Blucher might gain in holding her."

"Good," Hopkins said. "We're hurt, but the techs are already working on the damaged equipment. We'll have another lance or two operational in sight of a week."

"Thanks, Darius," Archer said, rolling his shoulders slightly to relieve some of the tension he felt.

"You're going to have to fill in as my intel chief until we can find and recover Katya."

Hopkins gave him a big smile. "Now *you're* talking like you're convinced she's alive."

"Like you said, I have to." He lifted the flap on the field tent serving as his headquarters, then turned back to his old mentor before going inside. "Sergeant Major," he said slowly.

"Sir."

"Get word to Prince John through our usual chain of contacts. I want to know what's happening in the Lyran camp. Make contact with all of our cells. Let them know that we beat back the Guards, but that they should be treated like a wounded animal.

"If I were Blucher right now, I'd be considering making some changes. And in our business, change can be bad."

Felix Blucher looked out from the blast door of his command bunker, watching his techs work furiously to repair the 'Mechs out in the courtyard of the fort. As of now he had only two lances of operational BattleMechs and armor. Many of the 'Mechs were severely damaged, which the techs were now hustling to repair. Other machines had to be abandoned on the field during the retreat.

He reflected on the battle and its aftermath. His force had stumbled onto mines the rebels had laid, which had slowed his assault. He'd countered with a flanking move that inflicted heavy damage on his enemy, but he hadn't foreseen that Archer would strike at both satellite relay stations at the same time. Now they were in ruins. He still had the field units. Each one was able to control two satellites at a time but with only limited data download possible.

Blucher still believed his own plan had been sound. His air support had given him the upper hand, which he thought would let him punch through the rebels. Then Christifori's aerofighters began to attack the fort, and Blucher had to divert his fighters to stop them. The fighters tangled for a bit, then the Avengers retreated. The damage to his command bunker wasn't serious, but he'd been forced to play away his ace card—air superiority.

Archer was probably thinking he'd won a tactical victory because he'd held the field. Blucher, however, had crippled the Avenger's main base of operations, which gave him a strategic victory. He massaged his sore leg, wondering if a strategic win was enough. It had come at a high price.

Now he was holed up in the fort, digging in, forced into a defensive posture. That wasn't good. No army ever won a war bottled up on the defense. Yet here he was, his battalion down to less than a company. And by holding the field, Archer could salvage and recover many of his own losses. Blucher and his Guards were fighting a kind of war that was almost alien to them, against a commander who was a native of this world and loved by its people. It was probably a miracle the Guards weren't in worse shape, though Blucher doubted that would count for much with upper command.

He heard the sound of bootsteps coming up behind him and turned just as Leutnant Sherwood, his arm in a sling, clicked his heels smartly and saluted. Sherwood had done well; his *Hercules* had taking on a Galleon tank and a *Javelin* at the same time. He'd dished out some heavy hurt before getting pummeled by a rebel SRM carrier. The wave of missiles had devoured the *Javelin*, and he'd injured his arm in the fall. Somehow, though, Sherwood had managed to drag what was left of his BattleMech away during the retreat.

"Reporting as ordered, sir."

"Well, did you find out anything?" Blucher asked.

"The techs say the missile warheads were disabled

by removing a juncture from the arming circuit. Our autocannon rounds were apparently defused. A pfenning coin was inserted into the fuse mechanism so the rounds couldn't explode. Our inspectors never spotted it, but that's because no one could have without prying open every round. I've got a crew checking every round in our inventory and re-arming them, but it's going to take a while."

During which time, Blucher knew he didn't dare attempt to break out of here. "How did this happen?" he asked, shaking his head at how cleverly he'd been tricked.

"From what Leutnant Fisk was able to determine, the ammunition was sabotaged during transit."

"What?" Blucher shouted angrily, but his voice was hoarse from exhaustion. "This is treason! We'll seize the assets of that company. I want their owners arrested immediately." He was edgy from lack of sleep, and all the coffee he'd consumed only made it worse.

"I'm afraid that's not possible, sir," Sherwood replied carefully.

"Why's that, Leutnant?"

"It was Christifori Express."

Blucher wanted to scream, but instead he slowly closed his eyes and drew a deep breath. He was fighting a man who knew as much as he did about things military. A man who had bested him in battles mock and real. A man who had managed to force him to hole up inside the fort, digging in like a mole. He considered, for a moment, giving up and leaving Thorin, but that was not a real option. In his long military career, Felix Blucher had never fled from a fight with his tail between his legs. Now was not the time to start.

Besides, he wasn't out of ideas. One of them had the makings of a real plan, though it would be risky. Because it would operate on a strategic level, it stood a good chance of catching Christifori off balance. Blucher had already beaten him once strategically. Perhaps that was the arena where he should engage him.

Luther Fisk had also joined them by now. His black hair was unkempt, and he had bags under his eyes. Oddly enough, he was smiling, a stark contrast to the grimness of the Guards' situation. "What is it, Leutnant?"

"I've got a present for you, Colonel." Fisk seemed to have recovered some of his old cockiness. "I just got back from the medical ward. We captured some of the rebels who attacked the relay station outside the city. They were injured so I had them brought here in case Archer tried to rescue them."

Sherwood cut in before Blucher could get the words out of his mouth. "Was one of them Christifori?" he asked sharply.

Fisk grinned even wider. "Better. We got Hauptmann Katya Chaffee."

"Will she live?" Blucher asked.

"She got the wind knocked out of her and took some shrapnel in her shoulder, but otherwise she'll be fine."

"Good work," Blucher said, surprised that Fisk was capable of such a thing. "He will come for her."

"What makes you think that?" Sherwood asked.

"Intuition and intelligence reports. She means a lot to him. He's already rescued her from the jail once. He'll do it again. Maybe we can use her to make him sit down and try to put an end this fighting."

"He'd never do that, Colonel," Fisk said.

"Maybe not. But my orders are to end this revolt. If I can do it at the peace table, so much the better. Otherwise, it's only a matter of time before Archer tries to rescue her."

"But we're not up to dealing with a full assault except from inside the fort," Fisk said. "Don't get me wrong, sir. Christifori's rebels got hurt, too, but from what I've seen of the BDA, it sounds like they got off a little easier."

Blucher rubbed at his forehead. "Which means we've got to change our strategic premise. I'm going to send a message to Muphrid, ordering Second Battalion to mount up and get here as fast as they can. Christifori's tactics have cost us personnel and 'Mechs, but he won't stand a chance against us plus another battalion." He looked at Fisk, and almost smiled for the first time since he'd known him. "And this time we have the perfect bait—Katya Chaffee."

Sherwood looked excited. "Sir, I'll be glad to start on those orders."

"Contact Hauptmanns Von Keiver and Gotteb. I'll need their input to work out the timing." Now that he'd put the idea into words, it seemed right. He believed it was a plan that couldn't fail, and it gave him a rush of confidence that almost instantly raised his spirits.

"Mark my words," he told the two junior officers, "in a few weeks the battle for Thorin will be over."

BOOK THREE

Civil Warriors

Despite the Archon's ban on non-military use of HPG transmissions, there are other ways to learn and report information the state would like to deny us. It is true that some worlds in the Federated Commonwealth are embroiled in guerrilla-type combat, but others are already engulfed in open warfare. Word has made its way out of Nanking that pro-Davion forces spearheaded by the First Kestral Grenadiers have seized the planet's vital manufacturing facilities and now control an important strategic world on the Federated side of the Terran Corridor.

—From *And Nothing But the Truth*, radical underground news sheet distributed widely throughout the Federated Commonwealth, 7 January 3063

= 23 =

The loss of Arthur, my beloved younger brother, has been made even more painful by my brother Victor's grandstanding and unforgivable accusations. I am appalled and outraged that he would dare even hint that I am to blame for Arthur's death. No one now doubts that he was cut down in his prime by enemies of our realm. Though I do not like to believe it, all the evidence currently points to Combine involvement in his death. I vow to my brother's memory and to all the people of our realm that I will not rest until the truth is uncovered and the real assassins brought to justice.

—Official response by Katrina Steiner to Victor Steiner-Davion's call to arms, Palace Ministry of Information release, Tharkad, 7 January 3063

Command Post Epsilon
Remington Forest, Thorin
Skye Province
Lyran Alliance
11 January 3063

Archer leaned over the portable holographic projector and watched the information scroll in the air in front of him. The air in the tent was heavy and, despite the slight chill to the morning air, held a trace of mustiness left by the rains the day before. He ignored it. It wasn't any worse than his own musky aroma from days in the same uniform. None of that was important. What mattered was what he saw on the holographic image displayed before him—the Fifteenth Arcturan Guard deployment orders.

"The boy took serious risks to get us these documents," Darius Hopkins said.

Archer nodded, but continued his intense study of the data on Blucher's latest "surprise" plan.

"You aren't worried by the numbers he'll be massing against us?"

Archer turned to Hopkins. "I take the news as it comes, Darius. Yes, the good colonel intends to throw his second battalion at us. What else is new? The odds have been against us from the start, and look how far we've come."

"Could it be the news that Katya is alive has improved your spirits, boy?"

"I won't lie, Darius. I'm *very* happy she's alive."

"Just don't let it cloud your decisions."

"For now, it's enough to know she's unharmed. Right now we've got to concentrate on the real threat of Blucher pulling in his Second Battalion."

"You said it," Hopkins grumbled. "A battalion of fresh troops is the last thing we need. We've been able to whittle down the one he came with, but it's worn us down as well. Three companies of fresh troops might be just too much for us."

Hopkins rubbed his lower lip and stroked his thick mustache as though putting his next words into understandable form. "So far we've played this like a chapter out of Robin Hood. We've irritated the enemy, captured them, and given as good as we got, if not better, when we fought them—though you'd never know it to listen to the news. Now the odds are really stacked against us. One possibility is for us to fade into the woodwork and wage a more traditional guerrilla war against the Lyrans. Those kind of tactics aren't your style, but you can't deny that history shows they can work. We can torment them for months, do what we did before, wear them down."

Archer knew he had to keep an open mind, but he wasn't convinced by Hopkins argument. His people were good, but they were also weary. Trying to get them to fight a more down and dirty guerrilla war would just not be possible right now. Besides, he didn't have the stomach for that kind of fight—bombings, assassinations, terrorism, sabotage. More innocent people were likely to die in such a war, which could turn the populace against him. As it was, his fledgling army couldn't have survived this long without partisan support via supplies and foodstuffs. Ordinary Thorins also spied on the Lyrans for him, bringing rumors and useful intelligence. If the people turned against him, the fight would be doomed.

"Not acceptable as a strategy," he replied.

"Then tell me what is, sir."

Archer didn't even want to put the truth into words, at least not out loud. He was just as weary of this kind of war as his people. Now, just when he'd hoped to drive the enemy off the planet for good, Blucher was upping the ante.

Archer looked at Hopkins, an idea seeming to form even as the words came from his mouth. "When I was getting ready to leave for NAIS, you told me there were a few keys to winning a battle. One was to concentrate your forces. Two was always hold the high ground. And three, take the initiative and grab them by the balls."

Hopkins nodded.

"I'd say it's time for number three," Archer said.

"And just how are we gonna do it?"

"Look at the timetable Blucher has laid out. There's some time before his Second Battalion leaves Muphrid. What if we go there first, link up with whatever rebel forces exist on planet, and take the Second out before they ever get here."

There was a pregnant pause between the two men, dead quiet. "You're talking a lot of coordination," Hopkins said.

Blucher had beat Archer once at strategy, now it was time for Archer to show he could play the same game. "It's doable. Look at these orders—the Second won't be loading up until the twenty-second. If we can catch them as they're loading or loaded, our targets are immobile—the DropShips. Their base on Muphrid isn't a hardened fort like he's got here. It's only a field firebase that they'll have to dismantle. It won't take a lot."

"There's two battalions of troops on Muphrid," Hopkins reminded him.

"Yes, on two different continents."

"If you go there, you'll be handing over Thorin to Blucher on a platter."

"Not if some of us stay here. How about if you stay and use my BattleMech to run some small operations that will get you some media. Blucher will never know I'm gone." Archer spoke faster as the idea took shape in his mind. He thought it just might work.

"How will you coordinate with the Muphrid rebels? Have you forgotten that there's a blackout on all HPG traffic except for military use."

"We can work around that with the help of Prince John," Archer said quickly. "As an aide to the colonel, he can authorize an encrypted transmission to Muphrid."

Hopkins stroked one side of his mustache with his fingers. "Colonel, the risks with this are fantastic. We don't know the terrain on Muphrid. Our intelligence there is going to be paper-thin, at best. You'll have to coordinate with rebels we don't even know. Not to mention that our timing will have to be exact."

Archer grinned. He knew all that, but he still thought it could work. "Darius, let's look at this from a different angle. Do you think Colonel Blucher or his officers on Muphrid would ever expect us to pull something like this?"

"Hell, no. You're fighting a war to drive him off Thorin. I'd expect you to stay here and fight on your home soil. And with all the risks of trying to take the fight to Muphrid that he'd probably figure you'd never take the chance."

"Precisely." Archer pounded his fist against the portable holographic unit, making the image in front of him wobble from the vibration. "If I were Blucher, I'd think the same way. His troops on Muphrid won't be expecting us to drop on top of them, either. I've got two DropShips, and I think I can also convince one of my business contacts to help out. We can do this, Darius. We can catch them with their pants down and pound them into snail snot." Archer felt a rush of power, a surge of raw energy.

Hopkins couldn't help but grin. "I know you when you've got your blood up, Archer. I couldn't talk you out of this wild idea even if I could prove to you how it will end up, could I?"

Archer shook his head. "We have a lot of planning to do, old friend, and not a lot of time. Get Captains Gett and Snider over here from their bases. Tell them to pass the word to their techs. We need every available BattleMech operational ASAP. We've got a rebellion to win."

Katya woke from a kind of half-sleep and saw the form of Colonel Blucher standing at the foot of her hospital bed. His arms were crossed, and he looked as if he had been watching her for a while. It gave her the creeps. Just how long had he been standing there, staring at her? She pulled the sheet higher on her body.

"I trust, Hauptmann, that you find our medical facilities satisfactory?" he said, with a slight Germanic lilt to his voice.

"I'm fine," she said, which wasn't a total lie. She felt better than she had yesterday after finally regaining consciousness. Every bone in her body ached, and the stitches in her shoulder blades itched madly, just out of her reach, but she wouldn't give him the satisfaction of knowing that. She would have liked to tell him she was now known as Captain Chaffee, but decided to save her strength.

"Good. I like to think of you as a special guest," Blucher said.

"If I'm a guest, then why are there armed guards at the door?"

"Guest *would* be a misnomer. Technically, you're a prisoner of war. Leutnant Colonel Christifori sent me a copy of your commission the day after the fight, just in case you'd survived your attack on the relay station, I suppose. Though I don't recognize Prince Victor's little army, I will grant you the dispensation due a fellow officer captured in battle."

"Colonel," she said flatly.

"Yes?"

"No. You called him Leutnant Colonel. He's a full Colonel now, sir," she corrected.

Blucher bristled. "As I said, *Hauptmann*, I don't recognize the army that Prince Victor has rallied to his cause."

"Do you visit all of the POWs?" she asked, changing subjects but not attitude.

"No. In truth, I've come to ask a favor of you."

Blucher moved to her right side. "You see, you are a good friend of Leutnant Colonel Christifori. I'm hoping that you will act as a liaison. Perhaps you could convince him to sit down and negotiate a peace."

"Does that mean you'd be willing to take the Fifteenth Guards off Thorin?" She ended the question with a flash of a smile that took more energy than she'd ever thought a mere smile could.

Blucher chuckled. "I'm afraid not. But I would be willing to offer him generous terms if his Avengers would stand down."

"I'm afraid I can't help you, Colonel Blucher. Colonel Christifori will never lay down his arms until the Lyran influence over Thorin is removed or the Archon steps down. If you're willing to negotiate those points, I'll climb out of this bed right now and take your message to him."

Blucher was not amused, and she saw that her cocky attitude had finally gotten to him.

"I'm sorry you feel that way, Hauptmann. Once you're better, I'll be transferring you to one of our detention camps."

"Very well," she said, slumping back against her pillow. "But know this, sir . . ." She paused to get his full attention.

"Yes?"

"I'll be more safe in a detention camp than you will anywhere on Thorin."

· And in global news today, a recent Reeves poll shows that sixty-three percent of the population strongly support Archer Christifori's opposition to Archon Katrina. Surprisingly, another fifty-one percent reportedly support the Archon. Reeves officials offer no explanation for the inconsistency.

—From *Thorin Week in Review*, Ecol City, Thorin, 11 January 3063

Lake Sprague, West of Ecol City
Thorin, Skye Province
Lyran Alliance
13 January 3063

The slightly frosted dew changed instantly to mist as the sun rose over Lake Sprague. Instead of a sandy beach, the lakeshore was covered with small polished stones, a loop of nearly fifty meters ringing the deep blue waters. A thick pine forest also ran along the shoreline, with only one trail leading to the water's edge. Not a breeze stirred as Archer and his command waited near the shore.

Archer, who was standing on the ground, glanced up at the 'Mechs that held the rest of his command and couldn't help thinking the machines definitely looked worse for the wear. Most showed dull gray replacement armor plates, while others had been equipped with weapons salvaged from fallen 'Mechs. Archer was proud of them. Despite the battle damage, his unit was still a viable combat force. They'd worked hard, and now he was asking them to take this war to another world to free their own. Not one of them even questioned the command. If anything, they were behind him more solidly than ever. He only hoped he could live up to their faith in him.

Then a rumble came from the depths of the lake, followed by an enormous shape rising from the waters. It was round, with stout legs and big enough to make the 'Mechs look like toys in comparison. Water rolled off the immense hull of the ship, pouring into the lake like a miniature rainfall. Its fusion engines roared with white-hot flame that pushed the water away like a perpetual ring of force.

It was the *Angelfire*. Though it had been a combat DropShip once upon a time, the ship had been converted for commercial hauling. Lee Fullerton had hidden the vessel in the deep waters of the lake, and the dense iron deposits had all but shielded it from sensor scans. Archer could see the emblem of Christifori Express on one side of the hull as the ship lifted into the air toward the shore, where it touched down on the stones. The sight of the logo made him feel suddenly old, as if it linked him to a previous life. He couldn't help thinking of his sister, and he wished she could have lived to see this.

Some hundred kilometers away a similar scene was being played out with the DropShip *Shiloh*. The smaller *Leopard* Class vessel had been hidden in a small valley that had been a strip mine centuries before. Another *Leopard* Class ship, the *Black Fox*, was at another location, on loan from Carlos Centrini, who was also in the transport business. It was being loaded up with some of the ground armor and the pair of aerospace fighters Archer was taking with him.

"Ready to load, sir," came Captain Fullerton's voice over Archer's wrist communicator.

"Copy," he replied, then turned to Darius Hopkins. "I take it you're ready," Archer yelled loud enough to be heard over the distant roar of the *Angelfire*'s fusion engines.

"Define the word, 'ready'," Hopkins replied.

Archer grinned. "All you have to do is keep up the illusion that I'm still here on Thorin."

Hopkins nodded. "Wait till you get back. I should have Blucher just about bald from pulling his hair out." He and Archer had planned some highly visible raids that should be more than enough to convince Blucher that Archer was still alive and well on Thorin. But other elements of the scheme were stickier. When they neutralized the Arcturan Guards Second Battalion on Muphrid, Archer would have to make sure they didn't send out an HPG alert to Blucher. They also had to return to Thorin as soon as possible.

Those problems seemed insurmountable to everyone but Archer. Prince John—otherwise known as Leutnant Sherwood—had been able to get a message to an importer-exporter Archer knew on Muphrid. Both men had served in the Tenth Lyran Guards, and the message was encoded with one of the old Guards ciphers. Sherwood had gotten the message through under the guise of needing backup data for an invoice on military supplies. Archer knew it was a risk in case his old friend Dale Koin was a Steiner loyalist, but he didn't really think so. Before the interstellar communications interdiction, Koin had been the one keeping him abreast of events on Muphrid.

Things had changed since then, though. It was as if the war was entering a new generation, a new chapter. Archer had saved Koin's life once, which had to count for something even if his old friend felt torn between friendship and loyalty to his government.

"With the Guards still trying to figure out how to control the satellites one at a time, we'll be on radar for only a few minutes on our burn outbound," Archer said. "Once we take off, you're on your own."

"It's been over two decades since I piloted a BattleMech in combat," Darius said as the *Angelfire*'s loading ramps thumped and clanged down onto the rocks along the shore. "Now I know the reason I stuck to the infantry."

"I always assumed it was because the infantry drew less fire on the battlefield than a 'Mech," Archer said with a grin.

"I'll try not to break her," Hopkins said, referring to the *Penetrator*—Archer's *Penetrator*.

"Good. I may need it when I get back. Just do me a favor, don't get yourself caught. If Blucher figures out I'm not on Thorin, things could get messy—fast."

Two hours later as the *Angelfire* burned toward the Thorin system's nadir jump point, Archer was down in the ship's 'Mech bay. While the fusion drive of the DropShip thrust to accelerate, there was minimal gravity in the bay. He felt the slight drift and lightness in his walk, as if he'd been wearing ankle weights and had suddenly removed them. Waiting for him was the rest of the assault team as well as the officers from the *Black Fox* and the *Shiloh*, who had shuttled over. The group had been talking among themselves, but fell silent as he approached.

"Good morning," he said. "As you all know, we're on our way to rendezvous with our JumpShip, *The*

Twilight Run, which will transport us to a pirate point in the Muphrid system." JumpShips traveled between star systems, moving almost instantaneously between the nadir or zenith jump points above system gravity wells. Pirate points were mathematical "holes" in the gravity of a solar system; arriving at one of these rather than at either of the standard jump points could cut travel time to the planet as well as add to the element of surprise. Pirate points were risky to hit since their positions changed and they required some serious skill to accurately reach—intact.

"We'll have a two-day burn in-system. Second Battalion of the Fifteenth Arcturan Guards has established a fire base in the equatorial jungles of the planet's northwestern continent. It's not a permanent base, but conveniently places them in the middle of three of the planet's major cities.

"I'm not here to blow sunshine up your kilts on this one. We don't know a lot about the Second, but our contact on Thorin did get us a full listing of their table of organization and equipment. They've got three *Union* Class DropShips, two companies of BattleMechs—all top-of-the line gear—a company of ground armor and supporting infantry, and a lance of aerospace fighters."

"Sir," said Alice Gett, the stout armored commander. "On paper, we appear outnumbered—slightly." Archer knew Gett well enough to recognize her sense of humor, but no one else seemed amused.

"The battalion will either be fully loaded or in the process of loading when we hit them. By then most of their strength will be strapped into the DropShips. We'll have the advantage of surprise. Our ships will be posing as simple merchants making for the spaceport at New Dublin, when we suddenly make a low-level diversion and hit their base."

"What's the plan of attack, Colonel?" asked Captain Paul Snider, a spindly officer in the front row.

"The straight story is that we're going to have to improvise as we go, Paul. I hope we can hit the Lyrans so fast and hard that they surrender rather than fight, but there's no guarantee. We know from intel we gathered before the blackout that the base is in a long, narrow valley that's been cleared on all sides. On the perimeter is a trench lined with mines. Their base consists of some prefab huts reinforced with sandbags and light shielding. Inside the defense perimeter is a landing strip. If they follow standard military procedure, the DropShips will be at the end of the strip so their takeoff blasts won't mess up the ferrocrete on the whole strip."

Archer thought that was enough said. His veterans had seen the same kind of fire bases many time in their careers. The rookies hadn't, but it wasn't too complex for them to handle.

Archer moved closer to his people. "We'll deploy our aerospace support on approach," he said, giving Subaltern Officer Andrew Hackley a nod and getting a thumbs-up in return. "The *Black Fox* and the *Shiloh* will go in first, carrying our infantry and armor and one lance of 'Mechs. They'll come down the runway and deploy in front of the DropShips. Their job is to keep those ships bottled up so they can't deploy any forces already loaded into the ships."

"*Union*s have six bay doors," piped up Captain Gett. "We'll be a pretty thin perimeter."

"Right, but you just have to hold them until we drop-deploy our 'Mechs. I'm going to designate one of the DropShips as a primary target. We take out or at least cripple one of them, and we're knocking out a third of their combat strength. Also, our infantry troops will carry enough explosive charges to disable the ship deployment ramps. And we'll use our ECM gear to keep the base from communicating with

Third Battalion, though we can't guarantee no message will go out. That lets us focus on the DropShips as our targets. If we concentrate on their ramps and keep the turrets busy, we should be able to even the odds and whittle them down as they try and deploy."

"You really think the Lyrans will surrender, Colonel?" asked Leftenant Basil Hawthorne.

"It's hard to say. We're going to be hitting them pretty fast. If our timing's good, they'll be bottled up in those DropShips, unable to get out and maneuver, and that's half the advantage of a BattleMech in combat."

"DropShips can dump a lot of firepower, sir," Captain Fullerton said. "The *Angelfire* is a good ship, but only half her turrets are operational—and it's not like we get a lot of target practice while transporting cargo."

"The *Angelfire* is going to come down less than seventy-five meters from the Guard ships. A blind man couldn't miss them. Besides, they won't know how lightly armed we are. We'll tag one of the ships as a primary target, incapacitate it, and then move on the others. Let's hope their lance of aerospace support is also loaded when we arrive. That will give us air superiority for once, which means some firepower advantages in hitting those DropShips."

"Are we going to get any help from the locals?" Gett asked.

"Good question, Captain," Archer said. "And in all honesty, I don't know. I've sent them a message and a code phrase if they decide to join us, but we have no way of knowing what the people of Muphrid will or won't do until we get there."

There was a long silence. Even the technicians who'd had been busily working on the 'Mechs had stopped and were listening from their perches and workstations throughout the bay.

"The Guards Second Battalion is a top-notch unit. They're loading up because Blucher's ordered them to come to Thorin to kick our butts. I can't speak for all of you, but I'd rather serve them up a little defeat on Muphrid than let them hunt us down like animals at home.

"Yes, our intel for this operation is limited. That's the nature of the beast. Yes, we're going to have to make up a lot of this as we go along. Yes, they outnumber us. But can we take them? Ask me and the answer is, 'Yes!' "

A resounding cheer rang out in the main 'Mech bay of the *Angelfire*. Every tech, MechWarrior, aerospace pilot, and crewmember in it raised their fists and voices in support.

Kommandant Constance McCoy has announced that Second Battalion of the Fifteenth Lyran Guards has been ordered to rotate off Muphrid. When questioned about whether the unit was destined for Thorin, she stated that this was only a routine rotation and that the Second's official destination was classified. When asked if that meant she denied reports that the rebellion on Thorin had escalated beyond Colonel Blucher's control, she replied, "No comment."

—Holoclip from *Channel 7 News*, Muphrid, Donegal Broadcasting Company, 20 January 3063

DropShip **Angelfire**
Inbound approach vector, Muphrid
Skye Province
Lyran Alliance
22 January 3063

From the bridge of the *Angelfire*, Archer watched as Muphrid came into view through the clouds. It was a brilliant world of stark greens, with jagged, snow-capped mountains showing in the far distance. Sum-

mer was just peaking in the steaming jungles near
the equator, their destined landing zone. The oceans
were more green than blue like Thorin's, and the
light from Muphrid's yellow-orange sun danced off
the waters.

"We're only seconds from diverting from course,"
Lee Fullerton said. He adjusted his weight uneasily
in his seat, a hint of his nervousness. "As soon as
we swing off course, the ground controllers will
know we're not simply merchants."

"It'll be fine, Lee. You'll just tell them we're experiencing mechanical difficulties with our nav system."

"You watch too many holovids Mister—er Colonel
Christifori. That stuff works in the movies, not in
real life."

"I know that, Lee. But every second you buy us
with radio chatter will give us some advantage on
the ground."

Fullerton nodded and leaned forward to give the
DropShip pilot the necessary commands. The massive ship lurched. Under the new pressure of real
gravity, Archer had to grip Fullerton's chair back and
hang on tight to keep from getting knocked to the
deck.

A light flashed on the arm rest. Fullerton glanced
at it quickly, then at Archer. "Well, there it is. Incoming transmission from planetary flight control."

"Go ahead, Lee. Give them a good show."

"This is Captain Fullerton of the *Angelfire*"—Fullerton shut the commlink off for a second, then continued—"experiencing problems with"—he shut it off
again and looked over at Archer for a full second
before turning it back on. "Diverting from primary
landing at spaceport."

"*Angelfire*, this is Muphrid Control. We do not read
you. Return to primary landing zone immediately."

Fullerton glanced at Archer. "I told you so."

"Just keep talking, Lee. Stretch it out."

"Muphrid Control, this is the *Angelfire*. We are experiencing primary power failures on three decks. Repair crews are working on it, but it may be a breach in the fusion reactor coolant system on the lower decks. You know what that means. I don't think you want me dropping this beast down in the middle of a crowded spaceport with a reactor that's running amok. If we lose containment on this unit, we're going to have one hell of a me—"

The controller's voice cut him off. "Our recovery and emergency crews can handle you here, *Angelfire*. Return to course immediately or planetary defense will be notified that you are hostile target."

"But our cargo is armaments for the Arcturan Guards. If that stuff gets hot, it'll blow and take out half the city in the process. I'll divert, but you're going to take full responsibility for what happens if this crate explodes and kills people!" The drama in Fullerton's voice was only semi-convincing, but just enough to buy another few seconds.

There was a slight pause. "Stand by for coordinates for an emergency landing site outside the city," the controller said. Fullerton ignored the figures that scrolled by on the navigator's screen as the *Angelfire* dropped lower and faster by the second.

"Well?" he asked Archer.

"I think we've strung them out as far as we can. Good work, Lee," he said, giving his old friend and former employee a wink.

"Muphrid Control, this is the merchant DropShip *Angelfire*. We have received your coordinates but are unable to comply. Primary navigation is off-line, and we are in an emergency landing sequence."

"Crudstunk you are, *Angelfire*," came back the angry voice from the speakers on the bridge. "I'm turning you over to planetary defense. You got this far, Captain, but I don't think the Lyrans are going to put up with any more of your theatrics."

Fullerton turned to his communications officer. "Send a command-coded message to the *Black Fox* and the *Shiloh*. Commence landing sequence. Assume a hot LZ."

The comm officer began to key in the message for transmission, then asked, "Anything else, sir?"

"Contact our aerospace jockeys on the bridge speakers." The comm officer nodded.

"This is Specter One to Saber Two," Archer said.

"This is Saber Two, go," came back the disembodied voice of Andrew Hackley, the ranking aerospace pilot. Francine Culver had stayed behind to provide Darius Hopkins with at least some aerospace support.

"We're going to paint you a target in ten seconds. You and Saber Three pump everything you've got into the target. I want it crippled beyond repair. Oh, and planetary defense knows we're not exactly friendly. Assume that Third Battalion is going to send some fighters to pester you."

"Roger, Colonel," Culver said anxiously.

"We need a broadband communication to anyone listening in the area," Archer told the comm officer. "The code phrase is 'Friar Tuck,' and I want you to repeat it over and over. Got it?"

The comm officer nodded and began to repeat the phrase into the system.

"If the rebels on Muphrid are with us," Archer told Fullerton, "they know we're about to attack."

Subaltern Andrew Hackley began to pull his *Chippewa* out of a dive some distance up the jungle valley so he could get a straight run at the target. There were three *Union* Class ships at the end of the tarmac, and the *Angelfire* had designated one of them as the primary target. The *Angelfire* was on descent, along with their pair of *Leopard* Class DropShips, sweeping almost straight at him from the other end of the valley.

At his wing was Subaltern Fawn Dougherty piloting a fifty-ton *Corsair*. She hung on his wingtip only five meters away, maintaining perfect distance and poise. This was Hackley's first time in command, and it was a doozy. His orders were to blast the target DropShip to provide some cover for the landing forces and to do a quick survey of what was on the ground. With only limited intelligence, the Avengers couldn't be sure exactly what they'd be facing or the state of the Guards' readiness. If the enemy battalion wasn't already loaded or in the process, this would be the shortest invasion in the history of the Inner Sphere.

The targeting reticle on his heads up display shimmered, and a tone sounded in his ears as the DropShip came into view. Below him the firebase sprawled in a cleared jungle valley. Several sand-bagged bunkers and buildings rose up from the light-colored soil, and barbed wire protected the trench line surrounding the base. And sitting on the tarmac were the three bulbous shapes of the Arcturan Guard DropShips.

He fired, as did WO Dougherty. Her lasers stabbed into the ship long before his thirty long-range missiles got there. The heat spike in his cockpit was sharp but faded fast. Switching to his second target interlock circuit, he brought his own bank of four large lasers to bear, while Dougherty cut loose with her mediums. The DropShip hull, dull gray and marked with the upright fist of the Lyran Alliance, seemed to shudder under the impacts. It was impossible to miss such a huge target.

The *Chippewa* quaked as Hackley leveled it off in flight, then switched to his short-range missiles while his LRMs clicked through the reload cycle. He sent the burst of six missiles down-range just as Dougherty's *Corsair* fired its quad set of small lasers. The missiles twisted into the blasted armor plating on the DropShip's other side, while the scarlet laser beams stabbed through the smoke bellowing from the previous hits.

"You juke left. I'm heading right," he told Dougherty over the tactical frequency. He barely heard her "Roger," as he swept across the landing zone and saw, at the far end, both *Leopard* Class DropShips starting to touch down. His short-range sensors swept the firebase. He prayed to whatever gods there be that the Guard BattleMechs were not out in the open, that they were already loaded onto the DropShips.

Then he started counting the BattleMechs and vehicles his sensors picked up. *One, two, three, oh my God . . .*

Archer's fingers flew through the start-up sequence for the captured *Blackjack BJ-2*. The cockpit was older, out of date compared to the streamlined one of his *Penetrator*. He'd done simulator training in the *Blackjack* program during the *Angelfire's* burn in-system, but that wasn't enough to put him totally at home with the 'Mech. Until you actually piloted an unfamiliar 'Mech in battle, it was a lot like a first date. You both knew each other a little, but couldn't always be quite sure how the other would react. The GM 180 under him throbbed to life as the *Angelfire* began its final burn to the landing zone.

"Saber Two, paint me a picture," he said into his neurohelmet mike, looking straight ahead at the dull gray of the DropShip's loading door.

Hackley sounded nervous but not out of control. "Colonel, there are eight targets on the runway. We've caught them just like you wanted them."

"Yes!" Archer said and raised one fist in defiant joy. Then Hackley spoke again. "We've also picked up a lance of BattleMechs on the firebase's outer marker, and they've opened up on the Lyrans. It's not much sir, but I'd say that our brothers and sisters on Muphrid have arrived."

So much the better, Archer thought. "Excellent work, Saber Two. Keep concentrated on the primary target. Continue your runs."

Then it was Alice Gett coming over the command frequency. "Sledgehammers One through Four on the ground and engaged."

Captain Paul Snider also reported in. "Spiders One through Four attacking. Heavy fire from the DropShips." Suddenly the *Angelfire* rocked, and the metal groaned. *A hit.* Archer checked his tactical display. The short-range sensors flickered to life and started to project the landing zone. The DropShips were positioned in a triangle. The one he'd designated as the target was in the middle relative to where the *Angelfire* was dropping. His battle computer overlaid the fields of fire, and it looked as if all three Lyran ships had brought their turrets on line and were blasting away wildly.

On the ground two lances of heavy BattleMechs were pulling back to the other two DropShips. The Muphrid rebels were still too distant to do much more than lay down a pattern of support fire. Archer checked the altimeter readout on his secondary display. It was another minute or so before the *Angelfire* would deploy. Archer's Avengers had been damn lucky so far. If only their luck could hold . . .

The air was alive with long-range missiles as Subaltern Hackley banked the *Chippewa* for another run. Ten of the warheads clipped into his port wing, but did no more than mess up the paint job on his armor. The *Chippewa* rocked slightly under the impacts, and he leveled out from the bank to get more room for a better run.

Out the corner of his eye he saw Saber Three attempt to mirror the maneuver, but the missiles caught her almost squarely in the cockpit and wings. The black and gray explosions were but wisps in the air as her smaller *Corsair* was battered like a leaf in a hurricane. His tactical display told him that she'd lost almost half of her armor in just seconds as the DropShips seemed to target her alone.

"Saber Three, are you okay?" he asked

Fawn Dougherty's voice was shaken as she responded through a hiss of static. "Saber Two, I'm more holes than ship up here," she said. He heard desperation bordering on panic in her voice.

He was about to reply when his warning alarms went off. "More missiles! Juke low and left!" he commanded while thrusting the *Chippewa*'s yoke as far over as possible to boost its power. The fighter rocked as another handful of long-range missiles pockmarked his lower fuselage, grinding armor plating to worthless waste. Fighting the controls with all his strength, he came in low, a mere fifty meters from the ground.

Black smoke hovered in the distance, but he saw no sign of Dougherty. His tactical display didn't show her in the air either. Then her emergency beacon rang off from several kilometers away. She'd hit the ground so fast she'd never had a chance to punch out.

Fawn Dougherty was dead. No screams. No cries. Just gone. And it happened his first time in command. Hackley drew in a long breath and brought his targeting reticle up on the primary DropShip target. "Time for you to die, you Steiner bastard!"

A dull thud echoed through the *Angelfire* and in Archer's cockpit as the ship slammed onto the ferrocrete tarmac. The drop door that filled his front field of vision suddenly lurched outward. Light poured in as the bay door opened. Archer moved the *Blackjack* forward, then down the ramp, pivoting the arm-mounted-weapons upward in defiance.

Before him were the three Guards DropShips. Laser and autocannon fire from their turrets slashed and burned toward the *Angelfire*. At the feet of the DropShips were the Guards BattleMechs. One was already a burned ruin, a pile of debris littering the runway and a pair of charred metal feet still standing. The others were under attack by Alice Gett and her armored forces, with Paul Snider joining in. In the distance, the lance of Muphrid rebels, now down to three 'Mechs, was still moving forward, pouring every bit of fire they had into the DropShips and the defending BattleMechs.

Archer lit his jump jets and made a short hop away from the *Angelfire*. His cockpit got just warm enough to remind him that using the jets would be risky once he started firing all his weapons. "Specter One to all commands, deploy as planned and get some distance from the DropShips. Pour it on!"

He landed almost gently on the tarmac. With his joystick, he raised his targeting reticle and dropped it onto a Lyran *Wyvern* that was trying to cut off the approaching Muphrid rebels.

His extended-range large lasers sent crimson beams of energy downrange at the shifting foe. One beam missed, but the other dug into the 'Mech's right arm, and it stopped to see where the attack had come from.

"That's right, bitch, it was me. Come on—let's dance," Archer muttered as he brought his short-range Streak missiles to a pre-fire mode.

Without warning, the center DropShip erupted in a massive explosion. The shock wave pushed the *Blackjack* back several steps, throwing him hard against his seat as the restraint straps bit into his shoulders. A ball of orange seemed to spread out toward him and stop just short of his position. Armor plating and debris rained down as the ammunition magazines of the Lyran ship exploded outward with raw fury. One of its massive strut legs caved in under the force of the blast. The explosion damaged the other two DropShips as well. Burning pieces of debris from the destroyed ship could be seen poking out from the hull of one of the other ships.

Archer glanced down and saw that the *Wyvern* and several other defenders were either gone or lying prone on the tarmac. Through the dense black smoke drifting from what was left of the DropShip, he saw the shape of a *Chippewa* roaring upward.

"Good shooting, Saber Two," he called. "All commands, let's keep the other two ships bottled up. Let's move." At that moment a wall of long-range missiles hit his *Blackjack* with such force from the side that Archer almost lost control and fell over. His head ached as his biofeedback attempted to compensate for the change in balance through his neurohelmet.

He lifted his head and saw the form of the *Wyvern* emerge from the smoke and debris of the blasted DropShip. It was moving away from him, firing at the Avenger *War Dog*. He opened the broadband frequency and began to speak even as he brought a pair of his Streak SRM packs to bear.

"Lyran commander, surrender your forces or prepare to be destroyed!" he said, then punctuated his words by firing the four missiles. They plowed into the rear-torso armor of the *Wyvern*, forcing the 'Mech to dodge for cover as the last shred of its aft armor flailed off into the distance.

"Who is this?" demanded a female voice in his earpiece as he came closer to one of the DropShips, then a oblong Guard *Jackal* fired its extended-range particle projection cannon at him just within its minimum range. The jagged white-blue bolt of energy slammed into the *Blackjack*'s right arm, twisting the armor into a jagged and blackened shred.

Archer continued forward, then up the ramp of one of the DropShips, bringing his targeting reticle down on the *Jackal*.

"This is Colonel Archer Christifori," he said, then triggered his large lasers at the smaller 'Mech. Both shots hit the 'Mech's right torso, and its shoulder-mounted PPC barrel contorted backward under the fury of the blasts. The MechWarrior lost her footing and fell over on the tarmac, crushing even more of its armor.

"Surrender now or we'll wipe you out," Archer said again. Off in the distance he saw the ramps and doors of one of the other DropShips explode with satchel charges, mangling the ship horribly. The *War Dog* he'd seen a few moments ago was down, hit by the Guards who were attempting to debark and deploy. Twisted pieces and parts of the *Wyvern* were everywhere, as if it had exploded from within.

"Impossible," the woman's voice continued in disbelief. "Christifori's on Thorin."

Archer started up the DropShip ramp as he saw Alice Gett sweep her *Burke* tank into position and fire her three PPCs at the ship's turret. The deadly blue bolts of death streaked just over his 'Mech's head.

"Surrender now or you'll be destroyed," he called again. Archer had never even imagined being in a fight like this, a fight against his own people. How many more times would he be forced into such a battle before this was all over?

He charged up the gangway right into the heart of the ship's 'Mech bay. A barrage of laser and missile fire poured at him through the door, but he didn't care. He went in with every weapon blazing.

$$=== \mathbf{26} ===$$

Government officials refuse to comment on how many citizens are currently being held in the recently established detention camps near Ecol City. Nor will Colonel Blucher or his staff comment on how long he plans to detain them or under what conditions they will be released. The Thorin Planetary Ruling Council, empowered by the Duke while away at court, has issued an official protest to Freedom Theater Commander Komandant-General Sarah Joss.

—Holovid clip, *Thorin News Tonight*, Ecol City, Channel 43, 22 January 3063

Bristoe Detention Center
Thorin, Skye Province
Lyran Alliance
23 January 3063

The sensors in Darius Hopkins' borrowed *Penetrator* blared out a warning and, despite his many years away from a 'Mech cockpit, he recognized the tone—an air attack warning. Glancing down at his tactical readout, he saw the pair of *Lucifer*s and the *Stuka* beginning an attack run on the Avengers' position.

Bloody damn great! he thought. I was already too old for this back when Archer first left for NAIS. I must be nuts climbing into a cockpit at my age.

Things had gone wrong and gone wrong quickly tonight. His force had punched through the fence of the Bristoe Detention Camp to free the prisoners, hoping Katya Chaffee would be among them. Driving off the hired security force had been easy, but then came these aerospace fighters out of nowhere. Now, as the prisoners fled into the surrounding dark, the Lyran fighters were coming in, guns a-blazing.

"Specter Ten, get moving now," Hopkins ordered, picking up speed and taking the *Penetrator* forward in a long turn. Armor and speed would be his only protection at this point. One *Lucifer* was peeling off to strafe Hogan's *Battle Hawk*, while the hundred-ton *Stuka* and its *Lucifer* wingman were making their run against him.

"This is Icepick One to all commands. Time to bug out," he said, breaking away from the camp in a dead run. He could make out the forms of the escaping prisoners racing toward the dark surrounding forest, and he stayed well clear of them as the Guard aerofighters began their strafing run. He didn't stop even to check his tactical display. It was just get out of here—now.

A burst of long-range missiles and large lasers lit up the ground around him, damaging the *Penetrator*'s arms and legs. A pair of large lasers also hit his rear, melting away armor into white-hot globs of metal that sprayed over his 'Mech's shoulders as he ran, casting an odd glow into the night. The *Penetrator* lurched forward under the impact, and he had to fight the foot pedals and throttle control to keep up enough the speed not to fall flat on his face. While the *Stuka*'s fire found its mark, the *Lucifer* pilot had mostly missed. Hopkins told himself he was too damn old to be counting on luck to survive. A part of him wished Archer hadn't left him behind.

Sweat was pouring down his face. He swung his large lasers up and brought the targeting reticle onto the *Stuka*. It was almost invisible in the night, but painted up perfectly on his targeting and tracking system. He fired both lasers, which sent a wave of heat over the cockpit. The extended-range weapons bore in on the *Stuka*, hitting its right-wing armor enough to leave a glow in the air as it swung away. You could say what you want about the Clans, Hopkins thought, but they made weapons he'd have killed for when still in active service.

He swung around an outcropping of rocks and continued into the forest. The *Lucifer*s peeled off after him. The first one made good its earlier miss. Its long-range missiles hit his right and left torso, blasting away armor plating and rocking the *Penetrator*. Hopkins triggered his medium pulse lasers and his pair of large lasers. One of the *Lucifer*'s weapons found its mark, the crimson laser beam stabbing into his right arm and causing the shoulder joint to freeze as the actuator melted away. The other shot missed by mere meters to his left, exploding a boulder that sent up white-hot steam into the night.

His medium pulse lasers also lit up the darkness with their green fire. Almost half missed totally, the emerald bursts seeming to race up toward the stars. The others gored the wings and fuselage of the *Lucifer*, leaving ugly gashes. Its wingman of the same class swept in, firing its lasers and LRMs. The lasers missed, but the LRMS hit all over the *Penetrator*.

Hopkins wanted to stand and fight, but this wasn't the time or the place. This was a raid. His goal was to free as many prisoners as possible and convince Colonel Blucher that Archer Christifori was still on Thorin. A glance at his tactical display told him that all the *Penetrator* had left was a few tons of armor.

The 'Mech was still functional, but not for long. Grudgingly, he nudged the badly mauled war machine into the forest, where he hoped the cover of night and the protection of the giant trees would force the fighters to break off their pursuit.

Colonel Felix Blucher watched from his *Atlas* as the Bristoe Detention Center's searchlights once again swept the area. He didn't really expect to find Christifori's 'Mechs, but signs of their recent presence were everywhere. The foot of his *Atlas* had just crushed a chunk of armor from one of the two 'Mechs his aerospace fighters had driven off. That had been two hours ago. By now, Archer's Avengers would be long gone.

"Status, Fisk," he said into his helmet mike. Leutnant Fisk and his security team were still securing the perimeter.

"It looks like sixty-eight prisoners escaped. We'll be rounding up many of them throughout the night. They won't get too far with no provisions in this weather."

"And what about our special guest?"

"Our bait is still secure," Fisk said. "Hauptmann Chaffee's guards kept her from going anywhere."

So, Christifori had come for her just as Blucher predicted he would. Out of all of the camps he might have hit, Christifori had chosen this one. Katya Chaffee meant something to him beyond military matters. He'd been married to his career until now, but it looked like things had changed. Christifori's feelings for Chaffee would be his downfall.

And it had almost happened tonight.

The colonel had downloaded some of the gun-camera shots from the aerospace fighters to his cockpit as he'd traveled from the fort to the camp. The *Penetrator* and the *Battle Hawk* had barely managed to escape into the forest, but the sensors of his aerofighters told the tale of damage. Very little armor remained on Christifori's 'Mech, and the *Battle Hawk* had lost one of its arms in the flight.

Christifori obviously hadn't expected Blucher to use all his assets the way he had. He'd set up a defense against infantry only, and the fighters had taken him by surprise. All alone in his cockpit, Felix Blucher smiled broadly to himself inside his neurohelmet. This time he was the one to walk away from battle with the upper hand. And once his Second Battalion arrived from Muphrid, he would crush Archer Christifori's little revolution once and for all.

If you believe the reports I've been getting from
the information officer for the Fifteenth Arcturan
Guards, this uprising will be over and done with in
a matter of a week.

—Holoclip from *News at Five*, Ecol City, Donegal Broadcasting Company, 31 January 3063

Melissa Steiner Memorial Spaceport
Ecol City, Thorin
Skye Province
Lyran Alliance
2 February 3063

From the cockpit of his *Atlas*, Felix Blucher sat
watching as the DropShips began their descent to the
tarmac. On either side of him he'd lined up his two
lances of functional BattleMechs at formal parade
rest. The mid-morning sun glanced off of their new
paint jobs as they waited to welcome Second Battalion to Thorin. Three additional 'Mechs had remained
back at the fort, in various stages of repair.

The battalion was late by a day and a half. He'd
received a data packet from them indicating that one

of their DropShips had been attacked and crippled by the Muphrid rebels. For that reason, Kommandant McCoy had commandeered a merchant *Union* transport to get to Thorin.

The news was disturbing. That there had been an attack did not surprise him, but that the rebels had managed to inflict enough damage to ground a DropShip was unnerving. If not for his recent successes against Archer's so-called Avengers, it might have been even more alarming. Two times in two weeks he'd used his aerospace forces against Christifori's raiders, both times driving them off the field in retreat. They'd damaged one of his *Lucifers*, but he still claimed air superiority and he savored it.

The ships, all three of them, became visible in the sky above him long before he heard the roar of their fusion-fired engines. The two Guard ships were painted a dull gray, and the confiscated merchant vessel was a somewhat lighter shade. He could tell it had a commercial logo on its hull, but that side of the DropShip faced away from view as it approached for its final descent.

The ships touched down one by one on the tarmac. The thunderous bellow of their engines tapered off as the large landing struts took on the mass of the ships and held them upright. It was followed by the white noise of the engines as they throttled back.

Blucher welcomed all the storm and thunder. This was a great moment for him and his command. Archer Christifori had put up a good fight. The odds had changed now, and his last two victories over the Avengers had proven that. With the arrival of McCoy and her battalion, the rebels couldn't hope to put up a sustained fight against Lyran control.

As the ships vented excess steams and ran coolant to their lower portions to cool the exhaust ports, the gantry ramps clanged open and began lowering toward the ground. Blucher opened a wide-band channel and sang out, "Ten Hut!" The BattleMechs on either side of him stood tall and proud.

The 'Mechs of Second Battalion began to descend the DropShip ramps and lined up in front of him in a broad formation. They kept on coming, followed by a platoon of infantry and now the tank forces that were starting down the ramp.

His commline hissed briefly, but the voice he heard wasn't that of Constance McCoy.

"Colonel Blucher," said a male voice he recognized instantly, "I order you to surrender in the name of Victor Davion." A chill ran through the colonel's body. His heart pounded in his ears. Then the two long, deep rows of 'Mechs in front of him raised their arms. Blucher's eyes widened at the sight, and in the distance he caught a glimpse of the other side of the merchant DropShip. Painted on it was the flying ship logo of Christifori Express.

This wasn't possible. It couldn't be happening. But it was.

"It's a trap," he barked to his units. "Fire at will. That isn't the Second at all. It's Christifori. Fall back at once to the fort. We'll fight them from there!" He throttled his fusion reactor to full power and swept his gauss rifle into firing position as he piloted his BattleMech backward toward the street leading away from the spaceport. With so many targets, he could hardly miss.

The command center of the fort was quiet as Leutnant Sherwood stood behind the corporal working the comm station. "Say again, sir?" the man said into his head mike.

"What is it?" Sherwood asked.

The young commtech looked up and pulled off his headset. "I can't make it all out. It was the colonel, something about the spaceport. Then it cut off."

Sherwood picked up the headset and put it on.

"Colonel, this is the duty officer," he said. "We do not copy."

"We're under fire here and falling back to the fort," came a voice through the crackle of static Sherwood recognized as the sound of close-range PPC discharges. His heart began to race, and his uniform felt warm and sweaty.

"What about Second Battalion?" he asked.

"It wasn't them. It was Christifori," Blucher said in a rush. "Open the gates and as soon as we're in, button up tight. Crank up your 'Mech, along with Kramer and Druhot. They're jamming our long-range signals. Contact our fighters and get them over here. We'll defend from the fort."

"Yes, sir," Sherwood said, then removed the headset slowly.

"What is it, sir?" the commtech asked.

Sherwood looked around the room. There were four soldiers present, none of them armed as they worked the various defense and comm systems. He pulled out his sidearm, a Sternsnacht pistol, and stabbed it into the mouth of the tech sitting in front of him. Then he pivoted both of them around in view of the others in the room.

"Now that I've got your attention," he said, "do what I say or this young man's brains are going up in smoke, followed by your own."

Archer jogged his *Blackjack* diagonally across the street, listening to the loading cycle of his short-range Streak missiles as he went. Things weren't going as well as he'd hoped. He'd expected Blucher to surrender just like his Second Battalion did, given the sheer numbers against him: wishful thinking. Instead it had become a running fight in the streets of Ecol City.

Blucher's *Atlas* was still two blocks ahead, where some of Archer's lighter forces were attempting to engage him on the way to the fort. Archer had been pursuing a Guards *Vulcan*, but it fell to a gauss rifle slug from a former Lyran *War Dog* just as Archer was about to fire on it. The silvery blur hit the *Vulcan*'s head with so much force that the 'Mech toppled backward into a building, virtually burying itself among the caved-in floors and walls.

He turned just in time to see another Lyran 'Mech attempt to break for cover. It was a *Salamander*, and Archer knew that Luther Fisk was the only Guards warrior who piloted one. He immediately raced after it. The *Salamander* attempted to dart to the right to lead Archer's fire, but without success. Archer fired his eight Streak missiles at it, slamming them into its back. The armor plating exploded off, leaving behind a puff of light gray smoke and exposed myomer bundles.

That had gotten Fisk's attention. He turned to protect his fragile rear and to fire his medium lasers. The range was too short for his long-range missiles, his most potent firepower. The medium lasers lanced out at Archer, one missing and one blackening his right arm with a scar.

Archer knew his heat would spike, but he swung his own ER large lasers on line and fired their brilliant red beams into the legs of the *Salamander*. Armor melted off, but the damage wasn't enough to stop the 'Mech. Fisk was about to turn and run, when an awesome barrage of weapons fire from all around Archer hit his 'Mech. Missiles, emerald and scarlet lasers, autocannon rounds, and the bright blue-white light of PPC rounds devoured Fisk's *Salamander* and the surrounding area. The pavement erupted into a crater as flames, explosions, and smoke swept over the 'Mech. It seemed to melt like a candle in time-lapsed motion, disappearing and dying into the explosions.

Archer turned his head and saw almost his whole unit around and behind him. They had all fired. He and they had taken Fisk down together in a single barrage of carnage.

"Avengers take care of our own, sir," said Alice Gett. "Now it's time to finish what we've started."

A lightweight Avenger *Assassin* landed off to Blucher's front right quadrant in a move to cut him off from the fort. Its jump jets were still glowing as it turned toward his *Atlas* and tried to bring its medium pulse laser on-line. Blucher, on the other hand, didn't have to wait. His targeted his ER large lasers and medium pulse lasers onto the smaller 'Mech and opened up. The boxy *Assassin* withered under the barrage, losing armor from all of its limbs and its chest. It staggered back down an alley, firing its long-range missiles as it retreated.

The missiles swept over the *Atlas*, mangling its right arm and torso armor plating. Blucher had taken hits several times since the fight began, but so far he was still functional and still had some protection everywhere. He'd taken out two 'Mechs so far and had pummeled several like the *Assassin*. He wanted to stay and fight, but the fort was near enough that if he and the others could get in, they could make their stand from there.

Moving alongside him was Leftenant Fitzwalter in her *Axman*. A sick green ooze of coolant leaked from holes in her lower torso from earlier hits. Suddenly she crumbled under a bolt of PPC fire, her whole 'Mech seeming to evaporate into nothingness.

Blucher only had time to register what had happened. He had to keep on if his command was going to survive. A glance at his short-range sensor readout showed the fort almost within reach even as a moving wall of Archer's BattleMechs closed in rapidly. Oh, you're fast, Christifori, but not fast enough, he thought. The fort was directly ahead of him now.

But when he looked through his cracked cockpit

canopy, Blucher saw that the gate was still closed. Why hadn't they opened it, per his orders? The massive gate was blast-proof and could only be opened from the inside.

"Leutnant Sherwood—anyone in the command center. Open the damn gate!"

At first he heard nothing. Then finally came the reply. "Colonel Blucher, this is Leftenant Sherwood. I'm afraid we can't comply."

"What?" Blucher fairly screamed as he cleared the last bit of ground to the gates. Confounded, he stood there staring helplessly at the implacable granite walls and the huge, ferro-fibrous armored door. He didn't have to turn and look to know that Christifori's rebel band of BattleMechs were racing straight for him.

The broadband channel lit up, and Sherwood spoke again. This time anyone on either side could hear his words in their cockpits. "Sir, I am with Colonel Christifori. Your command personnel are locked in the map room, and the control center is under my charge. Your fighters have been ordered to stand down. Colonel Blucher, I suggest that you surrender."

A block and a half from the fort Archer ordered his forces to stop and hold their fire. He sent flankers up the side streets in case Blucher thought he could still get away. The Guards had lost most of their forces. A lone Chaparral tank, smoke rising from rents in its armor, sat next to Blucher's *Atlas*. A war-torn *Kintaro* also remained standing. Its back was to the granite wall, prepared for a last stand. The only other combatant on the Lyran side was a *Centurion* that was missing most of its arm and chest armor. By now what was left of a battalion of Arcturan Guards knew the truth; there was nowhere to run, nowhere from which to make a decent last stand. Prince John had taken the fort all by himself.

Archer paused and drew a deep breath before activating a neutral channel to talk directly to Blucher.

"Colonel Blucher, this is Colonel Christifori. I've ordered my troops to hold their fire. I respectfully request your surrender, sir." The many times Archer had imagined this moment, he'd pictured himself gloating over the victory. Now, looking at the *Atlas*, still smoking in two places from hits, it was the last thing he wanted to do. This was one of those moments where he could show himself a man of honor, a proper warrior instead of a renegade. Do this wrong, and factions on Thorin might be fighting for some time to come.

"I would prefer to die here, in my cockpit, rather than surrender," Blucher said.

"I understand, Colonel," Archer said. "However, I have no desire to kill a man like you or those brave MechWarriors and officers who fought beside you. Too much blood has already been shed. Let us stand down."

There was a long pause, then Blucher asked, "How did this happen?"

"We learned of your plans, Colonel. We struck at Second Battalion before they could get here. We caught them with their pants down and they capitulated. As we speak, I imagine the troops I left there are already raising hell with your Third Battalion. I know they crippled the HPG to keep you in the dark, apparently successfully."

"In all of my years of service to House Steiner, I have never lost a battle and been forced to surrender." Blucher's voice was low, controlled, almost resigned.

"In all of my years of service, I have never had to ask someone I respected so much to surrender, either. But my duty requires it."

"And I must accept. As you say, duty requires it. You're right. Too many have already died."

"You'll find my terms reasonable. You'll be prisoners. Your arms are our possessions now. You'll be exchanged with other prisoners as soon as is practical or authorized by Prince Victor. As for your forces on Muphrid—"

"With all due respect," Blucher cut in, "your fight was here."

"And here it would have remained if you hadn't planned to bring in your Second Battalion. I would ask that you surrender your other unit as well, but I doubt you will."

"That is correct," Blucher replied in a monotone. "Third Battalion is still a viable force."

Archer spoke with the finality of a judge's gavel. "That is why it pains me to say that we will be taking our forces to Muphrid and doing to Third Battalion what we did to you here."

"If you will permit, Colonel Christifori, I think the Fifteenth Arcturan Guards have suffered enough going against you. With your permission, I will send them orders to depart Muphrid for a more friendly location."

Archer reflected for a moment. He'd wanted full surrender, but this was a victory, too. "Very well. Have them withdraw in good order."

"This never had to come to pass," Blucher said dully.

"I agree," Archer conceded. "And it's not over now. It's only starting. Katrina still holds the throne. She must be removed."

"I cannot agree with that," Blucher said. "But for what it's worth, I respect a man who stands by his convictions."

Epilogue

With Thorin and Muphrid firmly held by Prince Victor's forces, it's apparent that the war is moving into a new stage. It is no longer the stuff of guerrilla operations, but more of a true military campaign. One thing is certain—the Federated Commonwealth and the Lyran Alliance will never be the same.

—Reported by *Word from the Underground*,
  pirate broadcast, Thorin, 7 February 3063

Ecol City, Thorin
Skye Province
Lyran Alliance
9 February 3063

Archer's forces stood at attention in the main courtyard of the fort. On one side of him was a row of BattleMechs, many of them captured from the Arcturan Guards. On the other side was a row of tanks along with Sergeant Major Hopkins' infantry, some of them still wearing dressings on their wounds. All the vehicles showed signs of recent action, but had been repainted and repaired. All the 'Mechs bore the symbol "A2" on their shoulders and center torsos— the informal insignia of Archer's Avengers.

The line was straight as a laser shot. Archer's dress uniform, neatly pressed, had been hard to come by in the chaos of the last few days. But this was important enough for him to make the effort. At his side was Captain Katya Chaffee. Upon seeing her when she was first released, he let go a moan of relief. To both their surprise, he swept her up in his arms and gave her a long and strong hug.

The doors to the compound brig opened, and Archer snapped to attention. This was important for everyone, not just for his troops and Blucher's, but for the media observing on the fringes of the ceremony. Colonel Blucher and what was left of his battalion were being taken to more formal barracks for prisoners of war. Archer wanted to do it right—with malice toward none.

"Atten—shun!" he barked. Dozens of heels snapped into the ground, and the straight line of his troops became rigid vertically as well.

The guards, at full parade march, led the Arcturan Guard prisoners to their transport, moving down the entire line of Avengers. Archer could see from Blucher's face that he was moved by the gesture of respect. The colonel stopped when he came to Archer, which also abruptly halted the line of people with him, guards and all. With perfect military precision he pivoted right face and saluted. Archer returned the salute.

"You honor us, Colonel," Blucher said, loud enough that all present could hear him.

Archer smiled slightly. "We're not enemies deep down. We just believe in different leaders."

"Perhaps you're right. But to quote another military man, 'Time sets all things right. Error lives but a day. Truth is eternal.' "

Archer remembered the quote from his academy days. "General Longstreet."

Blucher nodded. "But remember this. Even centuries after he fought, his actions are still the stuff of controversies. May your truths be more constant."

Then the line continued out toward the waiting APCs that would transport the prisoners to more spacious facilities. As the injured soldiers passed, Archer spotted a stretcher in the line. He stepped from his place and went toward it. The two Avenger stretcher-bearers stopped as their commanding officer looked down at the man they were carrying. From the way the sheet hung on him, Archer knew he was missing an arm at the shoulder. His left eye was patched and most of his head was bandaged. His black hair was singed from fires.

Archer bent over the stretcher. "Leutnant Fisk, odd as it may seem, I am pleased you did not die."

Fisk looked up coldly with his one good eye. "I might as well be. I lost my eye, my arm. My knee is severely injured. I may never pilot a BattleMech again." His voice stung with bitterness.

"That's right," Archer said, "and I will never again be able to speak with my sister. She was my right arm as well. At least you have your life." Archer turned and started to walk away, but Fisk's voice followed him.

"Why not just let me die rather than leave me maimed?"

Archer turned back again. "I've been made into an Avenger. Consider it done."

Later that day Archer sat in his office, the one formerly used by Colonel Blucher in the fort. He stared at the hardcopy and disks piled in front of him. This was the part of the job he would never learn to like. He was about to pick up the top datapad to review some requisitions when a knock came at the door.

"Enter," he said, and Katya Chaffee came in. He gave her a grateful smile. "Thank God it's you," he said wearily, leaning back in his chair.

"Sir," she said with an odd degree of formality, "a DropShip landed an hour ago from a pirate point in the system. We've got a visitor."

Archer cocked an eyebrow and rose to his feet, resting his hands on the desk. "I'm not sure I like the sound of this."

"He says he was sent by a friend, and I've checked out his credentials," Katya said.

Archer nodded, and Katya went back into the hall to usher in the visitor. He was a small man with a receding hairline and wore the white uniform of ComStar. He also wore a Star League Medal of Honor like the one Archer had been awarded. They had met briefly once before, and Archer recognized him immediately.

"I bring you greetings from Prince Victor Steiner-Davion," said Alain Beresick.

"Thank you, Commodore Beresick, and welcome to Thorin." This man was as much a legend in the Inner Sphere as Archer was on Thorin. He had commanded the WarShip *Invisible Truth* in the strike against Huntress. No man alive could match his experience in WarShip combat.

"It's good to see that you are well," Beresick said. "Though I now go by another title, that of Precentor."

"I'm honored you have come to visit," Archer said, motioning to a chair.

With a wave of his hand Beresick indicated that he preferred to stand. Katya stood somewhat behind him, looking awed. The man's appearance was totally unassuming, yet he had about him a presence that commanded respect.

"I was 'in the neighborhood' on other business and so will not stay long. His Highness, the Precentor Martial, has received word of your successes here and on Muphrid. He asked me to deliver an HPG transmission to you in person, if time permitted. He also extends his deepest gratitude to you and your command."

"That is not necessary," Archer said, his face flushing like a school boy's.

"But it is." Beresick took a folded sheet of paper out of his pocket and held it up to read. "By order of Prince Victor Steiner-Davion, Archer Christifori is hereby granted the field promotion of Leftenant General." Then he reached into his pocket once more and took out the rank insignia and presented them to him.

Archer stared at the two and a half barred insignia in his hand for a long moment. "Leftenant General?" he echoed in total disbelief.

"Your service has proven an inspiration to others. And though this fight is still young, the Prince needs men and women like you on his side."

Archer pulled himself up to his full height and saluted. Beresick saluted back, as did Katya.

"Are you sure you must leave so soon, Precentor?" Archer asked.

"Yes, General. I have other assignments to complete."

"Then can you take the Prince a message back with you?"

"Of course."

"Tell him it's good to be home."

Precentor Alain Beresick tipped his head with stately formality. "That I will, *General* Christifori. That I will."

About the Author

Amissville, Virginia
United States of America
Terra
10 October 1999

Blaine Pardoe was born in Virginia, raised in Michigan, and now has returned to Virginia in an effort to flee from three words—"lake-effect snow." He lives in Amissville, Virginia, approximately six miles past the middle of nowhere, one mile past the blinking light on the main road.

He has written over forty-three books, including novels in the BattleTech® and MechWarrior® series as well as a best-selling business management book, *Cubicle Warfare*. In his "day job" he is a senior manager at Ernst & Young LLP in Global Learning Solutions.

Blaine has a wonderful wife, Cyndi, and two children, Alexander and Victoria. They have a dog that lacks motivation and, at times, a brain, named Sandy. His hobbies include playing the GHB (Great Highland Bagpipe), hunting for Civil War relics, and, of course, writing.

His favorite authors include Harry Turtledove, William Davis, Shelby Foote, and yes, he's a fan of BattleTech® and plays the MechWarrior® PC game. Blaine can be reached at Bpardoe870@aol.com.

Here's a sneak peek at the next
explosive BattleTech adventure:

Path of Glory
by Randall M. Bills

Coming from Roc in December 2000!

===== **1** =====

Battle Cruiser SLS Severen Leroux
Zenith Jump Point, Irece System
Draconis Combine
12 June 3061

When the unknown ship appeared exactly two hundred and forty seconds after the infrared radiation spike first appeared, Star Admiral Jorgensson had just reached the bridge. In the void of space, some ten thousand meters off the prow of the *Severen Leroux*, the emergence wave of an incoming vessel split the dark. The spindly shape blurred into existence, arriving almost instantaneously from some other star system light years away.

Antila, her second, glanced over at her. "Star Admiral, our aerospace fighters and the *Sacred Rite* have already begun a burn toward the ship."

Jan heard the note of pride in his voice and shared it. She and her crew had won the *Noruff* Class DropShip away from the Steel Vipers in a Trial of

Possession, a triumph that was one of their finest moments. Khan Leroux was so pleased to acquire this swift and fearsome DropShip for the Nova Cats that he'd allowed Jan to name it. The *Scared Rite* was the only ship of its kind in their entire Touman.

"Have a look," Antila said, gesturing toward the holotank in the center of the bridge.

Jan turned toward the laser-generated, three-dimensional image of a *Monolith* Class JumpShip hovering in clear detail over the tank. The largest JumpShip in service with either the Clans or the Inner Sphere, its seven-hundred-fifty meters could carry up to nine DropShips. This particular vessel had obviously seen some vicious fighting. Pock-marked craters and smooth, blackened troughs from autocannon and laser fire covered almost every meter of its hull. Even the DropShips docked in rings around the Monolith's cargo section showed the scars of the battle, with at least one ship having lost several decks to explosive decompression.

Only eight DropShips were docked to the vessel. What had once been the ninth docking arm was now a fused mass of metallic parts. Even more shocking was that the entire stern of the *Monolith* was simply gone. The place where the ship's critical parts had once been—the jump-sail array, the drive-charging system, the station-keeping drive—was now a gaping maw. Jan wondered how in the name of Kerensky the vessel had survived the jump.

"Magnify the extreme forward prow," she said, eyes glued to a spot on the blackened armor plating where she thought she had glimpsed an insignia.

The tapping of the holotank's keyboard console echoed in the dead silence of the bridge. Then the three-dimensional image of the *Monolith* seemed to zoom toward her, and she experienced the momentary sensation of falling into it. Several gasps broke the silence as one side of the hull became visible.

Though much of it was scorched and burned away, there was the unmistakable emblem of Clan Nova Cat.

Jan was stunned. "Star Commodore, scramble the second Star of fighters immediately and launch both *Promised Vision* and *Promised Sight*." She was outraged at the sight of a Nova Cat ship so devastated.

"With the station-keeping drive destroyed, we must stabilize the ship as quickly as possible before she begins to succumb to our star's gravitational pull. We must also send a message to Irene immediately, with instructions to relay it on to the SLS *Faithful* at the nadir jump point. Inform them of the arrival of the *Monolith* and instruct them to be prepared for possible hostile intrusion."

She thought of the DropShip on its way to her now, bringing her guest. "Send that message to the *Nova Cat Alpha* as well."

Jan walked slowly around the holotank, continuing her scrutiny of the ravaged vessel. "Have we been able to contact the ship yet?"

The communications tech looked up briefly. "No, Star Admiral. If you look closely, you will see that the communications antennae on the prow of the *Monolith* seems to have been sheared away. We will not know more until we board her."

She turned to Antila. "Any thoughts on where the ship came from, Star Commodore?"

"Ave, Star Admiral." Jan smiled slightly at the trace of smugness in his tone. True to form, her second had calculated an answer even before she had asked. Though the trait was maddening sometimes, it had saved the lives of her and her crew on more than one occasion.

"Using the number of DropShips carried by the *Monolith*, along with the duration between the IR spike and the vessel's actual arrival time, I can say with ninety-five percent accuracy that the ship arrived from the Outer Volta system. Outer Volta is within one easy jump from three different worlds currently occupied by Combine troops. I do not discount the possibility that the ship was attacked by the Draconis Combine, but it is doubtful."

Antila turned away from his console and looked at Jan. "The taboo against damaging JumpShips is still too ingrained in them. Pirates perhaps. But not Combine warriors."

Jan agreed with Antila—it wasn't the work of the Combine. But with her visitor arriving so soon, she could not take any chances. The *Monolith* was virtually destroyed. If not by the Combine, then who? There was only one way to find out. "When will our DropShips rendezvous with the *Monolith*?" she asked.

A new round of furious typing followed her question, and several moments passed without a response. "They should make contact in less than five minutes," the technician answered.

Silence fell again as the waiting continued. Several techs moved from console to console, verifying the status of the *Monolith*, as well as the progress of the *Severen Leroux*'s three DropShips and twenty aerospace fighters toward the wreck of a ship floating out there in an endless sea of black.

Penetrator

Champion

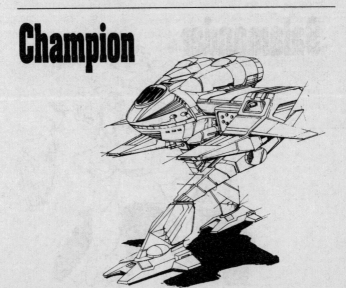

Battle Hawk

Salamander

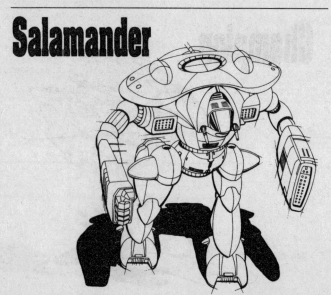

Hollander

Atlas

Lucifer

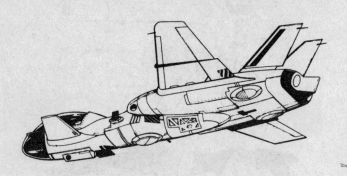

Chippewa